THE WILL OF GOD

JULIAN DE LA MOTTE

HISTORIUM PRESS

The Will of God

Copyright © Julian de la Motte 2025
Published by Historium Press 2025

Library of Congress Control Number on File

Hardcover ISBN
Paperback ISBN
Ebook ISBN

Historium Press 2025
A Subsidiary of The Historical Fiction Company LLC
Macon Georgia
United States of America

Dedicated to two of the greatest giants of the genre
and to whom I owe so much:

Zoe Oldenbourg and the inestimable Cecelia Holland

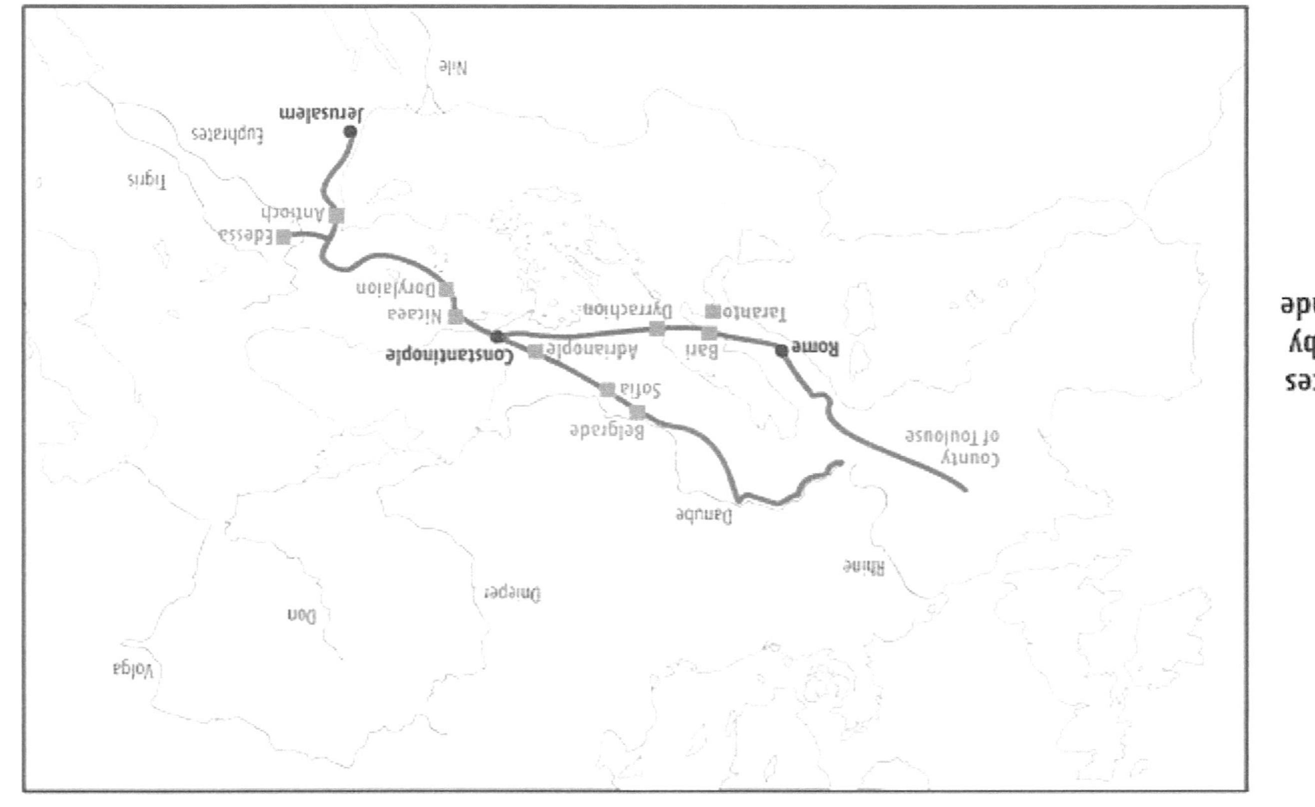
Volga
Don
Dnieper
Rhine
Danube
Tigris
Euphrates
Nile
Belgrade
Sofia
Adrianople
Dyrrachion
Bari
Taranto
Rome
County of Toulouse
Constantinople
Nicaea
Dorylaion
Edessa
Antioch
Jerusalem
Cities
Main routes followed by first crusade
River

Prologue: Rouen

"As I write these words, it is nearly time to light the lamps; my pen moves slowly over the paper and I feel myself almost too drowsy to write as the words escape me. I have to use foreign names and I am compelled to describe in detail a mass of events which occurred in rapid succession; the result is that the main body of the history and the continuous narrative are bound to become disjointed because of interruptions. Ah well, "'tis no cause for anger" to those at least who read my work with good will. Let us go on." [Anna Commena: *The Alexiad*]

The war horse, bred specifically to maim and to kill, first flinched and then shivered. Bucking violently, it threw the rider against the high metal encased pommel of the saddle. Small wonder that it should do so, for the whole town of Mantes was by now aflame. It burnt fiercely and freely to the accompaniment of the violent sounds of crashing timber as houses and store rooms collapsed to the ground in showers and bright sparks of crackling fire.

Mantes had been given over to fire and ruin since the first Angelus Bell of the day, and before full light, when the full fury of the raiding force of the man both King and Duke fell upon it. The whole town and the few men of the garrison, half starved and half asleep at the gate, were no match for the host of iron men who came upon them from out of the gloom. The giant horse was habitually a reliable creature and wholly biddable to its master, but it had good cause for its distress, placing as it had its forefoot firmly and squarely upon a section of timber fencing burning white and red in its intensity. It had burned beyond the dense matter of its hoof, around it and up into flesh and sinew as it danced and capered upon the cobbles before the Church of Our Lady in the main square. Sections of the building itself were already given over to fire, as indeed were most other buildings on all sides of the open space. Grim men, uniform and anonymous in their grey mail, roamed about freely, joyfully, in their various pursuits of wealth and the transitory pleasures to be derived from the cowed and terrified citizenry. The townspeople, those not already captive and herded, scurried and skulked in individual and mostly vain attempts at refuge from this terrible visitation, from this destroying devilish force come upon them in the dawn and which killed with neither mercy nor compunction.

The war horse, now flailing wildly and beyond all control, was contained within a small, tight group of riders, the other mounts skittering away from the clearly maddened beast, its rider now hunched forward and gasping, grey faced and in obvious extreme pain.

"See to him, there," commanded one of the companions and leaned across the withers of his own horse to snatch at the reins of the injured horse carrying the equally injured rider. Two others dismounted swiftly to hold it by its neck, seeking to still it, making reassuring clicking sounds of appeasement

"My Lord, your Grace. Have you taken a hurt?"

There was no answer from the stricken man, an elderly and impressive figure, richly dressed and very corpulent in appearance. His eyes were clenched tight, his mouth was working soundlessly and his face ashen. With a grunt he began to slide from the saddle, his weight and volume easing him over the high cantle of the saddle to fall with a noisy clatter upon the rain drenched and glistening cobbles.

While the town continued to crackle merrily and the supports of blazing buildings crashed with a flurry of flame and rising sparks, a table was commandeered from a gutted tavern and dragged to the stricken figure who gasped like a landed fish before the burning Cathedral. A knot of men were now gathered around him, kneeling, muttering and anxious. Around them, order of sorts was slowly emerging and in the early morning there came the cries and moans of dying men and the eerie and unnerving keening of women and children. This was of no concern to the anxious group clustered around the fallen man. Their apparent leader slapped a mailed glove into his palm.

"The physician, that Jew. Find him and bring him here," he ordered decisively as the injured man, now raised up and placed upon the table, continued to writhe and moan and as the offered wine trickled down the sides of his mouth.

The figure assuming command looked up and sniffed the air. "Coming on for a fair old rain," he remarked, seemingly quite inconsequentially. "Get him up and into the shelter of the porch, at least. Away from the gaze of the commonality."

From the porch they carried the table and the man upon it into the stone-built apse and the as of yet intact roof and laid their burden down. Brands of burning pitch were brought in the gloom, throwing nightmare shadows upon the walls of the spasmodic jerking shapes of the men gathered there. More men gathered, some to receive instructions and then to vanish, others anxious to be in the presence of great things unfurling.

The Jew, Ben Shimon, had at length been located among the baggage beyond the defunct walls of the town and bundled without ceremony to the Cathedral Church and into the presence of William, King of England and Duke of Normandy. He had, of course, come with his little sack of trickery, the tools of his trade, and had promptly applied a double dose strength of hemp and poppy seed with apple brandy and a funnel. It took a while before the injured man had quietened sufficiently to suffer a short preliminary inspection by the gentle probing hands of Ben Shimon.

The physician tutted quietly to himself and pursed his lips at the realisation that he had seen such injuries before in his service to wealthy patrons. His observations concluded, he retired to the shadows and held his own council whilst greater men argued and deliberated on what should be done.

William, Duke of Normandy and King of England, lay like a stranded porpoise upon the table, the greater part of his pain for the time being numbed. He was talking, his tone observational and rational. From the shadows, the elderly Spanish Jew knew that this would not last. The pain, in fact, was considerable and he spoke in occasional short bursts brought short by sudden gasps. He was assured that the town of Mantes had been taken and was receiving its just punishment, that a lesson had been taught to all traitors and people in rebellion, and, of course, to the King of France who had provoked this latest disturbance. William ordered the looting to cease forthwith and for all fires to be quenched, for even now punishment squads of men, terrifying in their mail and studded leather jackets and upon horses from some child's nightmare were carrying fire and death to the outlying districts. Tersely, the King ordered their recall. Hugh Grandesmil, the most senior man present, bent his head to listen as William uttered his orders in swift staccato gasps.

"Grandesmil," William muttered, "Our people here. They are to fall back upon Rouen immediately, and me with them. Our task is done here. It is finished. Have the cordon parties fall back and screen us." William fell back, gasping and exhausted. "This is to be now."

Grandesmil nodded and made to leave. William called after him. "A Council, Hugh, to be there when I return. Fetch me back that Jew, now; and my chaplain. At the very least a priest."

It was a journey of some distance back to Rouen, a difficult and slow affair of six days and nights in a steady stream of fine September drizzle. Outriders and couriers had long since sped ahead and a protective line of armed horsemen formed a screen as the wagons and pack animals made their painful and tortuous way back to the supposed refuge of the Norman border. The main body of infantry cursed and stumbled along in their muddy wake, sodden and steaming when the sun did shine; the pennants and banners drooping and lustreless in the damp.

A large covered cart, heavy and unwieldy, containing the restless and feverish King upon a looted bed, lurched and swayed and tipped its way along the deep ruts and potholes of neglected minor track ways. The patient oxen straining in the harnesses and goaded by men with sharpened sticks, were at the very limits of their endurance as they plodded through the mire. Ben Shimon had been taken aside on a number of occasions and at frequent intervals by senior figures in the party and questioned urgently. Of a certainty, he informed them, the King had taken a mortal wound.

It was a wonder he yet lived, he would die soon enough, so make your plans, my Lords, make your plans. On this journey, with these roads, it would be a chancy thing for him to see Rouen again in this life. The number of couriers and messengers peeling off from the column increased. In stumbling in that manner in the main square of Mantes, the horse had thrown the corpulent King heavily against the heavy iron cantle of his saddle. His internal organs, his vitals, had been ruptured and crushed.

"Note, my Lords, how he continuously bleeds from his mouth. I have seen this before. The outcome is always the same. Nothing is to be done, save for him to make peace with his God and to prepare his mortal soul."

Thus, in the heaving wagon, William, heavily sedated with poppy and hemp seed, spent those lucid moments that remained to him in valiantly diverting his pain to thoughts and acts of piety and statecraft. In an active life containing many bouts of illness and fatigue and pain he had had a deal of experience of this, he prided himself on this ability. In addition, he knew that he was in fact dying. This was not an injury he could hope to come back from, he knew this in his very bones and the intense pain served to remind him at all times. Through narcotics and extreme pain he attempted to channel this into action. Earlier on, the local Mantes priest had been dismissed and replaced by his own chaplain and an abbot from a nearby foundation, for William was ever a pious man. They, along with the inevitable scribe with his writing things, were now his constant travelling companions on the difficult journey back to the Norman capital. They swayed and jolted in the malodorous interior along with Ben Shimon; listening to the commands, instructions and prayers of the dying man as the procession moved into the more secure lands across the fluid border. Already, vengeful packs of freebooters, men from Maine and adventurous cavalry sections owing direct allegiance to Phillip of France, were nipping at their heels and planning mischief up ahead, well into Norman territory. There would be sudden alarms, flights of arrows. Few were killed or even injured in these stinging little raids, but notice was clearly served that whereas the men of Normandy had crossed the border like lions, they were now removing themselves like cowed and terrified sheep.

Of all this William was aware. The two men of God almost ceaselessly called upon Him, accompanied with the clicking of their rosaries, a constant muttering and murmuring that vexed the heroically patient Jewish physician. He preferred by far the scraping and scratching of the quill on calfskin as William dictated his latest thoughts, wishes and commands. The physician perched precariously at the very entrance of the covered wagon, preferring by far the cold and the rain of the damp autumn to that of the foetid interior. At intervals he ducked within the cover of his cloak and self administered that same poppy juice that was increasingly failing to keep the pain of his master at bay. The two clerics and the scribe were oblivious to his very presence. He was quite invisible, save for the frequent intervals when he leaned forward to dab the blood from the dying man's mouth. Intermittently he dozed, luxuriating in poppy inspired visions of the sunlit and cool colonnaded palaces, the trees laden with oranges, of Valencia. He knew a death vigil when he saw one. He had, after all, been present at enough of them to know.

For William, lucid moments became less frequent beneath the confining canopy. His blue lips moved with the rhythm of the intoned, familiar prayers and those of a spontaneous nature. The scribe, when bidden, scribbled upon the vellum, greatly hindered by the constant uneven motion of the cart. The Holy Mother and the ineffable wisdom and kindness of the Virgin Mary was a constant theme. The King of England had ever had a most particular reverence for Her. As he always had, he now called upon Her for guidance and protection; both now and in the hereafter. He prayed, also, to his dead wife, his beloved tiny Mathilde of Flanders, a constant companion and tower of strength in his challenging career. She had been with God these four years now and he missed her and the wise counsel she had given constantly. In their long partnership he had loved her more deeply than perhaps she or any other had appreciated. It was William's deep and silent belief that his resourceful and devious wife, ever the architect of highly elaborate schemes and plans of a truly Byzantine complexity, now carried considerable clout and influence in the Heavenly Kingdom itself. Of that he was certain and, as the Good Lord knew, he had plenty to seek forgiveness for; more so than any other living man. His feisty wife could certainly call in a few favours. The certainty of this knowledge gave him comfort. He smiled to himself and the memory of her brought on a further blood-flecked coughing fit that brought the Jew, elbowing the clerics aside, forward once more.

That night, somewhere between the settlement of Elbeu and the capital itself and still some distance short of their destination, William rallied somewhat, became more conscious of his temporal duties and responsibilities. Over the course of this last campaign his loyal and most trusted men had been scattered over a wide arc, obedient to his will and commandments. Those who had remained with him at that fateful sack of Mantes had seen their numbers further much diminished by legitimate and sanctioned instructions to move on with all speed to Rouen on this or that task and errand or by those who had absented themselves with spurious explanations and excuses and who, even now, were churning up the mud in their anxious and frenzied journeys to their own estates in the urgent furtherance of their own interests. Hugh Grandesmil and a few others remained with their doomed and blighted Lord. Outside the wagon, brands of pine and pitch were brought and lit, supplemented by braziers of dampened hay that emitted clouds of choking smoke to ward off the swarms of infuriating midges. There the remaining men of influence gathered for their dismal, wretched evening meal, their backs to the wheels of the wagons and coughing in the smoke. They met in little knots and huddles and muttered almost furtively amongst themselves over their salted meat and stale twice baked bread that was hard as stone. Grandesmil was summoned once more to his master's side.

Hugh de Grandesmil, once a youthful paladin and tyro of both the pitched battle and the private feud, a famed seducer of the beautiful women of other men and a much feared man, had since grown old and grizzled and halting in his step in the service of his Lord, William. Somewhat fearfully, and in the presence of a bevy of clergymen and the newly arrived abbot of Rouen, he made his way to the covered wagon, conscious suddenly of the fact of how much he could smell of both himself and those who accompanied him. In the damp his leg ached fearfully, the result of a wound he had taken at the fight at Senlac and which had so nearly done for him. The wound, taken in full view of the Duke, soon to be his King, had won him additional grants of land in the conquered country. They could not, of course, all clamber and squeeze into the wagon. So it was that Grandesmil, alone, who clambered in, blinking as his eyes adjusted to the dim light and his nostrils flaring at the scent of an impending death.

"Here you are then, Hugh," came the familiar voice out of the gloom. "And about time too. Do not worry yourself about trampling all over these others. I know that your days of moving swiftly are over and you are none too clever on your feet."

Grandesmil made what he hoped were appropriate sounds of apology and self deprecation as he trod heavily on the chaplain and upset the scribe's pot of ink. There was a familiar, and to his ears, welcoming tone of asperity in his Lord's voice.

"No matter, no matter. Time is short, Hugh. So listen to me, and you too, clerk, with your pen and inks. So, take note." There was a rattle in his throat and then a further, prolonged, bout of coughing which produced more blood. "In the Abbey at Caen there is in the safe keeping of the abbot my final Will and Testament. It is my latest document on the subject and it overrides all others. There are written my clear wishes of what is to be done. Clear instructions of who is to get what, and what is required of them. The terms and conditions are very clear. They are precise instructions, Hugh. Very precise. You are to ignore any other document."

William jabbed a stubby and calloused finger in the direction of the scrambling scribe reaching in his scrip to replenish his ink. "I am seeking to make my peace with my God, my Saviour and with the Holy Mother while there is time; and time is short."

Outside the wagon a small crowd had gathered, clerics and fighting men, anxious to hear and learn. The voice faltered, but in its intent and resolve there was no mistaking the voice of the iron conqueror of England. "For all my many sins and all my many faults may I be forgiven by all those I have wronged. I ask pardon of them. I repent and seek to make good."

Ben Shimon sighed deeply. He was content, felt exonerated in his analysis, justified in his prediction. These were the statements of a man only too aware of his imminent demise.

"My wishes and my Will are there in Caen," William reminded Grandesmil. "All there to be seen, and to be read and to be obeyed by all. See to it, Grandesmil, upon your honour. Lord Jesu, our blessed Mary, Mother of us all, take this pain from me and grant me Salvation." William sank back, exhausted by the effort, and spoke no more that evening.

That was the last evening, before a muted entry into Rouen the following morning. A large and jostling crowd of luminaries and curious observers and others with ostensible and mostly spurious reasons for their presence were in numbers sufficient to further hinder the dolorous and dejected procession on its way to the Cathedral from the city gates. A whole host of churchmen, headed by the bishop of Rouen and a brace of abbots led the way. The city itself, though muted, seethed like an anthill, the subdued citizenry lining the route, for it was quickly and generally known that their Lord was stricken. The city of Rouen, much as William personally disliked the place, had been transformed into a giant building site in his time, and much of the work was still in progress. On his bed, the Conqueror of England was carried with extreme difficulty into the new edifice of the Cathedral, consecrated in his presence just twenty years before, and laid before the Altar. William clung to life. The old Spanish Jew, laden now with a bag of silver, padded with leaves to remove any betraying clinking sounds, made himself scarce. It was time, he decided, to return to the south once more, away from this grey cold land reeking of piety. He had made his preparations carefully, an unobtrusive bodyguard and a pack horse. He would head for the land of the Bretons and make his careful way from there, edging down the coast. Lesser men, gentiles, gifted with less care and knowledge, took his place. They were an encumbrance, useless objects and certain of the veracity of their primitive practices and beliefs.

In the Vestry, the bishop of Rouen, guardian of a small and elaborately carved box of cedarwood, leaned back on his fold stool and surveyed his audience, his elderly and heavily jowled head nodding from some unspecified condition.

"Here," he gestured towards the box in his lap and tapped with his finger upon the lid, "my Lords and my brothers in Christ, are the thoughts and wishes of our Lord William." He shivered and pulled his thick ermine trimmed cloak about him, the Vestry was chillingly cold.

The canons of the Cathedral, the few noblemen gathered and the usual gaggle of clerks and scribes leaned in expectantly. The bishop continued in his portentous manner; a man clearly entranced by the momentous occasion over which he now presided and, indeed, was the pivotal part of it all. In one corner of the cold stone chamber lit by flickering candles and in the shadows, Grandesmil muttered to himself irritably. The bishop, in his view, was a saintly bore and an idiot.

"Perhaps, my lord bishop, we could proceed? He suggested. "Time, I fear, is short."

The suggestion lay hanging there for a moment. "Quite so, quite so," said the bishop hastily. "Our learned doctors are of one view, I fear, and inform me that his Grace is soon to depart this world. May the Lord have mercy upon his eternal soul."

There was a flurry and the slightest of breezes as all there made the sign of the Cross. "His Grace, mindful of the mutability of all things, made frequent changes to his wishes and intentions. I know not what documents there may be in the city of Caen, but here," and he tapped once more upon the lid of the box, "we have his last and final statement, made before he embarked upon this present and most unfortunate venture. It is signed and dated and witnessed. Of your courtesy, Pray allow me to read this to you." Grandesmil smiled in his beard, content in his secret knowledge, for he alone knew the document to be worthless.

The bishop reached into his purse for a key, a tiny object to conceal and reveal such a document of so large and of such import. He removed a rolled parchment bound with red ribbon and bearing the personal seal of William, King of England and Duke of

Normandy. He broke the seal with an audible snap and, with a flourish, unrolled the document on the table set before him. An acolyte scurried forward to secure the parchment with two candlesticks as weights.

The bishop cleared his throat, "More light here," and he set to reading in a sonorous voice, honking with a heavy head cold. "We, and our most Holy Church of Christ, are the executors of all that is contained herein," he announced portentously. "Let all know and respect this. Given this day on...on.." Irritably, he looked up and snapped his fingers irritably at an acolyte. "What day is it, man?"

The Church official had the day and the name of the saint honoured on it readily to hand, it could well have been chosen at random, but the man was confident it would not be checked.

The hurried meeting in the vestry was concluded and there was a general exodus. There was a further scattering of officials both secular and lay, from the building to either some place within the confines of Rouen or beyond as each set about their own tasks of either the preservation or else the furtherance of their futures. With the removal of the iron hand of the King there would be scores to settle, accounts to call in and acts both of personal defence and defiance to be taken. The various gatherings and meetings in the porch were hurried and furtive. All saw, as the Duchy crumbled about them, truly dark times ahead and little advantage for any save those prepared to act in any manner that might be held to be in some way treasonable. The King, meanwhile, was moved to a side chapel, a place less public and where it was presently discovered that he was in fact dead.

Grandesmil was one of the very few who remained. Grim-faced, he looked down upon his dead master and made a brief sign of the Cross as four cowled monks took station and began the death chants and the office of Vigil. He too then made his own exit from the building. He intimidated the few remaining who were still huddled in the porch into leaving and gathered his own trusted messengers in a huddle where he gave them precise instructions and, to each, a purse.

This done, he gathered his own entourage. Armed and mailed, they left Rouen in a body in a flurry of mud churned up beneath the iron shod horses. Ever thinking ahead, William had foreseen the possibility of this event and had privily instructed Grandesmil before ever he had embarked upon the task that had ended in failure and in his own death. Naturally, he had also seen to it that it was within the man's interests to see his instructions carried out. Grandesmil, as he laboured his horse along the sunken lanes and the towering hedges, could recall the conversation of a few months previously, vividly, word for word.

"When I do turn my old toes up, Hugh, my boy, be sure that everyone will know what is to be done; or rather, everyone will assume to know what I want to be done."

He recalled the scene, in a hunting lodge just outside Rouen, vividly. They had been out after snipe amongst the reeds on the river and had had a fine time of it early one bracing morning the previous October. Returning, William had been in jovial mood, for it had been highly enjoyable, and successful. He had poked Grandesmil, painfully, in the ribs, a habitual gesture.

"But they don't, see. We are neither of us in the first flush of youth, you and I, and I have a family to consider, now that Matilda is with God. The Good Lord knows, they have been a trial to me these many years, but family is family I suppose, and blood is blood."

He had then revealed to him the secret place within the Palace where specific instructions for his troublesome family were to be found. "The moment I am gone, dig it out and act upon it. Tell no other person, certainly no churchman. You will find also, a little something for your efforts."

And so there had been, far more than a 'little something' in fact. Grandesmil was carrying in his panniers documents that entitled him to vast swathes of new lands in the Cotentin and he was carrying in his head visions of the likely reaction to William's death of certain of his more immediate family. And thus, to Robert his eldest son: The boy had been with the King of France for four years now. Kept on a short leash and harboured by William's greatest enemy; a boy caught in rebellion and in open defiance of his father. To Robert then, full pardon and restitution and the bestowing of the Duchy of Normandy for himself; but no Crown of England.

And thus, to Odo, his half-brother. A man so steeped in sin and villainy and treachery that he could no longer personally enjoy his former high estate. While he languished under close but comfortable confinement for his unchurchly crimes, the bounty of Kent, his bishopric of Bayeux and a score of other properties and estates had gone, untasted by him and savoured by others. To Odo, then, forgiveness and a return of all his former glories and previous estate. To his problematic and scandalous second son William, called Rufus for his red hair and high complexion, the great prize of the Kingdom of England itself and all that it brought, good and bad. To Henry, his youngest and avaricious son, the sum of the weight of five thousand pounds of silver, to make of it what he would.

It was ever the fate of younger sons to make of themselves what they could. That, after all, was what the wild lands of Spain, of Italy and Sicily and the possessions of the Byzantines were for, so that determined men with horses and swords could take and make of them what they could. But the strange and cold and calculating boy would not embark upon the world empty handed.

And so Grandesmil's couriers pounded off on their errands to these and other recipients of the dead man's goodness and mercy.

Grandesmil himself was grimly satisfied. The world now belonged to men younger than he. For himself, he very much hoped, a life of ease and contentment. He no longer had anything to prove, not unless he became bored. He envisaged his future life, of days before the fire when the weather was bad, at the hunt when it was good. There were grand children to either cuff or admire as he struggled to recall their names, new comely young serving women to covet and take.

He paused in his headlong journey for a while to chew moodily upon cold mutton and stale bread, pausing for long draughts of thin acidic young wine, to which he was partial. Well, he reflected resignedly, Let them make of it what they will and the best of luck to them all. He had precious little regard for the whole pack of them. They could, he decided, be relied upon to make a complete dog's breakfast of the whole thing. From now on he would best shift for himself. They could go to hell in a hand cart, for all he cared. Something in him had sickened, curled up and died, along with his master.

Within the chapel in Rouen the corpse of William, Duke of Normandy, King of England cooled and slowly stiffened now that all the inner fires and fury had departed with his tempestuous soul. The four monks, cowled and sinister in their clothing and facelessness, had worked through the Office of the Dead and began, furtively to look about them for guidance and instruction, but the shadowed spaces beyond the chapel were full of rushing shadows and the rustling and swishing of robes as figures rushed past. They heard muttered conversations and voices raised in sharp imperatives or whines. They were, they individually understood, alone, ignored and forsaken. They were weary and had not eaten since early that morning, besides, they had their own duties to attend to. Would they be left here until night fell and beyond? Tentatively, one of them began once more upon the Office of the Dead and, presently, reluctantly, they all took up the chant. Well into the night, chilled and cramped, tired and hungry, they simply, as if struck by a collective single thought, abandoned the task and returned guiltily to their cells. Quite likely they would receive punishment for this dereliction, but at that moment they were beyond caring.

The body of the King of England lay truly alone in the dark and bitterly cold chapel. Beyond its confines and those of the Cathedral, the men of power and authority set about the securing, strengthening or the defence of their own positions. By a common consent, no curfew was put on the gates and the justifiably tense and fearful gate guardians witnessed a steady exodus from the city of men about their business.

The first intruder in the Chapel was the King's own half-brother, the intimidating Robert of Mortain. He was a huge and shambling bear of a man, amiable enough, but not to be crossed. Hours earlier, while William yet lived and was capable of speech, he had earned from him, reluctantly, a pardon for his brother,

William's half brother, Odo, bishop of Bayeux. His battered, brutal face with a nose spread half across it from the blow of a mace he had received years back, was composed into a respectful mask. Nonetheless, he stooped and with some force, for the body had stiffened, he removed the signet ring from William's index finger. Ever loyal to Normandy rather than to England, this he would give to William's eldest son Robert, now Duke of Normandy. Duke of Normandy, but not King of England. He made the sign of the Cross and paused in respect and filial affection for a moment for the man who had bestowed so much power and authority upon him before spinning on his heel to join the group of heavily armed men who would accompany him back to his lands of Mortain and his devious and calculating brother Odo, Bishop of Bayeux; there to release him from his exile and house arrest.

The brutal and fiercely loyal Robert was the first of a steady stream of visitors and intruders into the chapel. Far lesser men than he next removed all of the dead man's jewellery, fingering it, piece by piece and holding their spoils up to the light of a candle to admire before hastily, furtively, thrusting the stolen items into their purses A minor figure within the Cathedral first removed William's cloak, a difficult task for the body had stiffened. It was a fine prize, being blood red and of fine woven wool with an ermine trim at the nape. He scuttled off. An unknown knight made off with William's riding boots, fine things, knee high and of the best Spanish imported leather. And so it went on until the light of day, when staff returned to make the body ready for the final journey to Caen. These churchmen were horrified at the sight they found, of a vast and corpulent naked corpse, half pulled off the bier upon which it had once rested and left sprawling in ungainly pose upon the stone of the paving.

Churchmen of a higher authority were summoned. They, too were equally scandalised by the outrages of the previous night. While the chapel was hurriedly blessed and re-sanctified, along with the corpse, workmen were despatched to find a suitable container. When they returned it was not with a coffin but rather a very large and plain box, almost square, once used for the transportation of cloth. Into this the bloated body was placed, with as much reverence as was possible under the circumstances. William was now stiffened, with his arms splayed to either side, an inelegant posture, but short of breaking his arms, not one person there had any solution to the problem of straightening him. Bags of camphor were hurriedly fetched to place under him and whole bundles of lavender from the Infirmary gardens to further sweeten the box, a pious wish bearing in mind the long journey now to Caen, some eighty old Roman miles along indifferent and possibly dangerous roads.

The contingent gathered to accompany the late King was a scratch force gathered swiftly, reluctantly. They were a mongrel collection, to be sure. A contingent of church knights and men at arms, long since gone to seed in comfortable semi retirement within the Diocese. They were conscripted against their will and against all protestations for the duration. They were stiffened in their resolve with an additional backbone of hardened warriors thoughtfully on loan for the purpose from Robert of Mortain. This motley group would make the unenviable journey along roads possibly made lawless by the uncertainties of the time with a corpse that would certainly not become any sweeter with each passing mile. Almost at the last moment they were joined by two men from the household of the youngest son, Henry, there, presumably to see that deathbed promises made to him were observed and honoured. They were treated by all others as pariahs and kept themselves to themselves. After a long delay of irritable preparation, of hastily gathered provisions and the replacement or mending of ill kept harness and the gathering of ill tempered horses, the heavily laden cart drawn by four oxen and the accompanying retinue made its slow, noisy and dolorous way to the main gate and out of the capital.

Chapter One: Gilles

As they agreed he [Earl Waltheof] *rose, and kneeling with his eyes raised to Heaven and his hands stretched out he began to say aloud, "Our Father, which art in Heaven." But when he reached the last sentence and said, "and lead us not into temptation" such tears and lamentations broke from him that he could not finish his prayer. The executioner refused to wait any longer, but straightway drawing his sword struck off the Earl's head with a mighty blow. Then the severed head was heard by all present to say in a clear voice, "But deliver us from evil. Amen."* - Ordericus Vitalis: *On the execution of the Earl Waltheof*

When his father's handsome and youthful head was separated from his shoulders, his son Gilles was a sturdy and robust child just over a year old and able to sit up and take note of things immediately around him. His father's crime had been that of a complicity in a treason that he had failed to explain away with any degree of conviction or success. He may well, on this particular occasion, have been wholly innocent; but it had happened once too often in his brief political career to be overlooked. So, up the little hill just outside Winchester he went. The mother of Gilles, the beautiful Eloise of La Petite Flague, was, of course, devastated and it was said of that truly peerless beauty that her glance remained forever downcast and tragic to the end of her days.

Amongst the local people of the English, the former Earl soon achieved the status of an unacknowledged saint. Even days after the execution his head, or so it was said, when it was reattached to his body for the purposes of a fit and proper Christian burial, bore a sweet smile of utter serenity. Both the head and the body were fresh and bore the strong scent of rosemary and thyme, untouched by the corruption of death. It was not long before stories of miracles began to circulate. Nothing major or cosmic, there was no raising of the dead nor any parting of any waves, but, rather, a localised curing of warts and the removal of blinding headaches from an itinerant cleric in minor orders. As with many saints before him, Waltheof was obliged to start small in his saintly career.

If rumours of the English boy Earl's doings from beyond the tomb ever reached the ears of his Grace, the Duke of Normandy and now King of England these nine years past then he displayed no reaction nor passed any comment. In truth, he had been more than passing fond of the young Earl and over the years had gone beyond strict necessity to both protect and advance him, seeing in the popular boy a possible lever with which he might, if not win affection in the hearts of his subjected English subjects, earn a measure of tolerance and respect. The early days of his Kingship were fraught and beset with difficulties and very real danger and he required all the help he could get.

Waltheof had survived the bitter fight on Senlac Ridge by virtue of arriving at it a good hour too late. He had come crashing through the dense woodlands of the Sussex Weald that separated the place from London sixty or so miles distant at the head of his men and bearing a wound that had near killed him in the recent fight many miles away against the men from the North. As had been eminently sensible, the young Earl elected to make his peace with the new King of the English and to make himself amenable after a battle that had swept the majority of the native aristocracy from the board. William, for his part, was delighted with this formal submission and the early days of his rule, before the iron and ice truly entered his veins and gripped his soul, led Waltheof and his other English captives like so many bears on leashes on journeys and progresses throughout England and Normandy; to be seen and exhibited and to learn all due fear and respect. Then, at least, William sought at least a measure of support from his English subjects, a passive acceptance of the new way of things, a new way of doing things. Thus had young Waltheof been feted and treasured.

Very soon after, the Earl found himself a natural magnet for discontent, bordering on actual revolt; all the botched, half baked and malformed conspiracies of others that he would have done well to have left alone and to have steered well clear of. And for this, this unpardonable and apparent crime, the Duke and King finally demanded, and then taken his head. That ever passively inclined Churchman and statesman, the Italian Lanfranc, actually went down on his elderly and creaking knees on the eve of the execution and begged for the boy's life.

But William, a man who usually heeded the Italian's advice, was implacable. The Earl had proved to be a check to his progress, a thorn in his side, a poisonous asp in his bosom; he had to go.

"And what," the Italian had demanded when all else had failed, "what of the fair Eloise? What of the boy's heart's love? What of his infant son?" William considered. "Yes, the girl."

As if by magic, the old conjurer and stage manager had then ushered the girl in question in. Gratifyingly, she was clutching the child to her tightly as she collapsed in a flood of tears and in an outpouring of grief at her King's feet. It had been a gratifyingly heart-rending scene and William relented somewhat. Very well then, he would award her husband the axe and not the demeaning dangling rope, the fate of the common criminal. He further granted that a garland and a small psalter for his spiritual comfort be conveyed to the condemned man. Neither, in the event, offered any consolation. The May flowers were long since dead and brittle and he could neither read nor eat the psalter.

These, in fact, were gifts granted to the girl's dead father rather than to Waltheof, the saint in waiting. Gilbert of La Petite Flague had been a fine and powerful man with his best years before him.

On that bloody ridge nine years earlier he had strayed too close to his Duke and had heeded his call as the boiling mass of English before them had belched outward, spilling men down the incline, their fine Swedish axes whirling and gouging into William's mount and turning the creature into a red ruin. At that critical point Gilbert had swung from his own mount and surrendered it up to his Duke, ushering him up into the saddle before he himself was overwhelmed by the mob that trampled him into the mire and he was never seen in this life again. Fine noble acts such as these the Duke treasured and never forgot. When, a scant two years later, the roving eye of Waltheof first fell upon the bereaved and beautiful daughter of La Petite Flague, William, who had a well hidden sentimental streak within him, allowed the romance to blossom, unconsecrated as it was by Holy Office in the eyes of God. Now, nine years after the sacrifice, William remembered.

All in all, that busy year of 1075 had, like all his other years, been an extremely vexatious and tiresome one for William. From all points, east and west, north and south, he was assailed by mutinous subordinates, a precipitous attempt at invasion by boatloads of unruly Danes, the thieving Welsh and the barbaric Scots and the ever present rumblings and revolts of the English. It was no surprise, therefore, that he quite promptly and immediately forgot all about the fair Eloise of La Petite Flague and her child.

In fact it was a whole five troubled and troublesome years later that William had occasion to be reminded of the orphaned and bereaved family of his former willing sacrificial goat of Senlac or of his former once favoured Earl. He was, once more, in Normandy and in his capital of Rouen. Once more, also, his pestiferous neighbour, Fulk of Anjou, was happily involving himself in that fine old family tradition and pastime of fomenting trouble, difficulty and general unhappiness in the adjacent Duchy of Normandy. Anjou, with the passive complicity of France, was brewing up a fine little stew in the ever contentious little County of the Vexin. Far to the west, and taking every possible possibility and advantage from the situation, the fiercely independently minded Celts of Brittany were up to their usual tricks; anything from tax evasion to actual cattle raids across the border, resulting in loss and destruction of property and the taking of lives in their stinging little raids. Earlier that year William had brusquely, and in a fit of ill temper, refused to acknowledge full fealty for all his possessions to the Holy Father himself in distant Rome. The Pontiff might well actually lack the teeth to bite him, but there were plenty nearer at hand only too happy to oblige his saintly request and make the life of the King Duke as difficult and as onerous as possible by sinking their own teeth deep into his hide wherever and whenever the opportunity might present itself.

So, William was once more in his gloomy grey stone capital of Rouen, nestling by the Seine, half bastion and half noisy building site. It was, for him, ever a place of harsh and bitter memories and for which he felt no affection whatsoever. Here litigants and complainants made their way endlessly in a nagging line of accusation and counter accusation that left his ears ringing and his head aching from the morning to the night. The King's government, and his justice, was wherever the King might be found. It was also where the Queen was. He was with her now.

Matilda of Flanders, his companion, co-conspirator and help mate of many years, was a tiny doll like figure the size of a child. William, at one and the same time, both venerated and feared her. In his periodic audiences with her he would begin with unease and trepidation and conclude, exhausted, and with a fine collection of fresh and wise advice; as pungent and lingering as the scent of her store kept herbs. In all their years together, her shrewd and acute mind, sharp as a knife and full of useful filed and stored information, always seemed to be at least two full steps ahead of him; full of speculation and expert analysis, measuring the fine lines between possibility and attainment.

She was in full cry now in her roaring great chamber, a space seemingly made small by the vast impedimenta she had gathered and accrued over the years. She sat at the very centre of her world upon a once immaculate divan. Her nose was pinched and pointed and her hands, once long and slender, now all but crippled with arthritis. Her eyes glittered like diamonds packed in ice. It had been some months since his last visit. To William it seemed that his wife had grown yet smaller. Briefly, he smiled at her with a rare smile of genuine affection. Matilda was unmoved.

'My fierce little mouse' he thought fondly to himself. She was sharp as a weasel on a whetstone, a store of bulging information gathered in the recesses of her mind as her eyes sparkled with mischief and, possibly, malice. As ever, the old lady delighted in posing questions to which she already knew the answers, relishing the prospect of throwing a speculation into the air and then seeing where it might land and what might also come with it in its fall back to the earth, and then taking it from there. If, by chance, she did not fully know the answer to her own question then she had a rich store of information stored away in her fevered, busy brain to draw upon. Long ago, from the days of his tempestuous wooing, he had learned to treat her with respect and caution. Once in the early days of his exuberant courtship, back in her childhood home in Flanders and when an unseemly ardour had gripped him, she had actually stabbed him, quite severely, with a large darning needle. Or so it was reported. The story was commonly believed and reported, and indeed he could vouch for its truth but for the fact that it shamed him. The matter was never discussed within the hearing of the Duke and King. With Matilda, honesty was always the best policy. Do not presume to dissimulate and the treasure of her wisdom could be yours for the asking.

It was a scheduled morning appointment after the first Mass of the day and William had already been there some hours. The permanent throbbing of his temples had worsened under her onslaught. He knew, however, that a few hours spent captive in her company was of far more value and actual currency than whole days spent in the Council Chamber or in hall, blustering and issuing ill tempered threats. Already a problem of a land and inheritance dispute of two equally troublesome distant cousins had been made to vanish and a thorny little legal tangle, one of many raised by the French King's irritating council in Paris in the Ille de France, had been deftly averted, lured into a new maze of law, into a bog, a quicksand, a veritable legal thicket of Matilda's own creative design. William grunted his satisfaction and made a mental note. 'Sweet as a nut', it was a favourite expression of his.

William's eyes flickered constantly, restlessly, about the ruins of the room. The fortifying blast of local apple brandy he had taken as insurance had long since worn off and it would be the very worst of manners to risk a further nip. He decided against it, seeing as the old girl was in such fine form and performing valiantly. William perched uncomfortably upon a small and fragile footstool at her feet and well within reach of a sharp and admonishing little slap. He sat, marooned amid the clutter of the room, a thick set and muscular man, incipiently fat and all but bald beneath the stubble of his close shaven Norman skull.

William prided himself on a heavily regimented and imposed voluntarily regime of health, of fasts in excess of required religion and purges. His cold baths were the scandal of his churchmen.

Here in Rouen he was entrapped, a caged animal. Involuntarily, he yawned. Matilda's voice was shrill and reproachful, of late he had noted it had grown increasingly querulous. "You would do well, my Lord, to pay heed to what I say. No one lives forever, and I feel my time is short." It was a sharp reprimand and William started and uttered a brief yelp of apology. His eyes continued to roam about the room. There was indeed much to gaze upon.

Matilda's Chamber was a riot of seeming clutter, of rough pots of clay and glass phials containing mysterious liquids and powders of unknown provenance, giving off a miasma of contrasting smells, none of them to the benefit to the overall atmosphere of the room. Earlier he had, in his clumsy and maladroit fashion when around women's things, dropped a clay pot. It shattered upon the stone and foul rushes of the floor.

Matilda's shrill voice was triumphant as she peered over myopically at the additional mess. "Aha! The finger bone of Saint Aeinerberg! I had been searching for that. I had it from the abbess over in Bec. Do you recall?"

The pots and phials and their mysterious contents were all the more sinister for the reputation that Matilda enjoyed as that of a Wise Woman, as a healer and as an interpreter of dreams and a soothsayer for the future. It was a reputation she both relished and cultivated, along with the whiff of the occult that accompanied it.

Did you but have a condition or problem then an appropriate

payment, be it a bright jewel or a secret or some information, then the old lady would usually have a cure for the problem. Long and respectful queues used to form outside the door of her chambers, or else a discreet and faint rapping upon the stout wooden door after hours. One or other of her trusted women was more or less permanently stationed outside, to either repel or else to announce and admit visitors. There was a cure, it seemed, for most things, the chilblain, the still birth, the failure to procreate, the grief of unrequited love or the tooth ache; there was a price for everything and little gifts bulged out of every cranny or else were stored within the expanses of her head. The gifts jostled uneasily with the little scraps and strips of parchment covered with her tiny spider like writing, for Matilda, unlike most, was literate. She had long since given up in attempting to keep this her secret. There were drawings, for she was also a skilled and ardent botanist, and of embroidery samples, now beyond her art for her with her arthritic joints. In a corner of the room, that large place made small, was a further little pastime; a collection of animals she had stuffed, none too successfully. They too were making their own contribution to the overall fug and miasma.

The glass eye of a poorly stuffed badger caught William's own gaze and seemed to wink at him in the flickering light of the thick church candles. William shuddered at the sudden start he had had and rose hastily to his feet. He stumbled over the obese and irritable lap dog at his feet, one of a malodorous quartet of flatulent and yapping hell hounds, and then over the fine damask carpet of fine silk as he made for the narrow aperture of the unshuttered window. He gulped in a few welcome lungfuls of damp and icy Rouennais air. At the welcome window, the voice and its laden litany of enquiry and reproach followed him.

"William! That is the fine silk rug we had from the merchant of Porto. Do have a care, and mind the dog!"

William looked down at it with no fondness at all. "It'll live," he said with some regret as it continued to carp and snarl at his ankles.

"William! Are you listening to me at all? Where is she?"

The King of England and Duke of Normandy started. "Where is who, my sweet?"

Matilda's voice was exasperated, but with the faintest hint of fondness. "'I refer, to remind you once more, to that fair girl, the daughter of La Petite Flague. She who you permitted to breed with that young puppy, Waltheof." She ended with a prim and disdainful little sniff.

William was stung to reply. "Body of Christ, woman. How am I supposed to know?"

Matilda murmured softly. "I recall she was a sweet little thing. Like a faerie, she was. And such a fine eye and fingers for beautiful embroidery work. That is is what I miss, in my old age" William was not to be fooled. He had known Matilda for too long to be taken in by a casual enquiry regarding an obscure and distant person or object. There would be an additional purpose, an objective to the question.

"Well, I shall tell you where she is, and her brat, if it survived. She was with that senile old fool Warenne in his old draughty barn of a place, the old fool. Well, I would have her here, at my side, do you hear? for the sake of her skillful little hands and the sound of a fresh voice. The brat too, should it yet be living." William nodded his agreement. "I shall see to it. It shall be done," With a sigh he turned his attention once more to the fresh tide of questions that came flooding in and over him like the fighting axes of the Saxon.

The young child, Gilles of La Petite Flague, grew to be a sturdy and resolute child of a fierce and growing independence, and living largely, perforce, upon his own wits, initiative and means. From the time his mother's milk failed her and that of a reservoir of suppliers was no longer needed, he grew to live largely by himself, relying on those same wits, living on them in the dairies and outhouses and barns, in the fields and orchards of the little fiefdom of the old Lord of Warenne. A man grown old and scarred in King William's wars. The old man could often be espied with his beloved crouching stool about the estate, either glorying in the weather or else sheltering from it.

Gilles was a scheming and brawling little scrap of a towheaded creature, perpetually covered with the small wounds of recent and ancient encounters and powered largely by the principles of either fight or flight. He had learned a cunning beyond his years and, as with all the other wayward children of the sprawling estate, had become a talented thief of those things necessary to life; of bread and cream from the board and from the dairy, a scrap of cheese or a slice of bacon which he, according to expediency, either shared with or hid from all the other young savages roaming around in his crowded little life. For security and refuge he had a number of safe, warm and hidden places that he fondly believed to be unknown to all. He was, of course, a wholly barbarian creature, untutored and uncouth, his language an uneasy blend of the French of the privileged few and the native English of the many. From a very early age, he had acquired the art of switching from the one to the other according to the particular situation or circumstance where he found himself. In this challenging and occasionally perilous environment he encountered occasional well meaning and good intentioned protectors, touched by the child and moved by the personal circumstances of his birth. Many of his former wet nurses still clucked and fussed and kept a weather eye open for him as they laboured at their milking stools or churned the butter. They would cuff him and chide him fondly as he sidled by like a stalking cat, keeping to the sides of the room.

A chaplain to old Warenne, a shy, stuttering and diffident young man with a club foot from the orchard lands of Bayeux, favoured him, brought him food and taught the wayward child his French and stories of Our Lord, wincing at the barbaric savagery of the English the child used. Both the steward and the master of the pantry and various of the foresters and estate workers were kind enough in their own way and proffered gifts upon encountering the reclusive child as they stumbled across one of his many hiding places. In the main, Gilles was simply one of the many who patrolled and roamed the estate like brawling, feral cats.

His encounters with his mother grew less frequent as he grew older. His mother, the fair Eloise, never quite lost her looks, but her downcast expression never lost the appearance of a tortured saint; a countenance of resignation and of hopelessness. It was an expression well suited for the pacific calm of the place of the ladies, where conversation rarely rose above a murmur and the usual decorum was that of the Cloister.

The environs of the Lady was a place of calm, at the centre of all the doings of the state of de la Warenne. It was a place where the delicacy of her needlework and the skill of her never ending work on tapestries illustrating the life and works of Christ excited much praise and covetous envy amongst the ladies. They were ever conscious of the protection and distant patronage of the King himself, though he had himself long since forgotten where he had squirrelled away the young and still attractive girl. Thus Eloise was left largely in peace.

She, for her part, was perpetually in mourning for the day when her husband had lost his handsome young head on a small hill outside Winchester. She sat quiet and passive and observed piously the many observances of the rigid Christian day. She ate when all others ate and slept when they did, arising at the same hour for the first religious service of the day. Her thoughts were known only to herself and she spoke but rarely.

Occasionally the young wife of Warenne or some other person in authority similarly moved by Christian compassion, would note her silent misery and put the word out to track down young Gilles from one of his many refuges in the barns or the tall grasses of the fallow pastures or in the fork of a tree, places where he would store his purloined or endowed treasures of the larder and the pantry. The places where he was known to haunt in his evasions of either the attentions of the French speaking children of the privileged or the pack of the English speaking offspring of the subjugated English would then be searched. A damp rag would be dragged across his face and he would be reunited with his mother for a very short and uncomfortable spell in which the miserable and heartbroken Eloise would spill out her love in a torrent of French and the child would respond in uncomfortable English monosyllables, comforted by little tidbits always made available by the particular benefactor and sponsor of the brief reunion.

Eloise always found joy in these meetings, most usually conducted with an audience of cooing women. Gilles, for his part, found them disquieting, unable to return, in his pride, her love and thus breaking her heart all the more.

The Feast of the blessed saints and martyrs Perpetua and Felicity meant absolutely nothing to Gilles, brutal, coarse and untutored as he was. He knew it, rather, for a bitterly cold day in early March and with the high moaning wind ruffling and bending the trees and parting the winter barley in the fields. There was more than a promise of snow in the air. Gilles was in the vintry, one of his more especial and favoured places. More specifically, in a small gap behind the carefully stacked and balanced oak barrels set against the walls of the barn constructed of rough stone and the local flint. The timbers were sound and the roof recently re-thatched. It also had a stout oaken door, for the contents were valuable, but this particular locked door presented the boy with little difficulty. There were always ways in and out of a barn to a boy of resource and courage. The sound of the key jangling and clinking as it was removed from the busy and crowded belt of the vintner, alerted Gilles.

He was nestling between barrels, seeking warmth and nursing a bruise on his forehead that felt the size of a duck egg. His safe refuge was not as secure as he had imagined. He froze at the sound of a key in the protesting lock and as the heavy door swung open. He squinted through a gap, unmoving. Four figures; two adults, two children framed against the grey of the daylight.

He recognised the two boys immediately, Ernoul, the son of the fletcher, a sworn enemy and in fact the creator of the throbbing bruise of his head. He must have tracked him there, eager for further retribution. The other, a simple boy and pure English, he recognised as one of the numberless pack of children that roamed the outhouses, barns and surrounding countryside, doubtless drawn to the vintry out of curiosity and boredom. One of the adults was the vintry man himself, pleasant and accommodating enough. The other a complete stranger who strode forward and raised his voice, not a voice of a local man, his boots sounding loud upon the packed and compacted earth. Gilles' highly trained and expert ear knew they were riding boots, studded with reinforcing iron.

"Out of there boy, you are wanted. No time to be fooling around."

Gilles could see him now, stropping a riding whip in his palm. The vintner was more reassuring, positively conciliatory, for all the fact that his own personal fiefdom had been entered, it did not do to fool with strangers. "Now come now, young Gilles," he called. "No harm will befall you. Gentry is waiting upon you. It does not do to be wasting their time, now."

Reluctantly, Gilles rose from his place and stepped into the half light, head bowed in abject surrender and in expectation of a blow. Ernoul, one of his many persecutors, crowed delightedly. The stranger snapped his fingers impatiently and Gilles surrendered himself up to the two adults. Fingers like iron gripped an ear and he was ushered out and into the yard by the two implacable men. He knew better than to speak or voice any objection. The stranger dispersed the two accompanying boys with kicks and a volley of curses that Gilles did not recognise as he was led, inexorably, in the direction of the Big House. It would be another interview with his mother, he assumed, in the fine manor house, an aristocrat amidst the drab and lowly buildings that surrounded it; a swan amongst ducks. Quality was waiting.

The courtyard of the Earl Warenne was the usual clutter and muddle of people and diverse objects scattered about. Men and women in the dun and green and grey of homespun cloth blended with the earth colours of the ground, the quagmire, the swamp of churned mud and excrement. They either strode purposefully through it all or else attempted to skirt delicately around the more obvious mounds of rubbish and ordure. The more colourfully attired, house servants and retainers for the most part, avoided the area when they could, preferring other entrances and exits to the Great Hall.

A cart with one wheel off for essential repairs was proving a major obstruction and people cursed as they edged around it and the blaspheming wheelwright and his apprentices with their heavy hammers working on a broken wheel. Across the way, over in the corner of the yard a large pig lay sprawled upon its back, slaughtered out of proper season. For some reason, it had survived the usual November cull. Scrubbed clean of bristles, a butcher was busily at work with his knife and axe, delving expertly for the liver and kidneys.

Despite the cold of the day and the earliness of the season there was a halo of flies circling the butcher and at his feet a coil of grey steaming intestines were attracting the interest of a trio of dogs. Wretched creatures, ribs showing like the staves of ruined boats, they sidled towards the pile of offal and retreated again from the slaughterer.

The butcher's boy, no more than a child staggered away, burdened with a heavy bucket of blood that slopped over the sides as he moved. There would be blood pudding and sausages made of scraps of inferior meat stuffed within the intestines ready by the afternoon.

Some fine looking horses with rich and well maintained saddles and tack had evidently recently arrived, for their sides and backs were still steaming and covered in foam. They were attracting a good deal of notice and interest as they were led off to the stables by ostlers. Strangers were rare and worthy of comment at the Great House of Warenne. Gilles, taking this all in, made a mental note. Clearly, one of these belonged to the stranger. There were the usual crowd of idlers gathered about the blacksmith's hut, drawn by the gossip and the heat of the forge. A blacksmith was never starved of company, as long as the bellows fed air to the burning sea coals. The stranger strode purposefully through it all, still disdainfully gripping the boy's swollen and reddened ear. People backed away from him as he and the boy mounted the wooden steps of the Hall and approached the open doorway. Giles, stumbling and wisely uncomplaining, was thrust through into the interior.

The building was constructed like a barn. As with all the buildings of worth and note in that place, the walls were of rough hewn stone and jagged lumps of flint long since made smooth, treated with plaster and crudely whitewashed on the inside. Rafters supported the thatch of the roof, home to scrabbling rats and scratching birds. Set in the walls there were occasional gaps for light and air, narrow apertures that provided neither. The Great Hall was possibly fifty paces from end to end. It was dank and freezing, treacherous and greasy underfoot, a stinking mess of soiled reeds and rushes and bones trodden into an uneven form of paving.

Set against a wall at the far end was a fire pit below an imperfectly constructed chimney, a novelty that belched back choking smoke into the gloom and stench of the interior. Benches and trestle tables were stacked against the sides, brought out to the centre of the Hall for the occasional feast. The open space was thus left available for a drifting mass of people, such as there were now. The sides of the Hall were all jealously guarded places for sleep and for whiling away the daylight hours.

At the far end of the Hall was an attempt at greater state. A raised wooden platform and a ladder leading up to a further wooden floor supported by beams, the personal space of old Warenne and his beautiful Provencal wife. A screen of hessian hid the interior from all curious and prying eyes.

Upon the lower platform were further attempts at gentility. The rushes were changed every day and strewn with rosemary and thyme, a handsome carved table of bog oak, four ornately carved chairs, treasured and much coveted possessions, two braziers glowing with sea coals against the bitter early March weather. It was understood by all that no one stepped up to stand amongst all this finery unless specifically invited or called upon. There was quite a crowd gathered around and about the raised platform. Gilles could see this as they advanced up the hall, he scuttling like a surprised crab in the grip of the stranger.

A slender and richly dressed man lounged in one of the chairs, one leg stretched elegantly over one of the arms. He gave off an aura of exquisite and ineffable boredom. Gundrada, wife of Warenne, was a tall and elegant figure, Gilles remembered her well from previous visits. Fine boned and dark, she was speaking rapidly in her high pitched sing song voice, the musical tones of the south of France of her girlhood.

A few women of her entourage clustered about her. They stood motionless in attitudes of demure respect, as was fitting, proper and expected of them. There was the chaplain, whom Gilles knew as well as he could be said to know anyone, also present, He was clutching a document, summoned there for his skill of literacy. A heavy lead seal swung from it, attached to a narrow red ribbon.

Two more strangers stood below the raised platform, arms folded and looking out blankly into the Hall. They were armed, and dangerous looking, and there, completing the group, was Eloise, his mother. Her head upon its long and slender neck was drooped in its usual posture of submission, her hair covered and her eyes downcast. She was staring fixedly at the planking beneath her feet, shoulders raised and hunched. Her face was a burning red and she was weeping silently, shaking with suppressed sobs. She looked as if she had been struck repeatedly, which in fact she had. Gundrada was clearly vexed with her and Gilles rightly guessed that she had been the author of the blows.

The elegant man raised his eyes from the contemplation of his uneven nails at the sound of their approach. The boy's captor bowed and coughed deferentially to announce his arrival.

The seated man raised his eyebrows quizzically, "and this is the boy?" He glanced over Gilles appraisingly for a moment.

The servant nodded once more. "My Lord, I am informed so, yes," He spoke with a level of loathing and contempt for the boy that Gilles felt to be unwarranted on such a short acquaintance. Throughout their brief relationship he had not uttered so much as a word.

The man rose from the chair and turned to Gundrada, a flash of a smile that was elegant and charming and with most of his teeth seemingly present and correct. "Then, dear Lady, we need impose upon you no longer." His voice was the pure Norman of the homelands. "Our little errand is complete and we shall be about our business. This," he said, indicating the squalid little hall with a fine leather riding glove, "has been absolutely charming; a rare delight. Of your courtesy, dear Lady. And you,"

He turned to Eloise, mother of Gilles, "you, madam, and your brat there, have put us to some degree of inconvenience." The voice had turned icy cold and contemptuous, "But the Lady, our Queen, has commanded and so I obey,"

Gundrada clearly felt it time, as Chatelaine and controller of the Household in the absence of the Earl, to exert some influence upon affairs. "It is as you say. The command of the Queen is to be observed, Messire Yves. Do I have the name right?"

Again, the charming smile, "Quite so, dear Lady."

The Lady Gundrada appraised him in a cool manner. "It is so I might give full account to my Lord when he returns." The elderly Earl, as it happened, was away that day over to near Arundel, exercising his deer hounds and completing the protracted purchase of a prized fine bull for his herd. He was not expected until the morrow.

"Quite so, Lady, and the document your man there clutches, is yours to keep, for your records. But now we must be about our journey. I regret it."

Gundrada nodded rapidly, like a bird. It was a habitual and much imitated habit. "I shall make full provisions for your journey and arrange a mount for the girl. The boy can ride with her, or walk. It is one and the same to me."

"You are too kind. The horse shall, of course, be returned in all good time," the Norman voice was a conciliatory murmur.

Gundrada turned to Eloise. "And you, you have been most troublesome today. But I forgive you this inconvenience. I shall miss you, truly. You shall have a purse and some fine things for your trouble. My chaplain shall accompany you to your place of lodging. Go now."

Eloise spoke for the first time, Her voice, though faltering, was brave and determined. "And some warm clothing for my boy in this weather, Lady. He has never left this place before."

A half smile formed on the lovely countenance of the Lady Gundrada. "Quite so, my girl, he shall not go naked into the storm, like a beggar." She glanced at Gilles, as if contemplating a dirty object, which, indeed, he was. "It pleases me to grant this," and she clapped her little hands. She had spoken, and spoken last. Her control thus established, the meeting was at an end. She instructed her gathered ladies, "Make it so," she concluded.

Thus was Eloise whisked away, first to her tiny cell in an outbuilding to collect and pack her few belongings and then to a final audience with the Lady Gundrada and her blessing and the promised parting gifts. The small boy Gilles, of course, was completely disregarded and utterly at a loss at understanding what on earth was befalling him now, sheltered in his skill of anonymity and insignificance. He was vaguely aware that he appeared to be leaving that place. To where, and why, he did not know. He was much gratified, however, that his ear, reddened and smarting, had been relinquished by the servant. The kindly chaplain, himself dismissed, stepped down to him, but he was of no use in further enlightening the boy. He was a very tall and spindly man and as he knelt, in sections it seemed to the boy, to his own eye level, he resembled the spindly water boatman insects which skimmed across the surface of the millpond when the weather was good and the wind was still. He clutched Gilles' shoulders and spoke in French very slowly, for the boy was widely known to be simple and lacking in his wits.

"You and your mother are to go upon a very long journey," he said gravely, "across the water."

Briefly, Gilles' eyes widened. "Across the water." He had heard tell of 'the water'. He had never seen it, of course, nor the ships that were said to sail upon it.

"You are to leave all of this," the chaplain continued. He

indicated the squalid little hall with a vague gesture. "Your mother is chosen as a special companion to the Queen herself. It is a great honour to her, and to you, of course. I shall pray for you both," he concluded.

Sensing a response was required of him, Gilles smiled cautiously and nodded. It was clear he was not be offered the opportunity to make his own farewells of the place, that much was certain. There was, in truth, precious little to bid farewell to. There was no companion he would miss, or any treasure to retrieve save a hidden discarded arrow head and a broken spur. Fleetingly, and with regret, he thought of the half blind cat and her newest litter at the back of the hay loft. All he really owned were the ragged and dirty clothes he stood up in. His new enemy, the iron handed servant, stepped forward and the three of them exited into the courtyard, there to wait upon further developments. The servant beguiled the time by watching as the pig continued to be dismembered at the skilled and practiced hands of the slaughterer. Gilles, distracted, fretful and excited, took it all in with his wild and roving eye. From the pig to the smithy, to the frenzied activity of the stables where preparation for a journey were underway, to beyond the courtyard and the little hill beyond that and where two figures swung gently in the stiff breeze. His forehead furrowed in concentration. They had been there so long. A murderer and a persistent thief, he recalled. The chaplain simply stared into space. Perhaps, Gilles surmised, he was talking to his God.

Matters resolved themselves soon enough. The foreign horses reappeared, refreshed and fed, the handsome saddles and tack once more upon them. There was a further horse, by no means so fine, presumably for Eloise and her boy. It was bony and sunken-backed and did not move well, the best of its years were well beyond her and the saddle was cheap and the horse blanket rough and patched. Presently his mother herself reappeared, stepping cautiously down into the mess of the courtyard. She was accompanied by the man named Yves and the remaining two men of his entourage. They strutted into the open space like peacocks amongst sparrows. His mother looked quite borne down by the weight of two leather panniers and a blue cloak of fine wool. It looked new and Gilles noted that it was held by the prized and treasured clasp of her husband, his father, Waltheof Sigurdsson, an enamel bear in red and white. She was also clutching an additional bundle of clothing, perhaps for him. No one offered to assist her with the heavy load. The elegant man, Yves, swung his equally elegant leg over the saddle. His men immediately hauled themselves into the saddles of their mounts. No one offered the least assistance to Eloise. The chaplain knelt and clasped his hands like a step for her. Eloise swung aboard, with difficulty and absolutely no grace. Next, he reached for Gilles and swung him up before her like a bag of wool, like the encumbrance he truly was.

The chaplain raised his hand in farewell and benediction. "May the blessing and mercy of God be upon you both, always." He made the sign of the Cross. Yves uttered a brief command and the little group, four men, one woman and one small child, swung about, out of the swirling courtyard and into the open countryside where the labouring peasantry paused to straighten their backs from their labour upon the fields to gape at them. They passed beneath the swinging bodies of the hanged men, Gilles nodded a farewell to them in passing.

The child Gilles was just eight, though he had no means of knowing this, when first he beheld the Big Water. He was overwhelmed by the spectacle, grey water stretching on forever and forever. He was entranced by the hypnotic regular sound of the water as it swept across the pebbles and shingle of the shore and retreated once more with a scraping noise of protest which he found both entrancing and beguiling. He was entranced also by the sound and sight of the gulls as they wheeled and dived before his widened eyes, their cries sounding like lost and tormented souls. He marveled at the smell of it all, of the salt seaweed he liked to pick up to pop between his fingers, the reek of the rotting fish that caught at the throat. He wondered, briefly, why all those about him did not seem to share his wonder and delight.

There, in the daylight hours on the quayside of the mean little fishing settlement where they had fetched up in, he sought to make himself even smaller, even more insignificant than he already was.

It was a gift of evasion he had learned early, having learned also that anyone taller than he was most likely an enemy. This talent had served him well in the past.

Throughout, and for the period of their stay in this present place, his mother had, from time to time, remembered to place the occasional object into his mouth; a hunk of bread, a scrap of cheese, dried meat, for him to chew with his strong young teeth. Water he found for himself in barrels and puddles. His mother remained an island within herself, sharing her thoughts with no one. As ever, he was uncomplaining and stoical. It was thus very easy to overlook him. His mouth remained firmly closed and his eyes and ears wide open. Thus, he appeared to the world a strange and silent figure and was mostly taken to be simple witted, even by his mother. He invoked in some a sense of pity and deserving of small acts of kindness or, by the majority, deserving of a cuff or a curse.

At some point all the horses disappeared, sold or returned, he knew not. He awoke on the first morning and they were gone. Gone too was the man, Yves, to some place called Dover. He stored the name in his mind for future possible use. Two of the servants remained with him and his mother. He continued to stare out at the mysterious grey of the Big Water, never tiring of the sound it made upon the small stones and wondering at the regular way it rose up towards the land and then shrank away, leaving an expanse of foul smelling mud and lop sided and marooned small boats.

The wind was strong, constant, and blowing in from the sea. And then, of a sudden, it backed and blew out to sea. Around him, this excited much comment, Gilles merely shrugged, retreating further into his donated clothes. Whatever its direction, the wind was still bitterly cold. Eloise continued to shiver, retreating deeper into her fine new cloak of blue wool. She continued to display no interest, in either the people or the general bustle about her. Though early in the day, the two servants had acquired a flagon from somewhere. It was just about finished and they had sent for another. They seemed content enough, calling out loudly and lewdly to the passing women of the little village and throwing knuckle bones against each other interminably in some private wager. Gilles continued to absorb information, his eyes darting about him without ceasing, serving to confirm the general view that the boy was simple minded. The wind had not only backed, but had also picked up strength. He gazed out upon the Big Water. Far in the distance, from behind a headland, there appeared a tiny water beetle, identical to those creatures he had often observed up close upon the mill pond on the very still days. Four stick like limbs protruded from its belly, moving laboriously. This particular insect had a spike emerging from its middle, a mast with sail lowered as the boat struggled against the contrary wind. Perhaps Gilles was the first there to notice it, but soon quite a crowd had gathered and the two servants bestirred themselves. The object grew bigger, to the size of a nut, and then a vessel with human figures. The boat made the harbour wall, edging along it, furtively like an unwelcome and uninvited guest at a wedding party. It was a ship, Gilles now understood, a ship, to take him and his mother away from here.

Another March day; a year since a boat had carried its cargo up the broad majestic sweep of the Seine and the curve that revealed the citadel, Cathedral and the grey brown sprawl of the untidy and foul smelling city arising out of the smoke of hundreds of fires. Neither the boy nor his mother had ever seen the like as they were shepherded through the noisy crowded streets to the castle keep and home of Matilda, Duchess of Normandy and Queen of England. And now a year had passed. It was the day of the funeral and all the solemn trappings of the ceremony for the old Queen, a figure universally loved and respected and feared, and now with God.

Gilles was nine. It had been an exhilarating spiral of a year for the boy, one crammed full of dangerous and thrilling moments between the times of monotony and idleness. The old lady, clearly ailing, had taken to her new possession as to a bright, new and glittering plaything and they had spent many happy hours closeted away together in Matilda's apartments. Matilda would prattle away brightly for hours on end whilst Eloise laboured upon samplers, decorated cushion covers and the like. In particular, and with a surpassing skill, she worked upon a large tapestry that confounded all who beheld it. It was to be, when completed, a depiction of the Marriage Feast at Canaan. Odo, Bishop of Bayeux, the grossly fat and mountainous half brother of William, once visited; a rare occasion when Gilles also happened to be present. Clearly, there was no love lost between the Queen and her relative by marriage. Odo was an avid collector and lover of fine and beautiful objects, having greatly increased his own personal wealth by over a decade of roaming the length and breadth of England in his search for further acquisitions. Odo had a practiced and expert eye for such things.

The bishop approached and appraised the incomplete tapestry, fingering some strands delicately with his fat fingers as Matilda waited for a compliment.

"It is a fine work," he said at length. "It follows the English style, as it is termed. Much like the work my own people are working on, a project of mine, at Canterbury. This, I allow, is finer." He inclined his large ponderous head.

Matilda eyed him with neither appreciation nor liking. "I thank you, brother in law," she said. "My girl here is to be prized and treasured and set up above all others."

Odo knew enough of Matilda to assess this, with accuracy, as a threat. He cast his somnolent, sleepy and deeply pouched eyes upon Eloise, seated upon a small stool at the Queen's feet, her eyes downcast.

"Ah yes, I recall," he murmured. "The daughter of La Petite Flague. She married that Waltheof, the Englishman. She had a brat, I remember. Did it live?"

Odo was a man of many interests and pursuits. He had, in particular a flair and a passion for genealogy. He prided himself on knowing the antecedents of important people and of how they might promote or detract from his many plans and objectives. It was rumoured that he kept a man on his staff whose job it was to exclusively look into this and keep him fully up to date.

Gilles, in fact, was mostly obscured by the malodorous and moth eaten experiments in the stuffing of animals of the Lady Matilda, a pursuit mercifully since abandoned. Gilles found them fascinating. He was further amply screened by the presence of two of Matilda's attendant women. He knew his place and also decided that this was no time to be advertising his presence. It was, in fact, to be the first of many encounters with Odo, Bishop of Bayeux and Earl of Kent. It was the very year of the first major reversal of the Bishop's career.

Upon his arrival in the city and fortress of Rouen, provision was made for both the mother and the boy. Eloise promptly disappeared into the fastness of the castle keep and Gilles was given over to the protection and charge of an elderly man named Hugh, one of the three keepers of a small postern gate of the city walls. It was not a large or an important gate, but it was a gate, for all that. Hugh had been badly injured in the wars of William long before ever the Duke took England. He walked with a heavy limp and had received the post and a pension, not massive, but adequate. In truth, the duties did not appear to be especially onerous, consisting as they did largely of the opening of the gate at the Matins Bell and the closing of it at curfew. In between such times he occupied himself by peering into the contents of baskets and the tapping of barrels of the various carts as they came and went, earning a respectful additional income also in extracting bribes and protection money from known malefactors and infringers of rules. Gilles would often accompany him on his frequent meanderings about the city when Hugh wasn't dozing before a comforting brazier in the gate room when the weather was inclement.

Life with the old gatekeeper, a widower, and his three handsome daughters was a charmed one for young Gilles, unknowingly cushioned by a fatness of kindness from the old Queen. Hugh was kindly enough and the doting of his daughters an additional benefit. Gilles was permitted, with the strict proviso that he return by nightfall upon pain of a beating, to roam the streets and alleys and wharves with a wild group of boys. He did largely as they did, relishing comradeship for the first time in his young life. He fought, played dangerous pranks and stole as they did. He fished in the Seine, gutted and cooked his own fish and was deliriously happy. He also learned fluent French in the argot and patois of Rouen and quite forgot his English. And every evening a warm meal doled out by the three kindly and plump and handsome daughters of old Hugh the postern gate keeper, who devotedly worshipped the strange little boy.

Occasionally there came a summons from the keep to attend his mother. Hastily scrubbed, a damp cloth hauled across his face, Gilles attended, confident of some gift in departing. Thus it was, lulled into a sort of complacency by the regularity of his days and nights, the death of the old Queen in the sweltering heat of mid July caught him, and the majority of people, completely unawares and unprepared. One early morning the single death bell in the Belfry of the incomplete Cathedral tolled, and continued to toll. The note was taken up by the many little churches of the new city on their own poorly cast and cracked bells and wooden clappers; a dolorous clamour that soon brought people out onto the Square before the Cathedral. Word spread. Matilda, that constant factor in the lives of so many for so many years, had been taken by a fever and was now with God.

Along with hundreds of others, he was drawn by the Bell of the Cathedral and by the bells and wooden clappers of all the little Churches of the parishes, giving tongue as soon as the news spread. He eased and wriggled his way through the crowd and to the front, where he was afforded a fine view of what was and what was not happening. Curiosity kept him there all the day long. When he was hungry he stole from the tray of a passing baker's boy. As with all his thefts, it was adroit and unobserved. Always a busy place, the activity around the donjon and the Royal Palace became at times frenetic.

Over the days, and when the interest had abated to a dull curiosity, Gilles returned, this time fully provisioned with bread and a flask of water and on the fourth day was rewarded by the sight of an impressive cavalcade of mailed and armoured warriors with a small number of men of Holy Church. The King of England, informed and summoned, had come to pay his respects. A big man, sweating heavily in the unseasonably hot sun, he descended from his mount and swept through the gateway to the donjon, and was gone. Gilles returned to the home of old Hugh. He would tell them all that he had seen the King, perhaps they would be more impressed than he had been.

The very next day, he was summoned, and he was nowhere to be seen or found. Jacques, a cooper still serving out the seven years of his apprenticeship and the ardent suitor to one of the three women of the household, rather fancied he knew where he might be found. It was a shrewd guess. He was right, the boy was fishing off the quay where the grapes were unloaded. He bundled the boy home unceremoniously, where two burly and intimidating men, sweltering in their leathers, took him in hand. It was an intimidating and fearful moment for all of the family of old Hugh, but Gilles was hustled off to an unknown destination by the two grim faced and unspeaking men, with Jacques trailing after in their wake.

In fact their destination was a return to the Cathedral close once more and to the arcade of canopied shops that sold to the quality directly opposite the Cathedral. One of the larger shops had been cleared of the general public and beneath its awning, in the shade and away from the fierce sun, a table had been set, behind which sat an austere and truly intimidating looking noblewoman. Around were gathered women of her entourage and armed retainers. With a start, Gilles noticed his mother was of the party. She caught his eye and smiled tremulously, cautiously, at him beneath her lowered lashes. Gilles, often wise beyond his years, composed his features into an anonymous and unrevealing mask.

The woman looked very tall, elegant and slender as she rose briefly from her chair at their approach. She looked down her long, sculpted and elegant nose and surveyed him with a certain disdain.

"And this," she enquired, "this is your child, my dear?" Eloise performed a brief but polished curtsy there amidst the horse dung and murmured an affirmative.

"He is a most peculiar child in appearance," The woman observed. There could be no denying this and Eloise shrugged apologetically.

"Attend me, boy," the strange woman commanded. "The

Queen, best and most beloved of all my friends, now sleeps in Christ our Saviour, may her immortal and everlasting soul be blessed. Your mother, she entrusted to my keeping. She is now my responsibility, as, I suppose, you are as well. She will be a companion to me in my own declining years. She will be favoured and will want for nothing."

She beckoned Eloise to her. "The boy will be cared for. You may depend upon it. Make your farewell."

Eloise held Gilles tight to her and sobbed uncontrollably. The boy and the grand lady were united in their discomfort at the sight. Both Gilles and his mother had been totally unaware of any outside interest in their present or future welfare. They held themselves to be as chaff to the wind. But old Matilda had always had plans and any necessary further plans to fall back upon for just about every contingency and every individual that fell within her wide orbit. Eloise, with an additional life pension, was surrendered up to Matilda's oldest and dearest friend Blanche FitzOsbern, the wife of William's oldest companion and childhood friend, currently the governor of still troubled England. Blanche had long coveted the sewing, stitching and embroidery skills of Eloise of La Petite Flague. The girl, in her charge, would always be safe and comfortable, no doubt of it.

It was further decided that the child would enter into the service of Matilda's third son, Henry. It was not that the youthful

Prince had any especial need of further servants, but it would surely give the boy Gilles more advantages and prospects of advancement than elsewhere. Matilda, of course, could simply have left the child to fend for himself, but she had a rare fondness for Eloise.

It was decided, therefore, that Gilles was to leave Rouen and to travel to the west, to the region of the Cotentin where young Henry had large estates and considerable regional influence. He was largely separated and estranged from his parents, who in fact cared as little for him as he did they. Henry, it was generally agreed, was a bad lot. Shortly before her death the Queen, secure in the knowledge of her impending end, had sent for her old friend and had drawn up her Will and its many provisions and clauses and footnotes in great and exhaustive detail. Both old ladies were well acquainted with all the wickedness of the world and the document sought to protect and further strengthen Matilda's many projects from beyond the grave. Accordingly, the document, breathtaking in its diversity and scope, was drawn up by the two old ladies, often giggling at the thought of its various effects upon certain people of their acquaintance, signed, witnessed and secretly delivered to Matilda's favourite and richly endowed religious establishment in Caen, for she shared her husband's love of the infant city, and his dislike of Rouen.

Jacques the cooper's boy was dismissed with a purse that clinked. He was dismissed with the curt statement that the family of Hugh of the Gate need have no fears for the boy, for he was destined for finer things in life. Lady Blanche nodded to the two men, still sweating copiously in their reeking leather vests in the oppressive heat.

She spoke for the last time, addressing the distraught Eloise. "Your child, my girl, is the gift of the Lady Matilda, now with the Lord, to bestow upon whomsoever she deems. She has decided to give him into the care of her most beloved son, Henry. It is to be hoped that your child will rise and prosper."

Gilles was to leave Rouen and travel west to the region of the country of the Cotentin. Here, away from the court by mutual consent, Henry held a large number of estates and much territory. Matilda, in amongst all the other things preying on her mind in her last days, had found time to consider her little treasure Eloise and her strange child. The two old ladies had sat in perfect amity and divided up the spoils and treasures of a long and productive life.

Blanche surveyed the little boy one last time. "Well, little scrap," she said. "You are luckier than in fact you know. Embrace your mother and do nothing that would bring shame upon her head. May our blessed Mother and all the saints bring you many future happy meetings."

Without further ceremony Gilles was given over to the custody of the two red faced and sweating men. Blanche spoke for the last time, to Eloise. "Your son, my girl, is the Queen Matilda's gift to her beloved son Henry." There was a slight pause and an inflection upon the word 'beloved.'

"There he will be schooled in the manners of a gentleman. He may perhaps rise high. It has been made clear that he is the grand child of the man who gave up his life for our beloved King."

Chapter Two: Caen

"I have persecuted the natives of England beyond all reason, whether gentle or simple. I have cruelly oppressed them and unjustly disinherited them, killed innumerable multitudes by famine or the sword and become the barbarous murderer of many thousands both young and old of that fine race of people."
[Ordericus Vitalis]

William, called the 'Rufus' for his florid looks and his doubtful and uncertain temper, was long gone, racing for the coast and in search of a ship, a tide, and the Crown of England. He had remained just long enough to establish this much after the news of his father's death. There were, of course, many who deeply feared this division of Kingdom and Duchy, and between two such fickle and irresponsible sons as he and Robert, not considering young Henry, fit only, it would seem, for a rich purse. He could navigate his own future. All men of good sense held their own counsel. They pursed their lips in private. Affairs in the Duchy and the Kingdom were clearly going to Hell in a handcart. They set about their own plans and in affairs of defence or expansion.

Which left Robert and Henry, moodily and uneasily sharing a

room in a damp and draughty ante room of the Abbeye eux Hommes close to the Church of Saint Stephen in honey coloured Caen in preparation for the funeral. They had never, even as boys, spent any considerable time together and disliked each other's company immensely. Now resentment and envy were added to the stew. In that bare stone room sectioned off and away from the main hall, surrounded by a crowd of uneasy followers and retainers, they either ignored each other or occasionally flared up into shouted words. Robert, angered beyond measure that William the Rufus would take the Crown of England, leaving him to defend a bitterly divided Normandy and beset on all sides by vengeful neighbours, would not be staying for the funeral.

Robert placed his hands on his thighs and levered himself up to his full and inconsiderable height, grunting as he did so.

"Well, brother," He announced. "I am leaving, Paris or Rouen, a matter of indifference to me, whichever is safest."

Henry, aged only fifteen, he of the purse of five thousand pounds of silver, looked up at him and sneered. "So, you'll not stay, not even for our own father's funeral. A fine display of love and respect that is, for sure."

Robert brushed down his tunic. He was ever one for appearances. "Our father," he announced loftily, "would have his Duchy cared for, before any pattering of prayers. Things to do, brother, things to do. Spend your money wisely. I will have need of you and your services soon enough." He gestured to his men, four of them, and they swept out in a body into the chill early afternoon.

And that, Henry reflected to himself, was true enough. He stared at the bare floor moodily for a while. He was nursing a truly evil hangover. He called out to his squire, "Gilles, more wine here." He paused, inclined his head and sniffed. "Do you smell burning?"

The young boy rose from his crouched and introspective position and stepped towards the rough table where a flagon and a brace of rough pewter cups stood. His nose flared. Now he could smell smoke too and there came to his ears the sound of crackling and distant shouts of alarm.

The boy Gilles, in the intervening years and in his time with young Henry, had grown taller Admittedly. He still retained his wary and slightly hunted look, peering out at the world under the thatch of his fringe, his hair, a curious blend of yellow and red, cut brutally and shaved at the back in that peculiar Norman manner. His curious eyes darted hither and yon out at the world and he spoke only when spoken to. He had learned that it was safer and life was easier that way. Life since his service to the young Prince that he had very much grown up with had been crowded and unpredictable and he had been a constant source for bullying and harsh treatment, singled out as he was for his tainted English blood. He had, however, thrived and even prospered. He had learnt a wealth of new things and, with his sharp ears, quite a few secrets that he wisely chose to keep to himself. Now in direct service to Henry, he could put a sharp edge on a weapon. He could speedily butcher, quarter and serve a slain buck or boar or fowl for the table with all due respect and decorum. He had a skill and a natural affinity with horseflesh, could shoe and treat for illness the war horses upon which the Norman state owed so much for its strength and power. If he could survive the almost daily blows and assaults, the unspeakable rage of his master's frequent outbursts of temper, then he could go far and above his station. He was, after all, a squire and in training for his knighthood.

Gilles handed the Prince Henry his fourth cup of the morning. For one so young, Henry drank to excess. With an irritable gesture of the wrist he motioned Gilles to investigate the smell. When Gilles returned a short while later, he bowed slightly, an inclination of the waist.

"The roof, Sire, it would appear to be on fire," he said in the fine and urbane manner that he had practiced so hard at. "In fact there is a general conflagration round about. I would suggest we remove ourselves."

There was a general bundled exodus to the door. Fires were, of course, a frequent occurrence and an ever present danger. They gathered once more outside in the large courtyard adjacent to the Church of Saint Stephen and looked about them. The Church itself, containing the body of the Conqueror, was untouched, being of stone. Instinctively they looked up at the roof. No flames could be seen there, at least. In the rest of the courtyard the fire was general and appeared to be spreading even as they gazed upon it. The timber and thatch buildings around them and the thatch that roofed them, the beams treated with pitch as a preservative, invited the hungry, licking flames.

"The stables," commanded Henry. "The horses, get them out."

Outside the courtyard, the fire had become general. Much of the young, bright City of Caen, the beloved pet project of William and his wife, carved out of the fine local honey coloured stone resisted the flames. Much of the remainder appeared to be succumbing.

The stables was as of yet untouched. In a flurry of sparks, Henry's men led their distressed and panicked mounts out of the building and beyond the infant city walls where they sheltered them at a wayside Inn. Upon their return, some semblance of order seemed to be returning. Files of men had been formed, ferrying water from the many wells or else, more effectively, beating out the remaining flames with branches and blankets. Others were ripping great handfuls of thatch from the roofs or else raking the stuff away from the timbers. People were carrying merchandise and personal possessions and furniture and dumping it outside. Acrid smoke was everywhere. The blackened and shriveled body of an incinerated blacksmith was found in the shell of his ruined booth. No person mourned his death. He was the source of the fire and was known to have been a habitual drunk.

Within the Church of Saint Stephen and before the High Altar, the cloistered calm usually surrounding solemn occasions was heavily underlined by a rising atmosphere of panic unbecoming such a solemn and holy occasion. The eight monks, cowled and anonymous, were doggedly ploughing through plain chant, coughing furtively occasionally from the acrid smoke that had permeated through the Church. They were made of strong stuff and would continue until instructed to stop.

Through training and usage, they determinedly fixed their gaze upon their sandaled feet, thus sparing them the unedifying sight of the near naked, bloated, blue corpse of the former King of England sprawled before them next to an empty stone sarcophagus. The corpse had been dumped there before the steps by aggrieved workmen who had left hurriedly at the first cry at the outbreak of fire. There had been no conversation or discussion as to how to move the sarcophagus, or, indeed, to where, once the service was concluded. William had been on the road for some days now and the incense billowing out from the enthusiastically swung censer went only some way to masking the undeniable smell. The whole affair had all the hallmarks of a spectacularly botched job.

Scandalously, only one man of noble birth who had offered and agreed to escort the bier from Rouen to Caen remained; all others of rank having removed themselves. This man, Ernoul, known as 'the landless', resolutely remained with the monks during the fire; perhaps to ensure there was no backsliding and in reverence to his dead master. Equally possible was the desire for payment for his efforts, he being a poor man and of no estate. The entourage that had set off from Rouen with ceremony and solemnity had drifted off and away with each passing mile until, at the very end, only he was left. Rightly, he deserved recognition and praise. He also deserved payment. Individually and in small, guilty groups, the congregation assembled once more and the Church slowly filled.

Naturally enough, the three bishops present were given pride of place at the altar steps, placed uncomfortably close to the corpse. Saintly old Lisieux had made the journey out of loyalty and respect. A thoughtful and forward looking acolyte had packed a folding stool of canvas and wood for the old man. He sat upon this, head bowed and nodding and shaking with age. He was, due to his advanced years, as deaf as a post. There was a total of seven bishoprics within the Duchy of Normandy, only two others were present. When news of the King's death and of a state funeral to be held in Caen, his half brother, Odo, was in a comfortable semi confinement within the Palace of the bishop of Coutances. A courier from his full brother, Robert of Mortain, brought the news of the death, and of his own pardon and release. Odo had lost no time, of course, in prevailing upon the affable and highly impressionable bishop of Coutances of the necessity and the Christian obligation to attend. They had arrived the previous day and now the newly reinstated bishop of Bayeux stood erect and proud, attired once more in his full panoply, staring fixedly and piously at the simple crucifix nailed up before the altar. He was conscious of his tarnished reputation and of the hatred and fear he still provoked in so many men, so appearance and display was all. He had noticeably lost a fair amount of weight, but then he could afford to. Occasionally he stole a hurried glance at his dead half brother at his side. Coutances, for his part, glanced about amiably and even bestowed shy little waves upon people he recognised. A quartet of local abbots, principal among them being the abbot of Aux Hommes, whose property and living had been relatively untouched by the fire through the Grace of God. It would be he who would present the Eulogy after the Office of the Dead.

Other people drifted in, largely through curiosity or through the wish to be present whilst history was in the making. At the very last minute, when the little Church was three quarters full and before the Office of the Dead, the Prince Henry himself entered, striding purposefully to the front, exchanging a less than affectionate nod with his uncle. Unobtrusively, young Gilles took up a position at the rear of the Church. The Office of the Dead was commenced. The lay members of the congregation, having no Latin or perhaps only the barest minimum, stood in respectful silence, allowing the sonorous Latin to waft over and around them.

Had they understood some of the observations of Psalm Forty, the more cynical or humorous might have raised an eyebrow or even ventured a brief, wry smile: "For innumerable evils have compassed me about: *Mine iniquities have taken hold upon me, so that I am not able to look up; they are more than the hairs on mine head. Therefore my heart faileth me.*"

The all too visible corpse of William was an overwhelming distraction to all there; even as accustomed as everyone present was to the presence of death in their daily lives. Perhaps the corpse should have been placed in the stone sarcophagus prior to the ceremony. Someone, at least, had shown a little foresight in breaking the collar bone and upper arms of the grey blue corpse so that, once frozen and rigid and flung out like a crucifix, they at least were now folded more decorously across his chest. The service was, perforce, truncated. The more attentive and knowledgeable of the congregation would have noticed that, with the 'Magnificat', the end was in sight.

"Magnificat anima mea Dominum; Et exultavit spiritus meas in Deo salutari me..."

Those who were literate and aware in that largely privileged congregation may have sensed the hidden threats contained in the message: *Deposuit potentes de sede, et exaltant humilies. Esurientes imoplevit bonis, et divites dimiset inanes. "He hath put down the Mighty from their seat and hath exalted the humble and meek. He hath filled the hungry with good things and the rich he hath sent empty away."*

The service finally faltered to a halt. People cleared their throats and shuffled their feet, ready to leave. The abbot of Aux Hommes, equally anxious to be out of there and about, tending to his fire wounded foundation, stepped forward a pace to deliver the Eulogy. Everyone stiffened once more in anticipation. The address, delivered in French, was much as anyone would have expected. There followed a list of triumphs and achievements of the Great Man and the respect thus due to him.

The abbot spoke of the late King's love of God and of God's love for him. He addressed then those gathered directly. "Let any man present, speak!" he commanded sternly "Speak! if this man, now with God, has in any way offended him." It was, of course, a purely rhetorical question prior to the actual burial, following which they could all then be about their business.

From the very back of the Church came a single raised voice in angry and strident reply. "Thief! The man was a thief. I declare it!"

There followed a stunned silence at this outrage. The abbot, from the benefit of his raised position on the altar steps, scanned the crowd. His heart sank when he located and identified the source of the voice. The hairs upon the back of his neck rose up. The owner of the voice was a man who was a constant thorn in his flesh. Arnulf of the little farm, by God! It was not the first time they had clashed in the regional quarterly Court of Litigants, these two men. He winced. The man called Arnulf of the little farm had a grievous axe to grind, and it was not the first time he had done so, but at a funeral, at the funeral of the Duke of Normandy!

"Mother of God," he moaned quietly to himself. But the man was not to be stopped, as those about him sought to move away from him, as if he were tainted meat and that this would absolve them of any complicity, he continued remorselessly. "This land is my land, as well you know, my lord abbot. My father's land and his father before him. Stolen!" Arnulf's voice was now a hysterical shriek.

The man's dress, his posture, denoted a person of comfortable standing, well dressed enough and with a pendant securing his cloak. This was a man clearly not in fear of where his next meal was coming from, a courageous man nursing an old wrong done to him and his family and now his blood was up and he had caught his stride.

"Thief I call him. Thief." In the environs of the new city of Caen and the districts thereabouts, this was in fact a common enough complaint and a long held grievance. In the enthusiasm of their youth and their admiration of the location and its possibilities, young William and his new bride of Flanders, Matilda, had fallen head over heels in love with the place. Fully at ease, comfortably bolstered within their own youthful sense of power and immortality, their birth and privilege, the happy couple had set about the unremitting sequestration of all around, occasionally dispelling a judicious purse here and there. Thus, here will stand my new Convent, and here, dearest, a fine new Abbey. Here a new stretch of wall, there a gate and tower, there a fine new road. Soon the entire district had become swamped with enterprising building contractors vying and touting for business, making the air hideous with the shouting and quarrelling of the work gangs and the squealing of wheels. The area experienced a brief local economic boom, followed almost immediately, inevitably, by a spiralling and crippling inflation that beggared many of the local population. William's new found enthusiasm and passion for urban planning seemed boundless and there were many, monied and of high birth, only too happy to participate. Scores of families were thus made landless and impoverished and without compensation whilst this happy dream of release from gloomy and cobwebbed Rouen and all the bad memories had entranced the young and vigorous Duke of Normandy. Arnaulf of the little farm was one such victim, a man deprived of land and revenue.

And here he was now, positively warming to his theme, showing no caution or reserve in his passion.

"My land, this very church stands upon my land, the land of my father and his father before him." His voice rose in pitch. "And for this, I have received not one single coin."

Already, people were converging on him from all directions, intent, at the very least, to eject him. But Henry, son of William, was quicker than any other person there.

"Let no man touch him," he commanded. Henry, nearly at tall as his father but thin as a whipcord, strode to the entrance of the church. Undeniably, his was a dangerous presence and the man Arnulf cringed at his approach. Henry drew up before him, staring him up and down. "I do not wish to know anything about you, or your claims. I share the outrage of all here at this... this insult! I have a mind to set the dogs on you, in the meantime," he reached for a bulky looking purse tied to his belt. Contemptuously, he flung it to the flagstones where it made a dull chinking thump. "You will find in there, in silver, sixty shillings."

In the shadows, Gilles smiled to himself. Indeed, sixty shillings exactly, he had himself witnessed the transaction earlier that very morning. Henry had extracted the sum for petty expenses whilst waiting for the payment of his five thousand pounds of silver. The man dropped to the ground to clutch at the purse. It would have been very foolish indeed to attempt any assessment of the contents there and then. Instead, he scuttled out of the crowded doorway, sidewise and almost on all fours like a disturbed crab.

"If you have a mind to, then call on me at the next Sessions," Henry called after him by way of farewell. He spun on his heel. "And now," he announced, "let us finish this thing."

All present watched, necks craning, as four burly workmen moved towards the body, the plan being to place the corpse within the stone sarcophagus and then to drag it to a side door and ultimate burial whilst the congregation dispersed. Two monks with censers hovered expectantly, waiting to waft fresh clouds of the cripplingly expensive frankincense. William was first raised up by the head and feet and then the men knelt to place him within the stone coffin. They looked up and across at the Abbot, a questioning expression upon their faces.

"Proceed," the abbot snapped, somewhat peevishly. Clearly, none of them was accustomed to being addressed so directly.

Flustered, one replied. "Lord, your Grace, sir. the coffin is insufficient. It will not take him." Mercifully, the exchange passed largely unheard.

"Well," said the abbot, "Apply a bit of force to it, man."

From his vantage point, the abbot could see that, indeed, the coffin was far too small. The lower shins and feet of the defunct King overlapped the stone rim.

"Well, push," he hissed. There came a sound, now audible to all present, as the labourers pushed down on the chest of William.

The sound was similar to that of cloth ripping and then a very loud belch and the audible hiss of gas escaping. The men stepped back hastily, their faces green, as a foul miasma enveloped first them and then those nearest in proximity and then spread to the

Church in general.

To men reared and inured since birth and well accustomed to noxious stenches, this was the worst in life they had ever experienced as the bowels and the intestines of William, former King of England and Duke of Normandy, gave way and then exploded beneath the strong hands of the labourers. To a man, choking, the congregation made for the single exit and the purity of God's air outside. The Abbot, face ashen, muttered a brief Benediction before joining the choking throng outside. He breathed in moist smoke seasoned air, but welcome for all that, as he gestured to the hapless labourers to return inside and make good the havoc they had unwittingly unleashed.

To all others, the Church was uninhabitable. The abbot gagged once more. As he crouched, retching, against the wall, the giant figure of Odo, bishop of Bayeux, loomed over him. The bishop had lost only a little of his customary urbanity and presence.

"Well then, my good abbot," said Odo, "I take it that this is not the usual practice in conducting funerals here in Caen." He surveyed the dispersing crowd. "You are to be complimented. You have a good Latin about you, but remind me never to get buried here in Caen, or anywhere near to you. A very good day to you."

The Bishop of Bayeux strode off and it was several hours before the good abbot thought of a reply that was in any way suitable.

Chapter Three: Upon the Road of God

"For when the head is thus struck, the limbs at once are sick. If the head be sick, the other limbs suffer. Since the head was thus sick, pain was engendered in the enfeebled limbs; for in all parts of Europe peace, goodness, faith, were boldly trampled underfoot, within the church and without, by the high, as well as by the low. It was necessary both that an end be put to these evils, and that, in accordance with the plan suggested by Pope Urban, they turn against the pagans the strength formerly used in prosecuting battles among themselves." [Fulcher of Chartres: *Chronicle of the First Crusade*]

Young Gilles, a gawky and ill shaped boy of sixteen, trailed disconsolately in the wake of his lord and master all the way back to Rouen. He knew better than to open his mouth at any point unless addressed directly. In search of his five thousand pounds of silver, Henry was, predictably enough, in one of those moods that Gilles knew only too well, a youth to be dreaded and avoided wherever possible. He had witnessed his ungovernable rages often enough. Henry's public demeanour of choice was that of a figure, sardonic and aloof; a person permanently and remotely amused by all he saw and heard. In moments such as these, however, he reverted to that of an incensed adolescent, prickly and spitting with ungoverned anger. Mercifully, Gilles, for once, was shielded by a quartet of understandably glum and silent youths of Henry's own age and social background as they splashed through the mud and pot holes in a steaming rain as they resentfully made their way back once more to the capital in search of the hoped for munificence and protection of Robert, now Duke of Normandy.

If Henry's current mood could be best described as foul and unpleasant, then that of his brother Robert was truly murderous. He had not reacted at all well upon learning that his brother's first response to the news of their father's death had been to race to the coast and take ship to England, there to seize the Crown of that conquered land for himself. That this choice of William, his second son, had been his father's own decision came as a blow to the enraged Robert. Largely feared and unloved by the aristocracy, Robert had hardly endeared himself to his own father over the years. Unruly and ungovernable, he had had an unhappy history of backstairs intrigue and open rebellion. His own father had scant regard for him, sneeringly making unkind comments about his height, 'curtmantle' or 'short hose' being the least damning. Under the circumstances, Robert, his eldest son could hardly not feel more than slighted and overlooked.

So, here was his fulminating younger brother, seeking his own place in the sun at the court of his slighted older brother, seeking to secure his own uncertain fortune and his hopes of further land in the west of the Duchy and of his mother's promised estates in England. It was an uncertain and insecure hope, but in brother Robert lay his only chance. Gilles shrugged to himself philosophically, turning his collar up against the rain and as the mud churned up by the riders ahead of him was flung into his face. He had had worse. Doubtless there would be worse to come. This was no time to be raising the subject of his own elevation to the knighthood. In these uncertain times it would be wise to avoid the subject altogether and to consider alternative futures. Gilles was a great believer in going with the flow of things. It had come as no great surprise to learn that at some point Henry had, for reasons of his own, gifted both Gilles and his services to his older brother Robert. Servants were, after all, numerous and replaceable. Gilles had shrugged philosophically when brusquely informed, his not to question the decision. It was a matter of supreme indifference to the brothers and Gilles, for his part, had not cared for the company and the supposed protection and patronage of Henry in the least amount, having formed no fond attachment to the youth at all.

The greeting and welcome at Rouen had scarcely been filial. Robert had been drinking since early morning, not the red wine that tended to sedate him, but the fiery apple brandy of the region that always provoked in him an ungovernable fury. They had all been crowded into a dank stone room at the Tower, Henry's companions wishing heartily to be elsewhere whilst Robert roasted his brother in his anger.

"Two brothers," he raged. "And I want neither of them. Both as bad as the other. The one a hem lifting boy chasing thief, the other a good for nothing whingeing parasite. The Devil take you both."

Henry sat through the whole tirade with an admirable patience, waiting for if not an ending, then at least a pause for breath.

Robert, finally looked up. "All you others, out of here. There are things the Duke of Normandy, by which I mean me, wishes to discuss with his devoted and loving brother in peace, and in private. You, clerk, you shall stay; you may be needed." His embarrassed and fearful audience lost no time in making themselves scarce.

When the two brothers and a very chastened and clearly fearful clerk left the dank stone room some considerable time later, both brothers appeared slightly unsteady on their feet, but in far greater spirits. Robert actually slapped Henry on the back as they both made their way to the stables to set off on their separate journeys. Henry collected Gilles and the rest of his little entourage who had been loitering nearby and sent them off, scuttling away on separate tasks and chores in preparation for what they were told would be a long journey and Gilles was informed of his new change of ownership. As the group re-assembled some time later they were joined by a cart laden with provisions, two wagoners, a string of spare mounts and a score of men at arms One of the group ventured a question as they trundled out of the western gate. The man, an ill favoured youth from Brienne, fancied himself as something of a confidante of the young Prince Henry, though anyone in the company could have told him he had little cause to believe this.

"And where to now, my Lord?"

Henry favoured him with a withering stare. "The gate we have just passed through would indicate west," he said coldly and Guillaume of Brienne lowered his head.

Gilles, some way back in the group and wearing his usual cloak of anonymity, allowed himself a quiet little sardonic snort of amusement. As personal squire to the troublesome Prince, he was better placed than most to judge Henry's mood and to predict and react to his most likely moods and moves. He had developed this skill, along with both tact and tolerance in all his dealings with him, along with patience and forbearance. He had learned also to take each day as it came. His own moods and preferences and personal wishes, he understood, had no bearing or any relevance at all on any outcome. Gilles could well imagine that period of hard bargaining with brother Robert as if he had been a spider upon the damp stone wall of that room. He simply shrugged. What would be would be.

"Not you, Englishman," said Henry. "You are no longer my

concern. You belong to my brother now. Go to him, he is expecting you." And that was that. No fond farewells or words of thanks to Gilles Fitz Earl for all his hard and gruelling years of service. He watched their departure along the long muddy journey west without regret.

Gilles lay, legs crossed and arms behind his head which rested upon his saddle. He gazed up at the vast spectacle unfolded above him. His left side, facing the fire, roasted uncomfortably whilst his right side froze, one of the many vagaries of life on campaign. His mouth was sour and acrid from a combination of poorly cooked and very elderly mutton and local wine, thin, sour and acidic, unwilling gifts from the last village that he and his small command had visited.

In the jagged and flickering shadows on the other side of the fire his men also rested, seemingly oblivious to the splendour and majesty above them. Ralph, commonly known as 'the Contentious' was once more expressing his views and opinions to a largely uninterested audience. Ralph, a man from the badlands on the Normandy Brittany border, seemingly had a view and opinion on most things. Gilles allowed himself to listen for a while. Ralph had been on the lists of the Duke as long as Gilles could remember, as thickset and stocky as his master, he had been publicly whipped on a number of occasions for his views and the loose tongued manner in which he voiced them, particularly for those relating to dogma and religion. Currently he was treating his largely indifferent comrades to his views on the Holy Trinity. His almost casual remarks would have had a churchman apoplectic with rage and reaching for his bell and candle.

A flaring as a shrub of furze caught and crackled in the flames. Mixed with rosemary, it gave off a strong and aromatic scent amidst the brushwood, a further deterrent to the swarms of midges. Along with snakes, large black spiders with a life threatening bite and venomous toads that seemed to lurk under every rock, they appeared to be a speciality of the region. The sudden blaze illuminated the usually genial features of Ralph in stark chiaroscuro as he relentlessly continued to warm to his theme. Gilles surrendered his thoughts to the skies above him, a vast dome of black nothingness, blacker than anything else he could imagine and dotted with countless shining stars more numerous, it seemed, than grains of sand upon the beach. Despite the oppressive heat of the day, in this strange and alien country the nights were bitterly cold. Gilles shivered and pulled his riding cloak more tightly about him. The horses stood and fidgeted in the dark, tethered to a set of crude hitching posts hammered into the ground. Occasionally one or other of them stamped the ground or raised its ears in alarm. There were, after all, wolves in these high hills and they sensed their presence.

At the base of the posts there crouched a small and angry

figure, poised as if to pounce, eyes blazing in anger like the red hot embers of the fire. Cat! This, Gilles had decided, was the best name for the strange creature. Their paths had first crossed not two days since, but Gilles knew with all his being that he had seen that face before! He closed his eyes and then remembered the occasion vividly. It had been in a lonely, derelict and filthy hut on his journey through France.

The Lord Bohemond, Prince of Taranto, had entrusted to Gilles this his first truly independent command; to forage, loot and gather information. Ostensibly, his main task was to maintain contact with similar groups sent out ahead of the main force and to pool information for the common good, though in actual fact his task was to furnish the good Lord with provisions and even valuables wherever he encountered them in this bleak and hostile landscape.

His task completed, he would then return to the column, perhaps with a cartload of mouldering and fly-swept grain, a piglet or two, a brace of chickens or an ailing and emaciated milk cow, its ribs jutting out like a stricken boat wreck. Treasure he had yet to encounter, save for Cat! Gilles, knowing full well the proclivities and grasping manner if not of his master then certainly his subordinates, would not yet surrender up this particular prize. For the time being let the mighty and awesome Lord of Taranto be content with a stringy goat for his supper, to be grateful for a second pressing of olive oil in an old pig's bladder. Let him wait for the satiation he craved in the fabulous city of Constantinople, now growing every nearer. Gilles' mind whirled with possible stratagems and ruses to keep Cat well away from any rapacious Norman, though as of yet he had to come up with any suitable plan of action.

Two days since they had encountered the latest village, a miserable collection of mud and thatch clinging doggedly to a steep slope of treacherous and shifting stone and shallow rooted shrub. Predictably, and perfectly understandably, the few remaining villagers took to their heels at first sight of these dangerous looking Franks bearing down upon them. Word of these strangers was out in the countryside. These men spared nothing and nobody in their path, moving like a swarm of locusts. For the most part the villagers were as nimble and sure footed as the goats they tended in their scrambling exodus down the hillside.

Ever since the good warriors of Christ had received their personal instructions from the Holy Father himself the instructions to not persecute the foreign co-religionists through whose lands they passed were explicit, though widely ignored. These people were also in their own strange way followers of Christ, but this did not deter the army from widescale abuse on their way to fight the Turk. This dubious tolerance had certainly not been extended to the numerous Jewish communities scattered throughout the towns and cities of the Rhineland as the liberators of the Holy Land had moved by, joyfully putting the Christ killers to the sword, looting and burning their homes to the ground. Gilles setting out from Normandy and joining the other contingents from France, had been spared most of this brutality by following a different route that did not bring them into direct contact with the scattered children of Israel. As they slowly advanced upon the city of Constantinople the nervous Emperor received increasing reports of these outrages upon his land and his subjects with both anger and despair at these foreigners he had summoned like a genie from a bottle.

As the villagers made themselves scarce, Gilles and the men he led, sweating profusely under the blazing sun and cursing at the thorns that lacerated their flesh, took possession of their unprepossessing little prize. There were the predictable bins of sprouting corn, some loaves of stale bread, coarse and full of grit from the hand mill, a sack of dried raisins, all the predictable and disappointing plunder. Moodily, the men kicked about and began to fire the thatch, their normal practice.

They found a sole remaining inhabitant in one of the huts, an old man yellow with fever and covered in a sheen of sweat. Thin and emaciated and his chest heaving like a blacksmith's bellows, his eyes rolled upwards, his eyelids the colour of a duck egg. His breath rattled in his chest, clearly the man was close to death. Ernoul and Jacques, two men not marked out by their emotion or sensitivity, glanced at each other and knocked the old man on the head, killing blows, and set fire to the thatch. Gilles stood by the village well, scooping up water. He was unaware of this killing, neither would he have approved.

He approached the two men, a query upon his lips, as they emerged from the hut. From the burning thatch above them and screaming like a banshee, a figure leaped, colliding heavily against Gilles and sending him flying. The creature, briefly in his arms, lashed out with a raking hand, drawing blood from his palm.

The figure was that of a young girl. She screamed at him in an impenetrable language, her eyes blazing with an unquenchable anger that made him shudder. He dropped her to the ground like a hot stone where she howled and writhed like a snake. A girl of indeterminate age aged anywhere between fourteen and twenty. Through her ragged and filthy single garment Gilles could detect the movement of her small breasts as she struggled for breath. He grabbed her wrists to prevent further attacks and contemplated her more slowly. By the Virgin! He would not present the Lord Bohemond with this prize which had quite literally landed in his arms! Let him be content instead with shoddy wine and the goatskin of raisins. By God, he would not surrender her up. Short of dragging her at the end of a tether attached to his saddle, he instead had Demetrios talk to her. Demetrios was a wizened old Greek, skin as wrinkly as a sun dried fruit, on loan for the largely unnecessary purposes of translation. It was to be hoped that at least he could make some sense of the creature's ravings, but the Greek had to admit to failure.

So, for this particular phase of his limited career, Gilles assigned the girl to the care of his tall and laconic lieutenant, Benoit, a free man from the county of Maine. She rode now on his cropper, an unwilling captive, held and prevented from escape in his strong and implacable arms.

In the firelight Ralph continued with his monologue. In his theological speculations he had moved from mere rank heresy to the realms of the absurd. Who really cared about the exact date of Easter anyway? They have a problem with the Trinity? Well, have the Holy Father and their Patriarch of wherever, whatever, strip down and fight it out in an arena and we could all simply go along with the winner and get on with our lives. Gilles took a last covetous glance at the girl and prepared himself for sleep beneath the vast heavens.

In all fairness to Gilles and to his inadequate translator, the girl he had named Cat was a mystery to just about everybody, including her own community and family. This had always been the case and the only person who had been able to reach out to her, her mother being dead, was her father, now also dead and with his home burned about him. Artema, for such was the name given her, did indeed speak a local dialect as strong as a fuller's paddle. Indeed, much of her language was of her own devising. The villagers were in awe of her and gave as wide a berth as possible to this fey little demoness and her strange ways. Her father had been what passed for the head man in the little community and they respected her for that. It was commonly known that she had the second sight, and with hidden powers and abilities that came with it. A single malevolent stare from her and a cow would dry up, a goat would leap from its stall into the void from the cliff, wine would go sour and grain rot. A law unto herself, Artema was left alone and ruled supreme. Of her older brothers one had died of a gangrenous leg and the other two had been sucked into the ever expanding suburbs of the great city and were never seen again, a city as remote as the moon.

Two sisters had died in infancy and a third in childbirth along with her mother. The village was all that she knew and had. Knowing the hidden dangers that lurked everywhere, she seldom travelled far in her search for herbs, poisons and aromatics for the making of spells, remedies and curses, skills she had inherited from her mother.

The community was based on a subsistence economy based upon the crops raised from the grudging soil. People either slowly starved to death or drifted away. There was no money and traders rarely bothered to visit. It lay on no major routeways and visits from a priest on an elderly donkey and accompanied by a single acolyte were sporadic and rare, usually to bury or baptise or to join together in marriage. This Christos of whom he spoke was purely notional and more remote, less real, than the demons who lived in the communal well or the wicked fairies who lived in the rocks and stole eggs and milk and babies, less real than the nymphs of the trees and waterfalls.

With the imminence of a new century, a new millennium, the people of the Christian Europe Gilles had left, great and small, were affected in each their own way and according to their own circumstances. There had been a number of disastrous harvests in the countryside. Floods further destroyed the fields and murrains left sheep and cattle feet up in the unkept pastures. Famine was widespread and local gluts of produce also rotted for lack of transport or the dangers of bandits on the roads Ties and bonds, centuries old, were loosening or being thrown off completely or were else brutally enforced. Neither the Church nor the aristocracy were in any way inclined to temper their authority.

Throughout all of France, the lowlands, across the Rhineland and greater Germany, within the fast growing towns and where a sense of collective pride burned strongly there was the usual round of slump, prosperity and slump again. Prices rose and inflation spiralled, ruining merchants and artisans alike. The fullers and the weavers, the brewers and the masons, all the trades and crafts, dependent as they were each upon the other and their numbers increased by a steady increase in population from the countryside, fell into ruin and susceptible not only to disease, poverty and despair, but also to the stories and claims of any charlatan or mystic who happened to pass their way, and there were many.

The roads that linked them now teemed with the dispossessed

and starving and with crazed and fanatical hedge priests and their devoted followings and increasing numbers of armed bands. One took one's life into one's own hands for all but the shortest of journeys and it was prudent to travel only in large and well armed groups or else not at all. Local lords remained on their estates and waged incessant war on their neighbours over trifles and affronts either real or imagined. Mailed men, younger or penniless sons, haunted the crossroads and fords, extorting blackmail and dealing out violence to their hearts' content.

It felt like the worst of times, the end of days and with the seemingly very real prospect of the end of the world and of imminent judgement. Acts of excessive piety jostled with the violence of the times. The Church, both local and centralised, when it did concern itself, did whatever it could within its powers to denounce ill doing, to regulate and maintain order. Writs and denunciations flew from the pen and the pulpit, but the Church or the monasteries also had their own fish to fry and the sense of impending doom and the threat of damnation and the flames of the eternal pit was overwhelming.

Chains unbound, Satan was abroad and seeking whom he might devour. The Holy Land, the place of Christ's life, the places where he trod and preached salvation, was in the hands of Satan's servants, the despicable Turks. They stabled their horses, so it was said, in the Holy Sepulchre where once he had laid in his manger. They defiled the Cross and defecated and made water on the images of the Holy Mother of God herself. Everywhere in Europe there were reported instances of her weeping tears of blood. The good Christians of the Holy Land were everywhere oppressed and clamouring for rescue. In his unstable and insecure throne in Rome the Holy Father himself grew ever more indignant at these tales of horror, especially when he began to receive increasing numbers of embassies with requests for help from the Imperial Emperor Alexius himself in Constantinople, with his own secular territories and interests threatened by the Turk. The Holy Father began to formulate his own policies for action and at the Council of Clermont in 1095 he preached for a 'Sacre Bellum,' a Holy War, for the destruction of the Turk and the liberation of the Holy Land, which is how Gilles now found himself shivering in the dark in an unknown land and beset with his own personal fears and doubts.

Chapter Four: Beginnings

"Oh, how fitting and how pleasing to us all to see those beautiful crosses, whether of silk, or of woven gold, or of any kind of cloth, which these pilgrims, by order of Pope Urban, sewed on the shoulders of their mantles, or cassocks, or tunics, once they had made the vow to go. It was indeed proper that soldiers of God who prepared to fight for His honor should be signed and fortified by this fitting emblem of victory; and, since they thus marked themselves with this symbol under the acknowledgment of faith, finally they very truly obtained the Cross of which they carried the symbol. They adopted the sign that they might follow the reality of the sign." [Fulcher of Chartres: *Chronicle of the First Crusade*]

A brisk and cold October morning in the year 1095, when the spring felt a lifetime away and with months of bleak and unremitting cold and damp and want stretching ahead. Gilles had positioned himself at the main gate of the township of Evreux in Normandy overlooking the rough stone and timber bridge crossing over the river Iton, a rough and ramshackle affair, very old, precarious and seemingly only kept upright by frequent supplication to the Virgin and the saints. This was the latest location that the Duke's restless itinerary had fetched him and his followers up in. Evreux was a place that featured at least twice a year in the Duke's travels; for the hunt and the local boar, to dispense the law with his customary if not entirely predictable iron hand and to bed a favoured mistress. Gilles knew the place well as a result and was idling away the remnants of the morning at the main gateway to the town for lack of anything better to do to occupy himself with and running a cursory eye over the sporadic arrivals and departures. With his hunting knife he was whittling at a piece of discarded wood and whistling tunelessly. It was a favourite spot for Gilles, after the blacksmith's workshop where all the idle tended to gather for the warmth and the gossip. It was shortly after the hour of Terce. The morning now gone, the remainder of the day lay stretched out before him.

He glanced across the river to the slightly rising meadowlands with their usual complement of labouring peasantry to the ridge line and thick forest above and beyond, a forest he knew to take nigh on a full day to cross before open and cultivated land was reached once more. Gilles had sharp eyes, indeed, he enjoyed a reputation for them and was ever called upon on their many journeys to exercise his talent. There, on the tree line, he detected a movement. He squinted, a small black shape emerging on the track that led away from the shelter of the trees. He waited a moment to allow his eyes time to focus. No sound as of yet, too far away for that, but soon the vague black mass resolved itself into a knot of people, quite sizeable in number, advancing upon the town of Evreux as outraged crows, disturbed, wheeled above them. This was out of the ordinary, to be sure. No casual tradesman or visiting party of clerics, this. Robert, he knew, would be in the hall, drinking heavily and toying with his mistress, or else in the mews, teasing his falcons and making the lives of the stable hands a misery. Either place, the Duke would have to be informed. He stood up and threw the piece of wood aside. Alerting the gatemen of this new arrival, he spun around and made his way to the hall.

It being a physical impossibility to be alone and secluded in any hall, Duke Robert interviewed his strange and unexpected visitor in the full glare of public scrutiny, the man's equally strange mob of followers being confined to the keep under the watchful eye of armed men. In response to Robert's enquiry as to the nature of his visitor's journey, the strange man, emaciated and in rags that shone with dirt and grease and which scarcely covered his modesty, had subjected him to a tirade of hair curling biblical fury.

The stench of him was as palpable as his towering frame, the man was well over six feet tall and skeletal and people sought in those crowded confines to give him as wide a berth as possible as he raked them with a wild red eyed stare. The citadel's chaplain stood at the Duke's shoulder, absorbing the scene with an unusual fascination, a man widely held to be one of erudition and great learning and who had the Latin. The stranger was no local, though clearly a peasant. His French was not of this land, strange and rough and difficult to follow, but he was rattling off quote after quote from the Holy Scriptures directly from the Latin in his vernacular French! In the flood that was assailing the Duke's ears Robert had unusually acquiesced and was simply listening: to promises and exhortations and to direct and naked threats. He sat still before this passionate outburst, knuckles whitening as he gripped the arm rests of his chair and as the strange mystic continued remorselessly with his oration.

"The day of the Lord will come like a thief, and then the heavens will pass away with a roar, and the heavenly bodies will be burned up and dissolved and the earth and the works that are done will be exposed... behold, the day of the Lord comes cruel, with wrath and fierce anger, to make the land a desolation and to destroy its sinners from it..."

The chaplain, entranced, was amazed at the erudition of this extraordinary apparition, at the strange juxtapositions of Holy Writ emerging from the man's mouth.

"You also must be ready for the Son of Man is coming at an hour you do not expect... for there will be great tribulations such has not been from the beginning of the world until now... Children! It is the last hour, and as you have heard that the antichrist is coming, so many antichrists have come, therefore, we have felt this is the last hour... Just as the weeds are gathered and burned with flame, so will it be at the end of the age."

As if exhausted, the stranger lapsed into a silence. In the hall all was still. Duke Robert took the opportunity and leaned forward in his chair. "And tell me, Holy Man, if such you are. What do you want of me? What would you have me do?"

The mystic appraised him for a brief moment, a baleful red stare. "Feed my people," he replied. "Feed my people, and clothe them, for they are the elect of God. Renounce all your riches and follow me to Jerusalem, the Holy City of God. Help me in fulfilling all the sacred prophecies. Take back the city, and death to the Turk!"

There was the briefest of pauses, and then the Duke Robert began to laugh, uproariously. He turned and addressed his immediate cronies. "Which of you desires the Duchy?" he demanded. "Speak now, or forever hold your peace."

Dutifully, the people addressed smirked.

Robert turned again to the mystic. "You," he said. "Go in peace, for you claim to speak the word of God and I shall not lay a hand upon you, though you have offended me greatly. I shall feed and clothe you and your people, do not fear. But I command you to quit my lands. Spread your word where you will, but not in my Normandy."

There followed a further outburst that the Chaplain recognised as deriving from the Book of Revelation as the man was firmly ejected, to join his followers in the keep. His words, dripping with venom and with promise ringing in their ears, his voice gradually receding.

"...the cowardly, the unbelievers, the vile, the murderers, the sexually immoral, those who practice magic arts, the idolators and all liars - they will be consigned to the fiery lake of burning sulphur. This is the second death."

Robert, who could in fact claim ownership to a good percentage of this litany of sins, summoned his chamberlain and his seneschal to his side with an imperious gesture of his bejewelled hand.

"The food and drink, see to it."

He commanded the seneschal to send out couriers throughout the Duchy, to enquire of similar instances of such lèse majesté and investigate them. The answer came back more swiftly than he had imagined. Within the week, while his own particular soothsayer headed towards the border, there came reports of similar madmen abroad, in Normandy and beyond, and each with a more or less identical message. Now that it was generally known he was collecting information, alarmed local magnates from even beyond Normandy were citing instances. A new spirit and word of God was abroad and attracting people in droves. Renounce your wasted lives and embrace God's own Holy city! More alarming yet, there were instances of local aristocrats heeding the call and, setting off to the east at the head of their tenantry!

Robert, amiable and fast living spendthrift that he was, had problems of his own to contend with. He was indeed worried for the safety of his soul and feared damnation as much as the next man and was pious, often beyond convention. He abided by the daily liturgical constraints of the Church, observed the fasts imposed upon him and paid tribute above the odds to local religious foundations. Every so often he was brought up with a start at the realisation that he was fast running out of money. The Ducal Treasury was leaking like the proverbial sieve.

Across the Duchy there were scores of reported instances of civil disobedience and of flagrant tax evasion. In defiance of his law and authority, more and more of the petty nobility were throwing their hand in and hitching their wagons to his bitter rivals; to the King of France, to tiresome brother Henry and to his other despised brother, William, called the Rufus, King of England. Even earlier that year Robert had quietly opened up a channel of communication with the Rufus through the agency of the Holy Father in Rome and his instrument, the Abbot of Sainte Bénigne.

The man was now a regular presence at Robert's peripatetic court, an enigmatic figure, heavy jowled and unsmiling. Both he and Robert kept their own council, as well they might! For what they privily discussed was nothing less than the treachery of the mortgage of the entire Duchy of Normandy to the Rufus for the incredible sum of ten thousand silver marks! Indeed, a down payment had already been received. Not even his crafty and devious uncle, Odo, Bishop of Bayeux, had been able to gain any access to this particular choice piece of information.

But Robert had a balm, a salve for the wound he was prepared to inflict upon the Duchy of Normandy, a treachery that would set his own illustrious father and all his ancestors before him to spin in their graves. He had decided, pious and personally courageous man that he was, to become a warrior of Christ! In Rome the Holy Father, was busily spreading the word and calling for the Princes of Christendom to take up arms and embrace Holy War.

Through his agents, the abbots and the bishops, from the pulpits, all manner of incentives were on offer; the remission of debts, the increase of lands, payments to the cash strapped and the remission of sins and life everlasting to those who fell in the cause. For Robert, enticingly, there was also the offer of the Church's protection of his lands in his absence on pain of excommunication, thus making his pact with the Rufus a worthwhile risk whilst he himself enjoyed the various delights of campaign and acquired an untold fortune in loot, property and possessions, or so he fondly hoped.

To the increasingly entrapped Robert, the temptation was irresistible. In this February of the New Year of 1096 he arose one morning, prising himself away from the drowsy arms of his mistress, ducked his head into the all but frozen water of his ewer and at last decided to make his intentions known.

The teeming, seething city of Rouen once more. Gilles, answering Robert's summons, was curtly informed that important guests were expected and issued with a list of tasks to perform. These guests were expected to arrive imminently for a feasting and a mysterious announcement, to be made in hall when all were finally assembled. The rest of the day went by in a blur of activity, Robert's final words enjoining him to keep his own council.

"Important measures require the silence of your tongue, Gilles, my boy. There is advancement in this for you."

But Gilles, cynical beyond his years, had heard it all before. Dutifully, he hurried first to the stables, there to inform the stable hands and ostlers of a sudden influx of the quality and to be prepared for all events and requirements, at pain of the Duke's displeasure being visited upon them. He left the place buzzing with anxious activity as fresh straw and the best quality oats were sought out. Next, to confer with the chamberlain and the keeper of the Duke's board, two men grown old, crabby and petulant in Robert's service. Both men were inclined to cavil and grumble at these latest strictures and the further strains that this would put upon their limited resources, but Gilles had fully expected that.

"We'll all be beggars at this rate," the keeper of the bench observed mournfully. "We'll all end up with our arses bare and not a pot to piss in." His eyes flickered over Gilles nervously and he licked his lips.

"That's as maybe," Gilles said with some asperity to these two ageing and irritating men. "Might I suggest you share your concern and fears with his Grace?"

Which, of course, they would not, and they fell to the planning of an unseasonable feast in the depth of winter with ingenuity and a sense of growing enthusiasm. They were also given carte blanche to make free with the possessions of the townsfolk of Rouen and the outlying settlements, thus to some extent limiting the damage to their own resources. Fresh fish was seized in copious amounts from the boats at the wharf side and beer and wine from the breweries and vintners, grain and flour from the mills. Geese were strangled and hen coops raided, winter lean pigs were prodded into activity and turned out of the pens, as were prime heifers for the roasting. The grim faced Rouennaise looked on, powerless but with mounting anger, as mailed and intimidating men enforced the Ducal commands. In the countryside, this unexpected feast would make all the difference, they knew, between simply going hungry and actually starving to death.

The first of the quality began to arrive. First in, predictably, from his nearby estate was that inveterate free feaster at any man's board, Robert's uncle, Odo of Bayeux. A man, like his late brother, of formidable bulk and girth, and with a seemingly inexhaustible ability to consume and absorb all placed before him. Gilles noted his arrival with a personal distaste developed years before, observing his piggy eyes darting about from the vast dome of his head, taking in all around him as he was painstakingly assisted to dismount. Making an impressive entry through the gates of Rouen and with a full and sizeable retinue straggling behind them came Robert's cousin, Stephen of Blois and Robert, second of that name, the illustrious Count of Flanders. The Count of Flanders and Robert were well known for their deeply held jealousies each of the other and a long succession of tangled disputes, but, for this occasion at least, they had agreed to sink their differences. In Gilles' own hearing he had heard the Duke remark that it was important to keep your enemies close. The keep and the palace of the Duke became suddenly crowded with strangers and the streets of the city made dangerous and untenable with surging knots of boisterous and drunken soldiery. Sensible citizens kept their own council and kept themselves and their families indoors and their possessions close about them. These strangers brought with them disease, mayhem and murder and a dizzying spiral of inflation in prices. Other minor knights and dignitaries, each with their own followings, straggled in over the next three days in answer to the summons.

At the feast and at a moment he deemed appropriate and when his wife and her women had made their required departure, Robert rose majestically and with dignity to his feet, an impressive feat when bearing in mind the sheer volume of drink he had taken on board. With the bone handle of his eating knife he rapped on the table for silence and attention. Dutifully, the hall fell silent, save for the sound of an over excited nobleman being violently sick as he lay in the soiled rushes.

"Cousins, my most gracious abbot," he nodded to the unblinking abbot of Dijon seated next to him who was sweeping the hall with the stare of a harrier hawk. "Uncle. I welcome you all to my hall and I thank you for travelling to attend upon me in this most inclement season. I hope that the board is adequate recompense for your troubles." His gesture took in all the tables, laden as they were with meat, drink, fine white bread containing few impurities and winter vegetables.

A response was required and, dutifully, there were murmurings and thanks for his munificence. In the shadows, Gilles smiled to himself. Statesmanship was easy once you had the way with it.

"I have summoned you here as I have an announcement to make, and a boon to ask of you." He laid down his knife and leaned forward, taking the weight upon his arms. "My friends. We live in dangerous and troubled times. Let none of us doubt that the Lord of Hell is abroad and seeking whom he might devour. Have no doubt, his snares will take all within them to the pit and to eternal damnation. The signs are all of them out there for any who chooses to look."

The response in the hall was subdued, none there had predicted this rather sombre change of mood.

Robert allowed himself a dramatic pause for effect before

continuing. "But," he said, "through the good offices of Holy Church, I for one have been shown both my errors and the way free of these traps of the evil one." Dramatically, he stretched out his arms to either side, head up and jaw thrust out. "I hereby vouch myself as a warrior in God's Holy Cause. I am pledged to be a hammer in the service of our redeemer Lord Jesus Christ, whose wounds bleed afresh from the sufferings the Turk even now daily inflicts upon Him."

He raised his voice to a screaming shout. "Deus lo Volt," the old war cry that the Normans had made their own. "God Wills It."

In the main body of the hall men fidgeted and shuffled their feet awkwardly, cowed and intimidated by the moment. Then, to the left of Robert, the figure of Stephen of Blois rose to his feet and slammed the table with his fist.

"Here is my word on it too, by the Virgin and all the saints. Deus lo Volt!"

Stephen, a man commonly known to be even more enmired in debt than Robert himself. He looked across triumphantly at the Duke and the abbot, who gave him the briefest flicker of approbation, as, one by one, his followers too stood up and made their own vows to take the Cross. They remained standing, proud and self conscious as they enjoyed the plaudits.

The abbot rose to his feet to make a further announcement and set of incentives. "Be this made known," he announced, "for these are the words of our Holy Father himself."

He enumerated the list of benefits for those who took the Cross, the remission of sins, the protection of the Church for families and land, the prospects of wealth and, as he did so, four monks appeared on the raised dais with bolts of scarlet cloth. These they cut and tore with sheep shears to form crude crosses to be handed out to those who took the pledge to wear emblazoned upon their tunics. The cloth crosses were then sprinkled with holy water by the abbot himself.

"Come now," Robert urged the assembly, "who here will stand with us?"

Not wishing to be outshone or in any way demeaned, the bishop Odo made his ponderous way to his feet. In truth, he was feeling his age and his bones ached, far too old to go gallivanting about on some, to him, hare brained jaunt. But prestige and sense of honour prevailed. He was aware too of the powerful hatred of the Rufus radiating out at him from England and across the grey sea that separated England from France, of the power of his reach. Body of God, but Odo needed his allies too.

"I also," he announced briefly, and then suffered a fraternal and ecclesiastical embrace from the abbot. At least he could enjoy the transitory and genuine applause and praise from all those before him, a rare pleasure and experience.

Robert of Flanders, finding himself outmanoeuvred, was next

to stand and make his vow, along with those of his aristocracy who had accompanied him.

"My friends," the Duke of Normandy urged them all, "You are all my brothers now in this moment and for all time. Come, let us celebrate!"

Thus enjoined, those in the hall settled down for a bout of serious drinking as they admired the strips of crimson red cloth to be sewn onto their tunics the following day. There were those there of a more introspective and spiritual view of what had just happened and its significance. They knelt in prayer, heart felt mutterings up to God that came a poor second in volume of noise to the bellowing of old and much loved Norman war songs.

Gilles, noted all of this with his usual keen interest and sharp eyes. Later that night, as he sought sleep in a warm and pre-claimed straw nook in the stables, he reflected. It had all been, he thought, a little too smooth and polished an event to not have been in some way predicted beforehand. He liked to think himself a bit of an expert on the machinations of the Duke's mind.

And the next morning shortly after Matins he and others of the following were assembled in the main courtyard. It was a bitterly cold morning. their breath emerging in thick gusts of vapour as they stamped their booted feet upon the foetid mix of mud, ice and fractured flagstones. The thirty or so men so summoned found themselves thus inducted into the ranks of this holy army with only the briefest of ceremonies that lacked all of the panache and zeal of the previous evening. They, of course, and being the Duke's men, had no say in the matter and the reaction was mixed, ranging from almost indifferent acceptance in some to a holy fervour in others.

The Duke was accompanied by one of the abbot's creatures, a scrawny an unkempt monk named Martin. In his arms the monk carried a bundle of cloth, inferior to that of the previous night's celebrations, of crosses. Behind them two other men took up station, one trundling a small hand cart carrying a hogshead of wine and a collection of clattering cheap pewter mugs. The other had a bulky leather satchel on his chest.

The gathered men stirred expectantly and Gilles knew what was brewing, his own view was one of anxiety mingled with both of enthusiasm and excitement. Perhaps, he reflected, he had been too long in this often mundane and prosaic way of life. Here was a chance and the undeniable lure of the open road and wider vistas to explore and profit from.

There was also the coveted dangling prize of becoming a greater man; a Chevalier with a following of his own, a man of authority and means. And yes, the promise of remission of sins and the eternal salvation of his soul. Gilles was thoughtful, beyond his years, but was never given to excessive thought on matters theological. He of course attended the necessary and obligatory offices of the Christian day and season and he fasted and made penance when it was required of him, just like everyone else. Beyond that, he did not feel it especially to be his task to ponder on such matters unduly. These were issues best left to men chosen for such matters; the priests and the bishops, the monks and the growing number of wandering religious mendicants. Duke Robert could have adopted a hectoring and belligerent approach, one more familiar to his men. This morning, despite suffering from a crippling hangover, Robert had chosen to adopt a far more genial, almost avuncular tone.

"You are quite correct, my boys, in your conjectures," he began breezily. "We are bound together, you and I, and bound also to an even greater cause, to the liberation of God's own Holy City! You are all to accompany me on this, the greatest enterprise in our God given lives. You are to kneel."

Obediently, the men took the knee, there in that frozen courtyard amidst the filth and ice. The monk, thus directed, shuffled amongst them, distributing the coarse crucifixes of cloth into their calloused and chilblained hands. He muttered a brief Latin prayer to each man in turn.

They, of course, had no understanding of the words, only that they involved an obligation, a promise, a vow. Sensing a less than wholly enthusiastic response, Duke Robert announced, "and a drink on it, my boys. Strong drink. None of that piss they serve up to nuns and old ladies! And my man there, Hervé, has a silver penny for each and every one of you. Nothing debased, all of them unclipped. You have my word on it."

Half grudgingly, the men raised a cheer to their lord at these two welcome prospects. Gratified, he saw to the distribution of the strong drink and the silver penny, each to every man, and nodded to them as they passed him in turn and made their thanks. Thus did Robert the Short, Robert Curtmantle, make his own individual start upon the road to Jerusalem and to salvation.

Chapter Five: The Search for Redemption

"Oh, what a disgrace, if a race so despised, base, and the instrument of demons, should so overcome a people endowed with faith in the all-powerful God, and resplendent with the name of Christ! Oh, what reproaches will be charged against you by the Lord Himself if you have not helped those who are counted, like yourselves, of the Christian faith!" [Fulcher of Chartres: *Chronicle of the First Crusade*]

The departure took place at the gate leading south into the Ille de France and beyond on a brisk morning in mid march and with the promise of Spring and a sense of renewal in the air. The night before, the Duke had spent in prayerful vigil, in his chain mail and with his preferred sword of choice dedicated to the Virgin and laid upon the altar, his gauntleted hands clasped in thoughtful prayer. Gilles spent at least part of the vigil with him, seeking a deep sense of vocation, but finding none. That morning the Duke's wife, Agatha, stood, dry eyed and expressionless on the wall of the city, clutching her two infant daughters close to her as Robert made his farewells to the crowd gathered. It was common knowledge that there was little love lost between Robert and his wife. The good bishop Odo was there, booted and spurred and sweating under the weight of his mail. His following was squabbling and bickering with those of Robert's as they waited for the Abbot of Rouen to conclude his lengthy prayers and oration.

With them were the men of other contingents. Stephen of Blois and his people had recently arrived, Robert of Flanders would join them on the road south, but, all told, beside these great magnates were a combined array of some fifty knights and four hundred men at arms. Added to that were the servants, the cooks and ostlers, the bakers with their portable grind stones laden on to the carts, the blacksmiths with their travelling workshops, the fletchers and hunters, the squires and attendants, a stray apothecary and barber surgeon and, of course, the pious poor wishing to take the Cross. always the poor, accompanied by their own chosen or self elected holy men. Prostitutes and wives added to the throng and the abbot had to struggle to make himself heard above the din of the crowd and the small herd of cattle and flock of sheep kept on the hoof for provisions. Small children, infected with excitement, ran in and out of the crowd and played dangerously beneath the wheels of the wagons. Enterprising bakers and tradesmen plied their wares and opportunistic sneak thieves practiced their own covert skills. All in all, a veritable host numbering nearly two thousand souls.

As with other expeditions starting out all over France and the Low Countries with identical objectives, the host of Robert of Normandy was, at its head, all brave display and martial vigour.

Pennants fluttered in a stiff breeze that plucked at the tunics of men and set up a rhythmic jangling of the accoutrements of horses, dashing the cobbles with their iron shod hooves and striking up sparks. The deer hounds of the Duke and others strained at the leash and commands were barked as the horsemen, formidable in full chainmail, prepared to move off.

Next came the main column of infantry, more slovenly in appearance, carrying their weapons in roughly military fashion and with their possessions and supplies slung about them. Muster sergeants patrolled up and down their ranks, shoving men into line with vile oaths and rough blows. Thereafter, the brave procession degenerated into parody, a squalid circus of the poor, trudging along in the mire with the squealing wheels of the carts, with the barking dogs and the excited shouts of children. Above them there rose the thin chanting of psalms and dirges of a religious nature.

It took some considerable time for the column to finally clear the gates, by which time Robert and his companions were fast receding and tiny figures almost on the horizon. Gilles found time to wonder how his mother fared as he made his way in the wake of Duke Robert. He had not seen her for years, and he very much doubted that they would ever meet again in this life. He murmured a brief prayer before pushing the thought to the back of his mind. The Holy Father had made his thoughts known at a well attended Synod at Clermont in November of the previous year, hundreds of miles way in distant Aquitaine. Robert, of course, had not been present, but he, like many others, had certainly felt the ripples, felt the strength and the appeal of the message. The diplomat abbot had been quick to seize upon a transcript of the Holy Father's supposed exhortation to the faithful and Robert had it read aloud in his hall and had it proclaimed in the market places of his Duchy and from the pulpits:

First the dire warnings from Jerusalem and Constantinople: *"...that the people of Persia, an accursed and foreign race, enemies of God, 'a generation that set not their heart aright, and whose spirit was not steadfast with God' have invaded the lands of those Christians and devastated them with the sword, rapine and fire."*

An appeal to pride and to an elapsed glory followed; a direct appeal to the honour of men lessened by present wordly concerns. *"O race of the Franks, be stirred to bravery by the deeds of your forefathers and of the kings who have destroyed Turkish kingdoms, and established Christianity in their lands. You should be moved especially by the holy grave of our Lord and Saviour which is now held by unclean peoples, and by the holy places which are treated with dishonor and irreverently befouled with their uncleanness."*

And, while the listeners reeled at this grievous news, a timely reminder of the damning futility of their lives so far, there came a powerful and ringing warning and the promise of what could and should be: *"O bravest of knights, descendants of unconquered ancestors, remember what the Lord says in the Gospel: 'He that loveth father or mother more than me is not worthy of me and everyone that hath forsaken houses, or brothers, or sisters, or father, or mother, or wife, or children, or lands for my name's sake, shall receive a hundredfold and shall inherit everlasting life'. Let no possessions keep you back, no solicitude for your property. Your land is shut in on all sides by the sea and mountains, and is too thickly populated. There is not much wealth here, and the soil scarcely yields enough to support you. On this account you kill and devour each other, and carry on war and mutually destroy each other. Let your hatred and quarrels cease, your civil wars come to an end, and all your dissensions stop."*

And, finally, there came the ultimate promise. *"Set out on the road to the Holy Sepulchre, take the land from that wicked people, and make it your own. That land which, as the Scripture says, is flowing with milk and honey, God gave to the children of Israel. Jerusalem is the best of all lands, more fruitful than all others, as it were a second Paradise of delights. This land our Saviour made illustrious by his birth, beautiful with his life, and sacred with his suffering; he redeemed it with his death and glorified it with his tomb. This royal city is now held captive by her enemies, and made pagan by those who know not God. She asks and longs to be liberated and does not cease to beg you to come to her aid. Set out on this journey and you will obtain the remission of your sins and be sure of the incorruptible glory of the kingdom of heaven."*

There could be few in that immediate audience or amongst the many to whom it was subsequently proclaimed, who did not reflect upon the common routine sufferings that befell them on a regular basis. All, great and small, suffered the many hardships of the time, be it the total failure of the wheat or the grape crop, the seizure of lands or possessions, temporary or almost permanent hunger, the ever present spectre of death. 'A land of milk and honey', Heaven on earth!

These words had had a powerful and immediate effect. "There you go," Gilles remembered Robert proclaiming with a self assured shout. "The words of the Holy Father himself! Who cannot be anything but moved and compelled?" He reached for his wine.

Moved and compelled he may have been, as he then, for him, frenetically set about his plans, but others, thousands of others, took more immediate action. The much travelled priest Peter, him they called 'the hermit', had been at Clermont. He had also in his possession a holy letter written by God Himself in letters of pure gold dipped in a feather plucked from the wing of the archangel Gabriel! With the sanction of the Holy Father and the Patriarch of Jerusalem he had immediately set out to spread the message of evangelism and redemption, as far away as England and Flanders, and thousands had flocked to his banner and those who likewise preached. They came in their thousands in response, God's poor, with a sprinkling of lesser aristocracy. God's poor, rushing from the blights of war and famine, drought and disease, people maddened by the endemic ergot of the tainted rye and grasses they ate, the Fire of Saint Anthony, the curse of the Devil, that induced madness, hallucinations and mass visions. Even as Robert, and others, deliberated and planned, the poor were across the Rhine and tearing into the thriving Jewish communities in the cities. At Worms and Mainz, at Trier and Metz and Cologne, the cities went up in flames and they died in their thousands, pagan Christ defying victims of the mob. Even as Robert left the gates of Rouen they, in their turn, were forcing the border and flooding into the Kingdom of Hungary.

The road was thus set. To Pontarlier and the foot of the Jura mountains, a place of arranged rendezvous and one of the best available gateways into Italy and beyond. They moved with leisure along roads that varied from appalling to indifferent as the fledgling spring moved into summer. Robert and his uncle Odo and those others of noble blood could be assured of a welcome wherever they fetched up, far less so their rapacious followers. They were nobles and born to high estate, they represented the Church and the cause of God and hundreds of impoverished pilgrims, desired or not, flocked to their banners.The local quality gladly opened their doors and the contents of their granaries to them, masses were heard and songs sung. As they moved, came confirmation that they were not alone, fractured messages spoke of the progress of Count Raymond IV of Toulouse, accompanied by the Pope's own Legate, Adhemar of Le Puy. Out of the lands of

Lorraine came Godfrey de Bouillon and his brother in law, Baldwin of Boulogne. Unbeknownst to them, in the lawless lands far to the west and south, in the Norman controlled south of Italy and Sicily, Bohemond and his nephew Tancred were similarly moved, primarily not by any spiritual urges, to action. Little need to set the servants to scouring their mail for rust or putting an edge on their swords! They were as sharp and glittering as ever they had been. The transplanted Normans had been a thorn in the Byzantine flesh for years as they raided and seized imperial lands and enslaved its citizens, Here, now, there appeared a readily conjured Holy War as perfect justification for further deprivations.

A rare moment, almost of camaraderie, in a leaking barn south of Dijon. The group, habitually miles in advance of the main column, was sheltering from a sudden downpour that had turned the sky from a sky of brilliant blue to a sullen rain swept grey in an instant. Robert leaning precariously against a sack of sprouting grain, looked about him for support in removing his sodden riding boots, fine things of the best Spanish leather with embossed designs stamped upon them.

His eye fell upon Gilles, nearest to hand, and he summoned him over. Gilles sighed, it was one of a number of similar occasions, both before and during the campaign he had been called upon to perform mundane and servile tasks. He knelt in the filth of the barn floor and resigned himself to pulling off the Duke's dung encrusted boots. But the Duke, to his surprise, was inclined to be comradely and amiable.

"I would imagine," he observed, "that your father, the English Earl, would expect no less."

Gilles was taken aback to the extent that he actually rocked back on his heels. Over the years, the Duke had made no reference to Gilles' English blood. Indeed, he had no idea that the Duke was aware that he was the son of Waltheof, the martyred Earl at all.

"Oh yes," Robert continued, "many times."

He chuckled without malice, "and yet here you are, with the shite from my boots all over your aristocratic paws."

Gilles made to demur, but Robert held up one hand, still in its gauntlet. "No, no. it is the wheel of fortune, Gilles my boy. the wheel, it turns. And so shall it for you, mark my words. The time will come, and soon, when a man will do the same for you, and you will not remark upon it as anything out of the ordinary."

They watched together in silence as water dripped in a dismal flow from his boots and then Robert turned to other matters, instead talking to his uncle Odo, shivering and sheltering morosely in that same derelict barn. Inwardly, Gilles was elated, elated that his own lord, the usually unthoughtful Robert, had so sharply encapsulated his most inner desire. There was merit indeed in this Holy War.

There was, however, little merit to be gained from the enterprise for those not involved in it, for those who at best tolerated the passage of this host and for the many who in fact actively suffered from it. Approaching Pontarlier, the land rose dramatically towards the distant peaks of the Alpine ranges. The land through which they moved had changed dramatically, the ordered fields gave way to meadows of grazing sheep and cattle and then goats, settlements became poorer and scarcer, the people wilder and giving greater evidence of a transitory, more nomadic nature.

Where possible, they fled and hid their possessions from the approach of Robert's army as it made its increasingly more difficult way to Pontarlier and the appointed meeting place. The nights were colder and the Duke's control over his own men grew less as they began to loot and pillage where they could. There seemed to be no central authority present to prevent them, the land being disputed between the King of France, several local magnates and the Pope himself, Robert took upon himself to exert authority, occasionally stringing up various of his men whose crimes were too blatant to either disguise or condone. On one occasion it was to Gilles, beginning to rise high in Robert's esteem, he gave responsibility for justice to be done, and in so doing Gilles had his future, or at least a part of it, foretold to him.

It had been a squalid affair; an isolated village high above on its hill, a few huts of wood and thatch, a semi- derelict chapel, a barn, and a hen coop, the noise from which had first attracted the raiders. They came in the night in a rush, seven starving men who found chickens, eggs and a young girl to rape beside a warming fire. Robert upon learning of the crime chose to be incensed, he who had so far condoned so much. He raged and swore that these godless men had brought the whole enterprise into disrepute. The men had fled, leaving only three to face his wrath. This he visited upon them in the form of young Gilles and a hanging party and had them delivered to the same village to which they had brought ruin and shame.

The villagers watched in silence as the three hapless coop robbers were tied to a convenient bough of a tree and launched into space and eternity. Along with the villagers, his face impassive, Gilles watched the final struggles of the kicking men and as they voided their bowels and bladders, swinging blue faced and goggle eyed. He had seen death before, and doubtless would see it again. These faceless men meant nothing to him.

A hand plucked at his sleeve. The person who had had hold of him was a woman, tiny and withered and incredibly old, her face lined like a shrivelled walnut. Her eyes, however, were of a piercing blue and seemed to burn through him. Instinctively, he made the sign to avert the evil eye. She seemed to delight in this and chuckled, a sound of swift water passing over pebbles.

"Much good that will do you, my lordling," she said. Naturally, she was toothless and her particular form of French barbaric to his ears. Nonetheless, he understood and made to withdraw his arm from her grasp. "The likes of you have been this way before, and devil a doubt, will come again," she observed. "We thank you for this justice, but we would thank you more for new chickens and the eggs they make. You have the means about you, I know."

Gilles was at once on his guard, for he had a purse of copper coins in his wallet for this very purpose, to make amends. Robert had bestowed this on him not through guilt or penance, but because he did not wish for his supply of water to be poisoned or for his horses to be hamstrung, one of a number of ways in which the local populace could blight his progress.

"The girl was my granddaughter," the old woman continued. Gilles noted then that the villagers, who had all turned up for the spectacle of the three hanging men, treated her with deference and not a little awe. "She is just a little thing, and she will die in childbirth, cursing these men with her very last breath." She spoke with utter certainty and then winked at him. "This I know, just as I know that within your purse you have eight copper coins to purchase our good will. This money will be spent, amongst other things, on two milk goats and a billy. One of these goats will be lost over the cliff, but the billy will father good, strong young on the remaining one."

The men of the escort around Gilles repeated his gesture against the evil eye and, with a curse, one moved to restrain her.

"Let the old woman be," Gilles commanded and, intrigued, he

turned to her. "And what else do you know, old one?" he asked.

She cackled good humouredly. "Oh lots, my little prince," she said. "Most of the money you carry will be pissed away in repairing our chapel dedicated to saint Anne, not that she ever did us any favours. The church will be struck by lightning and burned to a crisp within the year." She fairly hooted with merriment at the prospect. "This I know for a fact, and also I know all about what is in store for you, my fine young prince. Would you have me tell you?" She gestured to the open doorway of a nearby hut, blue smoke trickled idly through a gap in the roof. He could smell cooking.

"In there," she gestured, "if you would have me tell you, in return for your coin, though that is already owing to us."

Gilles' companion, a man named Berthold, objected, making to restrain him. "I do not like this, Gilles. It has the reek of darkness and bad luck about it," he warned. Gilles shook him off, "and you were not, I believe, invited," he said to him, ducking his head and brushing aside a screen of rough sack cloth, he entered the hut.

Darkness, smoke and an overpowering and pungent smell of humanity and strange herbs. A young girl lay on some spread straw. She stared up and right through him, wide eyed and far seeing. She said not a word to him.

"My abused granddaughter," The old woman said by way of introduction. "Do not heed her, she will not be here long in the general scheme of things."

The girl nodded, not averting her wide eyed gaze. The old woman threw something on the small fire. There was a blue flash, momentarily, and the sound of crackling. "Sit," she bade him. "Sit, and later tell me what you see. Drink this."

She thrust a rough clay pot into his hand. The liquid it contained was bitter and foul tasting, like drinking mud. He wondered, briefly, why he had agreed to this. A sense of whirling smoke, the strong smell of burning, of ash. With his eyes clenched tight, he could nonetheless see debris swirling in the air, as if agitated by a tempest. The sound of fire catching and taking hold, a sound like the ripping of linen sheets. He could hear suddenly the sound of many souls screaming in torment, could feel their souls brushing against him as he seemed to fly, fly high above the spinning earth. And then there came a human face, but with the eyes of a cat, feline and almond shaped. It stared at him, unblinking, unwavering. The light from the face emanated, sometimes dimming but then increasing, but always there and at times too bright to look at. He knew then that he would never forget that face.

He was flying high above a rocky plain, not floating but flying, at some considerable speed, for the ground sped past below him. On the rocky plain was a city, tall with towers and high walls. He felt himself swooping down like an eagle, rising and then swooping down upon it and observing cracks appearing from ground level and spreading upwards in great cracks and falling masonry, great jagged lumps of it. In the midst of it all he was aware again of the screams of souls in torment. He could hear it and feel their pain, a rising and never ending pain and anguish. The face of the human cat that had been flickering at this point with intense clarity, and then he was awake, earthbound and blinking violently, attempting to clear his head in that dim and foetid interior of the hut once more.

"Do you wish to tell me?" asked the old woman, back in his vision once more and as his eyes adjusted to the light.

"No need," he assured her, "for I think you know already."

She nodded. "To be sure," she agreed. "I do. You have seen the destruction of one of the greatest things on what some call God's earth, greater even than the new Rome, to which you are heading. A great destruction, and you will witness the fall of both ordinary mortals and great men alike, and you will play your own part in their fall and damnation." She paused to allow him a moment of reflection and remembrance.

"There was," he said hesitatingly, "a woman."

Once again she chuckled, that sound of rushing water over time smoothed stones. "Indeed there was, there is, my little princeling. Mark her well, for she will be both your light and your darkness. Remember." She stood up briskly and rubbed her palms, as if to free them of dirt. "Then begone and trouble us no more. Those bodies on your hanging tree. We will dispose of them and give them their three feet of earth for them to lie in. I shall make the necessary words over them to prevent their wandering. Now, begone. Give me your purse, as you were bidden to do and leave us in peace, my little lord." There had been an element of pity and complicity in her voice, now there was only contempt.

Groggily, he stood and made to leave, all the while shaking his head. He reached for his purse and flung it at her.

"You made the sign against the evil eye, a while back," she noted. "I have one further thing for you," she said. She handed him a small envelope of kidskin with two strings of hide to place around his neck. "A little keepsake, princeling, a token. Perhaps it will keep you safe from harm; perhaps not."

She smiled at him through the ruins of her teeth, his last image of her. He spun on his heel and was gone and out into the light of common mortals once more. A later and subsequent scrutiny of the object contained in the little purse revealed a piece of bone, it looked like a human finger. He debated throwing it as far from him as was possible, but decided on reflection to keep it. He chose to believe that it would deter evil and bring him luck.

Chapter Six: Italy

"Jerusalem is the navel of the world; the land is fruitful above others, like another paradise of delights. This the Redeemer of the human race has made illustrious by His advent, has beautified by His presence, has consecrated by suffering, has redeemed by death, has glorified by burial. This royal city, therefore, situated at the center of the world, is now held captive by His enemies, and is in subjection to those who do not know God, to the worship of the heathen. Therefore, she seeks and desires to be liberated and does not cease to implore you to come to her aid. From you, especially, she asks succor, because, as we have already said, God has conferred upon you, above all nations, great glory in arms. Accordingly, undertake this journey for the remission of your sins, with the assurance of the imperishable glory of the kingdom of heaven." [Robert the Monk]

Pontarlier was the highest community that Gilles had ever seen. It was summer, but on the early morning that Duke Robert's own contribution to God's war finally clattered across the treacherous river Doubs thin tendrils of mountain mist were wrapped around the buildings and figures emerged into view as if from a fog. With the Duke's party, Gilles peered around at the town's central market place. Habitually, the town had a permanent community of perhaps one thousand souls, but new arrivals, visitors, travellers, merchants, were always a feature in the clement months of good weather. The town lay on the old Via Francigena and the old route between the north of France and the lowlands and Italy, encompassed all about by the crags of the Jura mountains. Now, the population was five times above the usual figure, swollen by arriving Crusaders. Robert's arrival had added perhaps two thousand more.

Others had already arrived. Robert's cousin, Ralph, the exiled Earl of Norfolk had quarrelled violently with the Rufus over some legal and financial matter, which made them allies of a sort, despite Robert's active dislike of the man. Still, their initial greetings were cordial and effusive enough. As were those of The Counts of Montgomery and Mortagne and the Duke of Brittany. They were obliged to wait for nearly a week, crowded into the narrow spaces available and fouling the river for miles around, dicing and quarrelling irritably over the faintest of slights as the days passed while they waited for stragglers and late arrivals. The latecomers slowly swelled the population to beyond breaking point; the men of Walter, Count of Montgomery and Mortain, the sons of old Hugh of Grandesmil, and the devilish Hugh of St Pol, to whom all afforded as wide a berth as possible; it being widely known that he indulged in ungodly practices and consorted with witches, jostled, brawled and argued incessantly. When the convened council of nobles finally met it was decided that they could wait no longer. Let late arrivals make their own way. Leaving aside the hundreds of servants and camp followers, the knights and men at arms numbered at least three thousand men. It was, all agreed, a formidable host, more than most there had ever seen gathered in one place. Let the Turk tremble, they were irresistible. Despite the usual predictable objections over precedence and lineage, Robert was appointed as head of this unruly army, sharing the honour with Robert of Flanders. The good folk of Pontarlier breathed a collective sigh of relief as the last of the army finally disappeared into the mountain passes that led into Italy.

It took very little time for rifts to appear, growing in size like the fissures and fractures of the rocks of the high Alpine pastures through which they made their troubled and disturbed progress. If the rich and favoured could not learn to govern their temper or passions then why should the ordinary man? Odo was universally loathed for his ever preening haughtiness, Robert for his fondness for drink, Stephen of Blois for his general disdain and his habit of taking the more comely of other men's camp followers, the Count of Flanders, likewise, for his light fingers with the possessions of other men and Hugh of St Pol for being simply who he was. By the time the sunlit plains of Italy finally emerged out of the mist, the army was fractious and so riven with mutual dislike and suspicion it was in danger of falling apart.

Speeding across the baked plain and towards Fidenza came an emissary of the Papal Legate, Adhemar of Le Puy. In the saddlebags of his labouring, froth foamed mount came oil for the smoothing of troubled waters and an extract from the Holy Father's statement at Clermont, the call for brotherly love, and, beside the lure, the goad: *"I am told you are so weak in the administration of justice, that one can hardly go along the road by day or night without being attacked by robbers; and whether at home or abroad one is in danger of being despoiled either by force or fraud. Therefore it is necessary to re-enact the Truce, as it is commonly called, which was proclaimed a long time ago by our holy fathers. I exhort and demand that you, each, try hard to have the truce kept. And if anyone shall be led by his cupidity or arrogance to break this truce, by the authority of God and with the sanction of this council he shall be anathematized."*

The Legate had had no means of knowing there had been dissent and division in Robert's own ranks, but it was a shrewd supposition and Adelmar, far away and travelling through the troubled Balkans with the Count of Toulouse was, in addition to all his other qualities, a truly shrewd man. The pilgrims listened to this timely admonition in a respectful silence amidst the rubble and dust of the foundations of the new Cathedral currently rising up to honour the local saint Donnino. Odo, in his best vestments, led the service and all exchanged the kiss of peace with solemn vows of brotherhood, save for Hugh of St Pol and the oldest son of

Grandesmil whose skin condition had worsened to the extent of all now believing he had developed leprosy. Out of the corner of his mouth, Robert muttered, "I would rather kiss the arse of a witch. Fresher and fairer by far." Gilles smiled at the ill-suppressed sniggers and guffaws. In a brooding mood of penance and guilt mingled with thoughts of a continued revenge, the group thus moved onwards on their way south.

As the combined group made its leisurely way south they encountered numerous fortified towns, first on the sun-baked plains and then perched precariously upon hill tops, their fortifications and towers thrusting upwards like aggressive fists. None disputed their passage, on the contrary, they were actively welcomed and encouraged to repeat their Crusader vows and recruit in the market places. The ever curious and acquisitive Odo took full advantage of the effusive welcomes and lost little opportunity to admire the ruins of the glorious past spread before him like a feasting table and to appropriate for himself and add to his growing collection of portable curios back home in his palace at Bayeux. He had long since discovered the true identity of lineage of Gilles and it pleased him, for his own reasons, to request of Robert the loan of his young servant and natural born son of an earl of England. Robert had no especial objection to this, though he was aware of his uncle's penchant for young and well formed men. Good-naturedly he would wave his assent. He had other matters with which to concern himself, the hunt and the feasting tables of an ever increasing number of followers and the sycophantic local aristocracy. There were the welcome blessings of the church and a free eye to wander over, and then select from, the equally large numbers of beautiful and well born women only too available to him. What Odo chose to get up to was of no concern to him.

"Bring him back safe, my uncle," he would say, "in much the same condition he leaves, with a little additional something for me for the loan." Robert was ever short of immediate funds.

And so Odo would mount his fine old grey mare and set off with an escort to spend an enjoyable day or two poking about the ruins and conferring with elderly abbots and local aristocrats and employing the remarkably fast growing linguistic skills of Gilles to smooth the way. Churchmen thrust much coveted ancient manuscripts in Latin and in Greek into Odo's arms, a local magnate would hand over a prized marble statuette of a nymph or goddess, chipped with age, or a still glittering cameo of a long dead Emperor. Odo would raise his hand in solemn thanks and benediction. Occasionally silver would change hands, most usually a blessing would suffice,and the knowledge that the approval of God was bestowed upon the donor, no payment was required. And on their expeditions the bishop would quiz Gilles of his past. Here, Gilles could tell him little. Indeed he knew little and was overawed by the man, but the bishop seemed content to have an earl's son as his temporary servant and cup bearer. It concerned Gilles a little that the bishop should know of his history, but Odo seemed not to care and, instead, spoke freely to him about his own life as they travelled from abbey to derelict castle or to some young and thriving commune.

Weaving their way down yet another perilous rocky path from one of the many hill towns that were to be encountered everywhere and with their panniers satisfyingly full, Odo was in expansive mood.

"Tell me, young Gilles, of your grandfather," he demanded. "He was a true Viking of the old stock, was he not?"

Gilles was understandably cautious in all his conversations with this elderly and dangerous warrior bishop. He grunted in a non-committal manner by way of reply.

Odo laughed at his discomfiture. "Oh yes, my boy. I know a lot of things that would amaze and discomfort you. I collect facts about all manner of things. I am, you see, a collector of fine things. Hence our little journeys together." He patted his full saddlebags by way of affirmation. "Speak, it amuses me and it serves to pass the time." It would be some time before their next rest and Odo sought diversion. Gilles paused, uncertain of what to tell and what to omit. When next he spoke, it was with pride.

"My grandfather was indeed a true Viking, your Grace. Of the line of the Danish Kings of Upland. They called him "Bigni", for he was a giant of a man. He was great in the service of the Danish Cnut who took all of England for himself and made him Earl of

Northumbria, which my grandfather took and kept against all comers. There was no greater warrior in the whole of England and beyond."

Odo nodded approvingly, motioning him to continue. "All knowledge is strength, and strength is power," he murmured.

"Your Grace?" asked Gilles.

Odo waved his gauntleted hand dismissively. "Nothing," he said. "Pray continue."

Gilles wetted his lips and continued. "It was my grandfather who took revenge upon his dead son by bringing the great Mac Bethad mac Findlaich of Alba, the slayer of his son, to combat, and who killed him."

Odo frowned. "The name is new to me," he confessed.

"Perhaps, your Grace, you know him by his other name, MacBeth."

The bishop smiled in delight. "New information, my boy. I shall make a note of it, you may be sure, continue," the bishop seemed to be staring into space.

"In the end," said Gilles, "death came to him in a plague that struck the host of the Northumbrians. Hundreds died, but my grandfather defied this death that loosened the bowels and stole the dignity of brave warriors."

How, the bishop wondered, had this boy acquired and retained this family knowledge? This brat, this little spawn of a rat, whose horizons been confined to the limited boundaries of the Lord Warenne's tawdry little fiefdom? Gilles spoke with fierce pride.

"So my grandfather jeered at death, and spat in his face. He had his best ring holders, those that yet lived, dress him like a Viking in his full armour. And, holding his battle axe and shield, he leaped from the walls and cheated this cheap and soul destroying little death by finding a greater and far more noble one worthy of him on the rocks below."

Odo was impressed. He had never heard so many words from the youth before. They rode reflectively in silence for a while. Ahead and below them they could see the encampment of Duke Robert's army at rest. Tomorrow the army would move on. Blue smoke curled upwardly in anticipation of the dusk that would soon fall.

At length, Odo broke the quiet. "A fine man by all accounts, my boy. He would have given us pause for thought, had he been at Senlac when we beat Harold and the English. I was there you know," he added unnecessarily, for all knew of the prowess of Odo, the fighting bishop. They had heard the stories time and time again.

Wisely, Gilles made no comment, neither would it have been his place to do so

"A Viking," Odo continued, "your grandfather. As were my own ancestors, when all is said and done, for are we not the Danish

Normanni who raided and took their land from the French at the point of the sword?" Clearly, no affirmation was required and so Gilles held his tongue.

"My late brother, William, King of England and Duke of Normandy," Odo spoke as if Gilles required reminding of who his brother was. "Yes, we are both of the race of Vikings. William's own father was a case in point, my boy. They called him 'the Magnificent', you know, or else, 'the Devil.' It largely depended," Odo chuckled to himself, "on whether you incurred his praise or his anger. Not a man to be crossed."

Their arrival at the camp had been noted, an outrider mounting to ride out to meet them.

Odo sighed philosophically, a long exhalation of breath. "One last thought, my boy, before we journey on to shame the Turk. Robert the Magnificent, or the Devil, call him what you will. He travelled out to the Holy City, you know. He did not make it back. His bones rest in some obscure graveyard somewhere. I am mindful of the fact that this is the fate that lies ahead for many of us." He leaned across the shoulders of his fine grey mare and fingered the collar of Gilles' tunic. "But you, my boy, I feel that you are destined for fine things. I feel this. Do not disappoint your fine Viking family."

And there the bishop let the matter rest. Once more Gilles was gripped by a sense of the future, as he had been by that eerie old woman and her own seemingly deranged predictions back in the high lands and the mountains. He shivered and felt her gift about his neck, the single bone in the kidskin pouch.

Another rise in the ground, affording another view of the land beyond stretching into another valley. As with all the others so far viewed, it looked prosperous enough to the eye. There were the expected heavily tilled fields leading up to the high lands dotted with vines above and the blue and heat hazed brim of mountains beyond, encircling them all like the rim of an upturned bowl.

At the head of his entourage, Robert, Duke of Normandy and thwarted King of England, paused to observe the usual scurrying figures of the local peasantry as, alerted by his presence, they rose from their stooped and labouring postures in the fields to scurry to the sides of the road in order to gawp at and note his passage. Robert, pulling his gauntlet off with his teeth, sighed extravagantly.

The day, near noon, was oppressively hot and he was weary, hung over and feeling the effects once more of a long day in the saddle, his mouth acrid with the acid aftertaste of the very young wine of the night before and left his head throbbing. The bright light hurt his eyes and only a sense of his own importance prevented him from leaning from the saddle and emptying the contents of his stomach onto the rocky path beneath. Duke Robert was feeling very aggrieved. He had spent his entire youth and adult life, it seemed, in racing up and down Normandy and beyond, defying and fighting his own father and his utterly untrustworthy and treacherous brothers. Denied the English throne, as was his right as oldest child of the Conqueror, he had seen both his own fortunes and the Duchy of Normandy dwindle as a result of his own excesses and the perfidy of others. Now, at last, he was a true prince of Christendom, a bulwark against the threat of the pagans. He loved and cherished this new lease of life. The mare he habitually used for travel took the opportunity of the pause to drop its head to crop at the sparse vegetation of the rocky track beneath.

Robert shook his head, regretting the movement as another wave of nausea struck him. A powerful prince, a defender of Christ! and yet... and yet a message from the Holy Father himself had been read to him only the previous evening in his pavilion as he feasted. The Holy Father regretted the act, but he was obliged to deny the Duke the triumphant entry into the city of Rome, now just a short couple of days travel away! Instead, he was to continue his journey unhindered and with all haste to where boats awaited him and his men to the lands of the Emperor of Byzantium and the waiting hordes of the pagan beyond.

This was a grievous slight indeed, but even Robert in his anger and nursing his hangover could detect the significance of the letter. The Pope neither wished the cost of either supporting or bribing this force of men of doubtful loyalty or of weaving them into his political schemes. His men, off the leash and loose in the crumbling and decayed city, were a threat to both the Pope and the existing uneasy alliances of Rome. Equally grave was the prospect of standing by, a helpless onlooker, as his own force, his pride and joy, became whittled away by violence, dispute and dissension in the back streets of an alien and threatening city. Such an event was unthinkable. Instead he was obliged to smile and nod politely and ply the Papal messenger lavishly with gifts, compliments and strong drink.

The other ingredient to this potent and unsettling stew was the ever present fact of the existence of the unruly and unpredictable tribe of Italian Normans who had been making their own mark on the shifting fortunes of the lands of Italy for close on to a century. Now, as his army moved out of the Marquisite of Tuscany and into the so called and highly disputed Papal states, Robert was to come up close to these troublesome distant cousins for the first time and be forced to recognise that one either ignored or underestimated this strange, proud and restless breed of men at one's peril. Far sighted Gilles, at the Duke's shoulder, detected movement along the valley far in the distance.

"There, your Grace," he pointed. Robert followed the gesture, squinting into the sun.

"Just so, Gilles. Thank you." He called out to his chamberlain. "Herve, we have guests. Let us prepare for them, a proper welcome and no stinting, mind. Inform his Grace and my lords."

With a sigh of gratitude, Robert dismounted, welcoming the opportunity to take his ease whilst about him his attendants scurried in preparation. Gilles drove three small stakes into the ground behind the Duke and draped a horse blanket over them, affording the Duke shelter and some relief from the baking sun. Robert licked his dry and chapped lips.

"A little wine, I think, Gilles, and some of those raisins with bread to break my fast."

Gilles nodded and withdrew while Robert focussed on the approaching group, now coalescing in the shimmer to reveal a sizeable force of mounted men.

Chapter Seven: Zoe

"But Bohemund, powerful in battle, who was engaged in the siege of Amalfi on the sea of Salerno, heard that a countless host of Christians from among the Franks had come to go to the Sepulcher of the Lord, and that they were prepared for battle against the pagan horde. He then began to inquire closely what fighting arms these people bore, and what sign of Christ they carried on the way, or what battle-cry they shouted. The following replies were made to him in order: "They bear arms suitable for battle; on the right shoulder, or between both shoulders, they wear the cross of Christ; the cry, 'God wills it! God wills it ! God wills it !' they shout in truth with one voice." Moved straightway by the Holy Spirit, he ordered the most precious cloak which he had with him cut to pieces, and straightway he had the whole of it made into crosses. Thereupon, most of the knights engaged in that siege rushed eagerly to him, so that Count Roger remained almost alone." [Gesta]

In a time and in a place that tended to create and throw out into prominence hard boiled and dangerous men, Jordan de Drengot was a man of such a bloodstained and diabolic reputation that even the far from saintly Drengot family held their distant cousin at a respectable arm's length. The man, to be sure, had his distinct and almost unique uses and talents and the ruling Norman powers of the region tended to employ him for the skills in which he excelled, as an assassin and a strong armed thug seemingly lacking in any scruples. Thus, from time to time, he would be enticed out of his rocky eyrie in the County of Aversa with his collection of cut throats to exact payment or punishment or to serve up justice to any number of locals who had in some way attracted the notice of the local powers that be. His name, as a consequence, was known and feared by the crumbling remnants of Lombard authority, Papal representatives and the church in general, and by the Moslem and Greek inhabitants to the south in particular.

Jordan de Drengot had become in his career an immensely rich man and now for the first time in his life he had been called upon not to display his usual skills but rather perform a task requiring tact, diplomacy and an array of subsidiary talents such as hospitality and the ability to be charming and entertaining. The man was understandably baffled, but the incentives, it had to be granted, were excellent.

Accordingly, Jordan had dressed fittingly, with a fine loose tunic over his chain mail and his prized Spanish riding boots buffed to a gloss. He wore his best cloak of striking crimson that almost matched in colour the leather of his saddle and the harness of his horse, a fine jet black creature of great spirit of rolling eyes and flashing teeth. Jordan was wholly aware of the figure he presented, alarmingly tall and thin and sinewy as whipcord, as he buoyantly paced ahead of his company. With him travelled his chaplain, almost as dissolute and lax in his morals as his master, a group of thirty warriors, armed to the teeth and carefully selected for their skills and all the impedimenta of the mobile camp, servants, wagons and mules laden down with panniers. Also travelling with him, and close at his side, as was only fitting, was his extraordinarily beautiful young bride, Zoe; for this was also an occasion requiring display and measured ostentation. Next to his string of horses, Zoe was the most prized of all Jordan's possessions.

Zoe was his most recent acquisition, and one which he displayed with pride. His new bride, not yet twenty, rode behind Jordan with her three female attendants, one holding a parasol valiantly above the head of her mistress to protect her pure and unblemished complexion. Upon his first glimpse of her, the headstrong warrior turned mountain brigand was determined to have her. This had been a first glimpse in the hall of her father, a minor Byzantine tax official with claimed links to the best blood that the ancient city of Constantinople could offer. Her father was a pragmatist and a realist. Realising that the man Jordan de Drengot was a basic fact of life and that he had to be accommodated if he were to hope for a reasonably comfortable existence, he reluctantly agreed to hand over his young daughter as a surety. Better, as he himself admitted candidly to his Jewish physician and lifelong confidante and friend, better by far to have the man inside his tent and pissing out than the other way around. So Zoe had gone, bitterly and regretfully, to Jordan de Drengot's high and arid rock, sacrificing the sea breezes and lemon groves of her blissful childhood for life with this strange and impossibly tall foreigner. The enticing beauty of the Greek Orthodox rite, the spine tingling and soaring voices of beautiful harmony replaced at one fell swoop with the terse and guttural worship of the Lord God in the vernacular and equally alien Latin. The beautiful Zoe, a reluctant prize bought for the sullen and grudging good will of the Greek speakers, sacrificed upon an altar like a heifer to some fearsome and vengeful God.

So she rode, squinting and eyes reddened and stinging, in the dust thrown up by the passage of the horses. Upon first sight of the large group ahead, passively awaiting his arrival, Jordan de Drengot had correctly identified them. He paused and summoned Zoe closer to his side. "Well, wife," he said unnecessarily, "here at last are our guests. We must prove ourselves to be pleasant and biddable at all cost." Privately, Zoe considered this to be rather a daunting requirement for her husband. Over the past few weeks of their partnership, her virginity ripped from her like her childlike innocence on their very first night together, she had grown from a state of unadorned fear to one of carefully concealed contempt, the fear was still there, of course. She listened to him attentively, his words like sounding like the crash and clatter of falling rocks when compared to her own language of babbling mountain streams. She had no idea, of course, that to him her own speech sounded equally strange and alien.

To Jordan's far from complete knowledge there awaited ahead of him a veritable host of thorny issues of protocol. He knew that he was due to play host to at least three dukes, of Normandy, Flanders and Brittany, along with any number of counts and senior land owners, a couple of bishops and the representatives of the Holy Father himself. Should he kneel, or would a stiff bow suffice? Whom to kiss first, if anyone? He had never in his life had cause to worry over such issues before. Life in his mountain fastness was much simpler by far, removed from any concerns over the niceties of behavior or the need for sensitivity for the feelings of others. The command of the Lord Bohemond, Prince of Taranto, however, could not have been clearer or more explicit. He would fail to comply at his own peril, it could not have been stated clearer.

In the event, he was spared the horror and the humiliation of flouting, even accidentally, the strict rules governing protocol. Long standing and bitter feuds had been known to start and lives to be lost over even the misplacing of a person at the banquet table. A short, elaborately dressed and stocky figure detached himself from the crowd and advanced upon him, arms held wide and face wreathed in a smile of welcome. Jordan de Drengot hastily dismounted and presented himself for an embrace that reeked of sour wine and the fumes of cheap scent. The hands grasping him did not even reach as far as the small of de Drengot's back. He had not had time for even the most cursory of bows. Robert of Normandy released his grip to stand back to survey the man. The language was strange and difficult to follow to de Drengot's ears.

"And you would be the sire de Drengot? Your reputation goes before you, we have heard much of your doings."

Jordan de Drengot recognised this as a cordial greeting, of sorts, and took the opportunity at last to bow. He did not yet trust himself to speak.

"Come, take your ease a while." Robert gestured expansively behind him, "for the morning is a hot one, is it not?"

Jordan de Drengot found himself propelled into a press of men, none of whom looking as affable as the man who now identified himself as Robert, Duke of Normandy.

"It is you, then, your Grace, that I am instructed to seek," de Drengot had found his voice at last.

Robert raised an eyebrow. "Indeed? And on whose instructions do you seek me?"

Already his gaze had rested appreciatively and speculatively on the alluring form of the Lady Zoe, brushing away the inevitable flies and uncomfortable upon her saddle after the long ride and wincing from the heat. Without averting his gaze for a moment, he said. "Well? I believe I asked you a question."

Jordan de Drengot, who had never had a man so frankly and openly ogle his wife in such a manner, was stung, torn between the need for respect and his own anger. "My instructions, your Grace, come directly from my Lord Bohemond de Hauteville, Count of Apulia and Calabria." He spoke woodenly, as if from some prepared statement. "He is presently concluding some business at the city of Amalfi," he gestured vaguely to the west, "on the coast there. I understand that he has been in conference with representatives from the Pope himself and that they are as one in this matter."

Robert frowned and, regretfully tore his eyes away from the woman, focussing instead on de Drengot. Up to this point, his Holiness, the Pope had always been a restraining, not to say, preventative block, on most of Robert's plans and ambitions. His blocking of a triumphal Ducal entry into the Holy City of Rome was a case in point.

Robert decided to retain his courteous and polite manner. "And what matter is it that they find themselves in agreement over?"

His voice was still mild and amiable. De Drengot shifted uneasily, such matters made him uncomfortable and ill at ease. Fighting and behaving in a riotous manner were more his fashion, not this slippery business of voicing statements of truth and half truth.

Robert, sensing this, sought to put him at ease. "Come now, man, drink. Simply tell me what you know and what is to be done, as you see it."

De Drengot took a lengthy pull of wine from the proffered goatskin and wiped his mouth with the back of his hand. He ploughed ahead. "I understand that the Count has had much contact of late with pilgrims come to this land on their way to the Holy Land, the place of our Saviour's birth," here he swiftly crossed himself, as if at pains to assure the Duke of his own piety, lest there be any doubt. "He has been much moved by their courage and by their devotion. He is of a mind, I understand, to take up his own sword and banner on behalf of our Lord Jesus Christ."

Robert smiled, as if to himself. "And devil a doubt to it, but the Holy Father himself may have helped to strengthen this resolve."

De Drengot shrugged, such matters were of no concern to him.

"And your instructions, then. What of them?"

De Drengot felt a burden lifted from him. Now, at least, he could perhaps deliver his message. "I am bidden to escort your Grace, and all your following, with the Count's hospitality in all things to his possession of Bari, and from there, perhaps to his possession of Taranto. From either port, ships will be prepared for your journey to the City of Constantinople, and from there to the Holy Land to do the work of God."

Robert's smile widened yet further. "And here we are, not even at Rome yet. Tell me, for I know little of such matters, is this a matter of a short journey?"

It was de Drengot's turn to smile. "I fear not, your Grace. I would hazard it to be a journey of at least ten days. In all probability, longer."

Robert nodded reflectively, aware that behind him the gathered group of noblemen were listening to every word exchanged. "Well," he said at length. "a tidy journey, to be sure, and in this heat. But then, we have travelled further than that to arrive here, I suppose. And doubtless there will be worse to come. This 'hospitality' of which you speak. Tell us more, of your courtesy."

Here, at least, de Drengot felt himself to be on slightly surer ground, for de Hauteville was truly a rich man indeed. And behind him lay the coffers of the Pope. By sending messages on ahead, he could summon sufficient wealth and resources enough to permit the Duke and his group of followers to travel in some comfort, if not in a state of high degree. There would be provisioning at least, and not all at their expense. Bread and meat and flour and grain and wine, food and drink and accommodation for this unruly gang without beggaring the countryside and causing it to rise up in bloody revolt against them. If they wanted luxuries beyond that, then, well, they could pay for it themselves. He relayed this information to the Duke with as much diplomacy as he could summon. Robert, for his part, felt a wave of relief. For some time past, finances had been a cause of discontent and a seething unhappiness amongst the camp fires and the discussions of the nobility now that they had arrived in a harsher and more remote land. Dissent could lead to defiance and fragmentation of his command, and worse! It could lead to actual rebellion and revolt. Leaving him stranded and in possession of, well, his own mortgaged Duchy! For all of his life Robert had, in the midst of all his spendthrift ways and his habit of living day to day, always had the eye and the view of a miser. Here, at last, was a lifeline of sorts; albeit at the possible cost of becoming the political plaything of another. Well, he decided grimly, time would be the judge of that. Let that lie, at least for the moment.

Not so much a pavilion, rather a screen of rough and patched linen hastily erected on four poles. Protected from the burning sun above, but open on all sides and the scrutiny of all who passed. Zoe sat on a rough stool surrounded by a press of men and the focus and interest of all. It was coming on for evening and the sun less vexing. Zoe's female companions, without the benefits that came from either birth or especially striking good looks, sought comfort as best they could outside in the general encampment. Their appearance was that of a line of parched and wilting flowers. In that crowd of large and intimidating men, Zoe shrank into herself, staring fixedly at her feet. She declined, again, a cup of wine sweetened with sweet cane. She had tried it and gagged, it was foul. It was as foul as these bearded and evil smelling men. They had all removed their chain mail and all those fiddly bits of leather that normally they seemed to be festooned all about with and, in that heat, and in that confined space, they quite simply stank. She focussed on a very large man in a loose tunic and wearing an impossibly large and cumbersome crucifix. Along with the supposed leader of these barbarians, he was quizzing her husband, who was luxuriating and basking in all the attention.

Already, and to Robert's regret, they had learned that the Lady Zoe was but a temporary travel companion. Jordan was escorting her to her father's estates for safety and comfort while he was occupied in seeing to the comfort and safety of these welcome guests of the Lord Bohemund de Hauteville. To Zoe, who had swiftly learned to neither question nor enquire, this was welcome news indeed. The comfortable security of her childhood home, albeit only a temporary refuge, was gladdening news indeed! She wondered if this might indeed in some way become permanent and if her new husband might meet in some way with a tragic and fatal accident. May the Good Lord and the Holy Virgin forgive her, but she felt nothing but hatred and rear of this man who had intruded so brutally into her life.

On the subject of Bohemond de Hauteville, Lord of Taranto, Jordan de Drengot was vague and, clearly, poorly informed. His own background did not make him privy to the background or doings of men set above him in station. But, between them, Robert and his noblemen already had a broad understanding, they could infer the rest. This de Hauteville was the natural son, though declared a bastard, of the awesome Robert Guiscard, one of the earliest Normans to have arrived to further stir the troubled waters of Italy and was native born, in Calabria. They knew a fair deal already of the man and of his growing reputation, a man with a towering ambition to match. They knew something also of his long standing and bitter feud with the Byzantines and of his various political arrangements with the Holy Father in Rome. None there, though, suspected for a moment that the man would come in time to eclipse them all.

"And when," enquired Robert breezily, "might we be honoured to meet our host? We all have, I am sure, so much to thank him for."

Jordan had no means of answering this question, his own orders were simple and plain enough to him. Again, he shrugged and swallowed his mouthful of raisins soaked in spirit. A man, he decided, could get to like these, and the flush of heat and high humour they invoked. He made a mental note to make them for himself once he had reached the safety of his high rock once more.

"Your Grace, I have no means of knowing. I am told that he is on his way from Amalfi to his ownership of Taranto. I have no doubt that he will cross our path sooner rather than later, and will advertise his arrival in due course." And with that, Robert and the others had to be content. In the meantime, having rested for the night, the camp would need to be struck and preparations made for their new course to the Adriatic coast, describing a wide circle around Rome and then to follow the old Roman route of the Via Appia, though little remained of that ancient enterprise, all the way to Taranto and the boats that were supposedly awaiting them. A more fitting place was erected for Jordan and his wife overnight, the rest of his command being left to shift for themselves. A hot and steamy night plagued by mosquitos and then the breaking of their camp for the difficult journey awaiting them. They set upon their laborious and slow journey south and west in search of the mysterious Prince of Taranto.

It had been decided that Gilles should be the point of contact between Jordan de Drengot and his motley band and the main column of the pilgrims. Chosen for his superb eyesight, his seeming flair for languages had also been already noted and Robert Curtmantle had come to trust and value his observations. It was an honoured post, and Gilles was duly grateful for it, freed as he was from the monotony and the clogging dust of the main column. He was to be the eyes and ears of the column as it moved through this alien landscape. It brought him too into sharp and direct contact with a host of new things, the strange countryside through which they passed, its odd vegetation and topography and its bizarre collection of inhabitants, Greeks and Moslems. It provided him also with a sharply focussed view of these wild and riotous Italian

Normans and also, of course, to the company of the breathtaking Lady Zoe.

Gilles was hopelessly in love, it was a type of love which he had thought he had observed often enough and to which he thought he had become sardonically and amusedly accustomed; love and worship combined together from a safe distance. Conveyed with gestures and soft words, little gifts and bad attempts at poetry. But this, he discovered, was far different. It was direct and up close, though hampered as it was by the intimidating, immediate and utterly masculine presence of the husband of the object of his desires; the undeniable and threatening presence of the man, Jordan de Drengot. This was a type of love that he had cynically witnessed many times in the past. Young men of good breeding mooning hopelessly over some languorous and utterly unobtainable young girl or, if she did prove to be obtainable, risking the consequences.

Despite himself, he smiled ruefully as he attempted to ease the itchy cloth of his shirt from his neck. The biter bit, by God! And here he was now, labouring under the hot and piercing sun, scratching at his neck beneath the confines of his chainmail, sweating and reeking as they laboured along yet another rocky and dusty pathway.

Out of the corner of his eye he was aware, as always he was, of the silent and uncomplaining vision of the Lady Zoe slightly to his rear. She was so close, and yet so unobtainable. To risk an unguarded approach was to invite a thrust of good old fashioned Norman steel deep within his vitals. So, wisely, Gilles forbore. He was not without experience in such matters, it had to be said. There had been the usual encounters with camp followers and women freely available for the price of a small coin in all the many places his duties to others better placed than he had taken him to. There had always been women of quality, older and wiser than he, women that he had admired. But this was another matter altogether, and so, with stolen glances at this object of his desires to console him, he writhed and itched in the high heat and strong sunshine. He wondered if it was much the same also for the man, Benoit, labouring alongside him, retained, with three others, for the role of conveying verbal messages back to the main column. He shrugged, he simply had no means of knowing. Calm and aloof, the man seemed likely to be proof even against any little dart or arrow of love. The man was the nearest that young Gilles had for a friend, a silent drifter from the bad lands around Maine and who had fetched up in Robert's gathering some years past. There had been a chance encounter back in Pontarlier, spilled drink, angry words and then an unseemly brawl in a tavern. Then the man had appeared as if summoned by a spirit to protect his back and see him safe away. Since then he had attached himself to the young favourite of the Duke of Normandy.

De Drengot was, as Gilles had known he would be, a far from

congenial companion, in any circumstances, he suspected. His statements were largely confined to instructions to his inferiors and brief and terse observations regarding the land through which they slowly passed, his eyes constantly roving about the barren hillsides in search of danger. Very few of his observations were directed at Gilles. On the second day of their travels Gilles did at least learn one thing of interest. They were heading, it seemed, for the ancient town of Benevento, some two or three days distant. From there the Lady Zoe, would be met and escorted to her father's estates nearby whilst de Drengot continued on his present duties to the Lord of Taranto. Benoit had been dutifully despatched to the column of Frenchmen labouring some way in their rear. Now he reappeared at his side once more, his usual collected and laconic self.

"Message received," he told Gilles. "Our Lords follow after and await further information." Gilles grunted a response and shrugged.

There was no further news to send back at present, neither would there be, not for mile after mile and as he shot occasional longing glances at the fine lady on her horse, seemingly oblivious to his presence.

A further uncomfortable day and another equally uncomfortable night plagued by flying insects. Gilles and his little command were instructed, a most novel command, to shake their boots well the following morning before forcing them once more over their blistered toes. The little black spiders of the region, they were informed, loved to nestle in them at night for warmth and comfort and their sting was the very devil! And so, another blistering day in the saddle whilst covertly glancing across at the deliciously swaying rump of the Lady Zoe. The following morning there came a diversion and an unexpected change of plan.

A messenger travelling at speed, coming from the west, his labouring horse sending up a cloud of dust in the early morning. De Drengot rode ahead alone to intercept him. The messenger dismounted, knuckling his forehead subserviently, and delivered a short message. De Drengot nodded and returned to the main party, summoning Giles forward, his face like thunder. Up to that point, de Drengot had largely ignored Gilles, barely registering his existence. He was to him an irrelevance, a necessary and unwanted presence.

"My presence is required elsewhere, for a spell," he said.

Gilles made a noise of polite enquiry in his throat. De Drengot fiddled with his sword scabbard. When he looked up, his eyes were dark and bright with a fierce anger.

"It is a small matter," He said. "A local tenant hereabouts," he jerked a thumb vaguely in the direction of the high hills, hazy and blue in the heat. "The man has quite forgotten his manners and his place in life, it would seem." He appeared quite puzzled. "The man owes me and yet he offers his defiance. This must, of course, be attended to." He gestured to his men, the gesture was clear enough and they began to busy themselves in preparation.

De Drengot drew Gilles aside, talking to him, not looking at him, his eyes fixed on the distant rim of hills. "It is doubtful that I shall be back before nightfall," he said. "Perhaps not even then. I shall leave you guides who will accompany you on your journey. I leave my Lady Zoe in your care. This is no occasion for women." He fixed Gilles with a direct and intimidating stare for the first time. "She will, of course, be safe in your care. See to it."

This was not a request, but a clear demand. With an impatient and imperious gesture he was gone, his men trailing after him in a noisy canter.

Gilles watched them leave, reflectively, and nodded to himself.

Benoit was once more at his side, gliding noiselessly into his line of vision. "It would seem," he observed rather enigmatically, "that all good things come to those who do but wait. I shall see to the necessary arrangements."

He gestured towards the woman, seemingly baffled, alone and vulnerable. "She should be informed of the change of plans, the Lady, perhaps?"

The Lady Zoe was indeed looking puzzled by her husband's unexplained and abrupt departure. Gilles approached her, speaking to her directly for the first time, briefly and in explanation. The fine and delicately feathered eyebrows rose in an unasked question on the perfect alabaster of her forehead. Gilles believed that he had never seen something quite so lovely.

"And so, what is to be done?"

Gilles had never actually heard the sound of her voice before, it made him think of pure mountain water flowing, sparkling and bright, down a hillside. He was wholly entranced. He coughed and stared at his boots.

"We must make shift for ourselves, good Lady, as best we may, until such time as your good lord returns to us."

The Lady Zoe considered this. "Yes, indeed. Quite so. I feel safe in your company, messire."

Clearly, the language was not her own and Gilles found the slight hesitations in her French charming. Thus dismissed, Gilles turned away and she fell into a long and animated conversation with her maid servant in what he took to be Greek.

De Drengot had left an escort of three of his men and a taciturn local man not given to any unnecessary comment who simply pointed out the direction in which they should continue. They travelled until past noon in a countryside totally devoid of any inhabitants. By now the news would have travelled. The devil de Drengot was unchained and at large and nowhere and no person was safe. The two villages they encountered were both of them deserted, with evident signs of a rapid evacuation by their inhabitants. It was clear that they too were being avoided.

They paused in a deserted village square, not so much a square as a space between huts of stone and thatch and a little chapel. Onions hung out nearby and bronzed brown in the sun, and a string of garlic, while flies buzzed noisily around a drying circle of cow dung and a solitary dog, tethered, bayed to be at them.

The lady Zoe commanded her woman to draw water from the well. The maid cautiously edged this towards him with an earthenware bowl of water and it paused its barking long enough to lap greedily at the water.

"Well," observed Benoit drily, "that is good enough, I suppose, but we aren't reduced to eating dogs, at least not awhile."

It was a timely and pointed reminder. A search through the village yielded up little. A crock of black olives, some dried and withered fruit and a pair of stale loaves, hard and unyielding as stone. They went through their own saddlebags. There was a quantity of twice baked bread, canteens of the local wine, warm, thin and sour, and strips of dried, cured beef to go with the water from the well. Good enough for them, they had all of them had worse in their time, but what of the needs of the Lady Zoe? In fact, she was already munching delicately and with apparent enjoyment on the olives and sipping well water. She had, spread before her on a cloth, a collection of sweet candied fruit and raisins and some nuts provided by her maid. She was sheltered from the sun by the shade of the low stone set around the well. Placed upon a travelling cushion, she looked comfortable enough, at least. She smiled up at Gilles as he approached. He had never experienced such a smile as this.

"Sit," she commanded. "You hurt my neck to look up at you so. Sit, tell me a little about yourself," She patted the patch of ground next to her encouragingly.

Gilles squatted cautiously before her, suddenly conscious that he smelled and that he must appear loutish and slovenly. He began to speak in slow, careful French, uncertain as to the full range of her understanding of the language. He found himself telling her of his childhood and what he could remember of it, at first with hesitation and then with a growing fluency. She appraised him, head cocked to one side and occasionally biting her lip in concentration at an unknown word. She raised her eyebrows at his mention of the Queen Matilda and her formidable husband, names she recognised.

What Zoe most wanted to hear, to have at least a broad understanding of, was the reason why all these unkempt and brutal men had descended upon her land, and in such numbers. What was the very nature of this thing, this Crusade? She already knew of pilgrimages. She herself had been taken on such things herself in her childhood often enough, purely localised events to a nearby shrine or grotto to pray to the Mother or one or other of the myriad host of saints and martyrs that crowded her young life. But this was something else altogether, she knew. Some strange and powerful alchemy that had caused hosts of violent foreigners to materialise as if by magic in front of her very eyes. She understood only well enough the allure and glamour of violence and the taking by force. Had this, after all, not been visited upon her by her unsought new husband, Jordan de Drengot? Taken, seized and abused by force.

This youth who knelt before her in the dust, touchingly young and not bad looking in his own coarse way, intrigued her. She knew then, and with a blinding certainty, that this boy was an embodiment, the very shape of things to come and that nothing could ever be the same again. He was, in a way, the unlikely looking key to an understanding of this new life into which she had been thrust. She appraised him between her lashes. He lowered at her beneath his unkempt and thatched fringe, like a promising young bull on display.

"And do you tell me?" she said, "that through this crusade of yours you will truly find forgiveness and eternal salvation?"

Gilles nodded earnestly, not having worked the thing through quite so far himself. That, through violence and wanton and unrestrained destruction, eternal bliss might be found? No wonder that her revered father had looked so worried! She very much doubted that her own unwanted and now absent new husband viewed life in such simple terms.

Gilles concluded simply, "...and so, Madame, we travel now to God's own city of Jerusalem. There we shall all wash our sins and be cleansed." Simply speaking the words, he found himself doubting them.

"And then?" she enquired. "What then?"

It was, Gilles recognised, a genuine question, one that he had not paused to ask himself. This beautiful creature was bringing into doubt so many things. He simply shrugged once more, a dismissive raising of the shoulders.

"Will this world then end, and all within it?"

He cleared his throat, would have spat in the dust, but thought that perhaps this might not be seemly and be taken amiss.

"Lady, I simply do not know," he said, staggered by this realisation.

"Well," she said, drawing herself to her feet and brushing crumbs from her gown and coming to a spontaneous decision. "Come walk with me for a while. Perhaps this will serve to clear your head." She indicated a small stand of ash and poplar trees a short way off and offering a cooling shade. She set off and he followed after, aware of a troubling and nagging ache in his loins.

Zoe leaned against the trunk of a young tree, choosing her

cluttered thoughts and her speech with care.

"We are both young, you and I, messire, and, indeed, you have seen far more of this wicked world than I." Gilles made no comment, nodding politely. This, after all, was true. "I have known only one man in my life, a man who took me by force and violently used me. I took no pleasure in the experience, believe me. Doubtless, I shall bear him children, indeed, I believe I carry one already."

Gilles believed that this was too much information to share and looked uncomfortable.

But the Lady Zoe continued. "In time, I shall be quite dried up, or else will die bringing another brat into the world. Perhaps, perhaps that man," she spoke with a very apparent distaste and dislike, "will then tire of me, discard me for another and have me packed off to a Convent somewhere to stitch and embroider prayer cushions for the rest of my days." She shrugged and then looked at him directly and unwaveringly. "I have had very little opportunity to sin, messire, as of yet. You tell me that all sin is pardonable. It would seem, from what you tell me, to require only the right words to make all good again, to gain forgiveness, and redemption."

Gilles cleared his throat awkwardly, "So I have been told, Lady, by men wise in such matters."

The young girl smiled, reflectively and thoughtfully. "Then let us sin together, you and I, and seek our forgiveness after. And beyond that? You shall continue on this journey of yours that you you are making to the Holy Land. Perhaps there you will find the redemption you seek. Perhaps you will die there, I fully expect this will be the case. And I? Well, it will be the grave for me also in God's appointed time and before that, either death in childbirth, the nursery or the convent. We shall, I have no doubt, never see each other in life again, after this brief journey." She gestured at the privacy of the young, green trees. "So here, let us take pleasure in this short life of each other, while we may. I have nothing further to offer, messire, than the gift I freely give, and with no questions."

She took him by the chin and kissed him passionately on the lips, "Come," she whispered into his ear urgently, "I am curious."

With one hand she scrabbled urgently at his crotch, scrabbling at the drawstrings of his breeches, and with the other she raised her gown, exposing the pure and lovely white of her lower body and legs. She guided him in to the place within to the tightly curled hedge between her hips and then they grappled together with a growing passion and competence and a growing level of ill suppressed sounds.

Gilles was lost in those moments, scarcely knowing who he was any longer. He lost any sense of real time as they squirmed and moaned together and he lost all sense of fear of the absent Jordan de Drengot in those stolen moments. They were both thoughtful and pensive on their short journey back to the village square. She held her lips to his mouth in a grave and mocking warning. She did not need to speak, for the meaning was clear. They must never speak of this again.

The square, in their brief absence, had become a hive of activity. The other messengers had returned from the main column, tracking them down to the village, and there was the smell of roasting meat. Benoit was there by the well to meet them. He said not a word to the woman, who moved away to her fretful maid servant. He did not need to speak and Gilles knew that the man knew and would keep his peace.

"While you were away," he said, "we found a young kid, not very well hidden. We are roasting it now and now we need to be off and away from here," he paused, "unless you have any further purpose in lingering."

Gilles was hasty in his denial. "No, no" he said. "We must move off without any further delay. Leave some money for the goat where it may easily be found. We know, both of us, his Grace's view of plundering."

Noisily, just before the dawn and the sky still black as pitch with just a suggestion of grey, Jordan de Drengot was back amongst them, cantering into camp with his tired but clearly elated followers. With the help of his local guide, he had tracked them down easily enough. He warmed himself at the fire and drained a whole canteen of wine down his gullet without pausing. He wiped his mouth with the back of his hand and spat into the fire.

"Well", he said breezily, "all well here?" He was in excellent spirits.

"Most certainly," said Gilles, "No problems at all in our journey," his voice schooled and easy in tone. Understandably, perhaps, he was feeling arrogant in his view of the man. He hoped that he didn't sound it, he with his new knowledge.

De Drengot, for his part, gave no sign of noticing anything amiss.

"Your lady Zoe is well enough," said Gilles, "though doubtless missing your company. And your business? Did all go well?"

De Drengot grinned, the flash of his teeth like the grimace of a wolf. "Most certainly," he laughed. "The man and his company were ignorant puppies, and sorely in need of a lesson in manners. This was duly served up to them." He patted a bulging wallet attached to his sword belt, "and there has been some excellent recompense for our troubles. My boys, too, enjoyed themselves."

This was evident, the men had several new pack horses with them, laden with what seemed to be all manner of things. They looked like happy guests recently returned from a highly enjoyable wedding feast. "And my wife, she is well?"

Gilles smiled reassuringly, "quite well. In excellent spirits, really."

De Drengot spat into the fire again. "I find that hard to believe. Well, I shall see for myself soon enough. The return of the happy warrior, and all that."

Gilles yawned and stretched. "Yes indeed, and I am sure that she will welcome your return and be all the better for it. Now I must make ready for the journey once more."

De Drengot moved to delay him. "Before you start, I have further news for you. The Lord Prince Bohemond is himself now at Benevento, and waiting for us. We must make no delay, and make a fine showing for him when we arrive. The Lord Robert of Normandy and the others have been informed and also make haste to the meeting place."

De Drengot himself strode off in the direction of the raised sheet that served as shelter for his wife and maid, his steps confident and steady.

Gilles and Benoit watched him leave.

"A dangerous man to cross, that one," observed Benoit, and he too spat into the fire.

Chapter Eight: Benevento and Bari

"The world is divided into men who have wit and no religion and men who have religion and no wit." [Ibn Sînâ: Eleventh century Persian physician and scientist]

The final journey to the old town of Benevento was short and without further incident, arriving in sight of it just as the dusk began to gather. By now it would of course be curfew down there and they settled down for the night within sight of its glowing and welcoming beacon of lights. Along the way there the men had been boisterous and much given to horseplay. There was frequent passing of wineskins, and snatches of song. The Lady Zoe was once more upon her delicate high stepping mare and without a single glance at Gilles.

"We shall be rid of her soon enough," Jordan de Drengot had said earlier that day. "It has been a troubling business to cart her about with me all this while. I have far more other matters to concern myself with, the Lord alone knows."

Gilles nodded politely, realising not for the first time how much he truly despised this arrogant mercenary. To de Drengot, the woman was a possession much like any other, though admittedly more pleasurable to look upon than most other objects and with the additional virtue of being the possible receptacle of a sturdy heir.

De Drengot slapped the pommel of his horse in evident high spirits. "Still, where we go, you and I, there will be women enough."

Gilles ventured a remark. "And where will the Lady go, in all of this?"

He indicated the vast expanse of nothingness that surrounded them. De Drengot laughed breezily, jabbing his thumb at the woman in question travelling a respectful distance to their rear.

"Where? Why to that fat old dotard of her father, of course, the pandering little Greek arse licker." It was clear that de Drengot enjoyed the very best of terms with his father in law. "The old fool has a fine place up there in the hills above Benevento, doubtless paid for with the Greek Emperor's money. He'll be meeting us in Benevento. Then let him take up the burden for a while." He paused a moment, "I may well touch him for a payment."

Descending the high ground of Mount Pentime, the prosperous town of Benevento lay spread below them, the river Calore snaking through it like a ribbon shining in the sunlight. Once an important controlling city on the now defunct Via Appia, though fallen on harder times, it still had the air of a natural fortress and a thriving centre of commerce, judging by the numbers of people entering and exiting its now largely derelict walls. Along with the rest of the crusading army, Gilles had been adroitly and diplomatically steered in a broad arc away from the city of Rome. He had nonetheless witnessed much of the ancient and imperial monuments of the ancient country through which he travelled. Here at Benevento, wherever he looked, the evidence of a once glorious and dead past was everywhere. De Drengot's party passed beneath a massive stone arch as it entered the town, crumbling now, its Latin inscriptions unclear and the many figures carved upon its surface scarred and blunted through the ravages of time or by damaging hands. Thick clinging tendril of ivy completed the look of utter ruin. The streets leading to the main square were dark and narrow, little direct sunlight ever made its way past the towering and oppressive tenement buildings. The sound of their iron shod hooves bounced off the pressing walls and back at them. Local people and visitors alike pressed themselves against the unyielding stone or scuttled ahead of them. None wished to dispute the passage of these dangerous mailed men on their giant iron shod horses.

They emerged once more into bright and brilliant sunlight, causing them to squint and shield their eyes. Opposite them was the Cathedral of Santa Maria Assunta, an impressing edifice rearing up at them in romanesque splendour and said to hold the bones of the blessed Bartholomew the Apostle. The square, usually a busy market place, was a riot of colour, noise and activity, coming as a shock to the newly arrived visitor. They viewed a temporary town of tents of bleached and tattered cloth, secured into the ground between the broken flagstones by pegs. A vast array of banners hung lifeless in the square, undisturbed by any breeze to set them fluttering. There were a multiplicity of horse lines and a crowd of men gathered in idle groups, tinkering and fiddling with equipment and harness or throwing knuckle bones against each other. As with most military men at rest, they were noisy and, many of them, half drunk. Their voices were a cacophony of noise and the strong smell emanating from them was tangible. As with the narrow alleys, the citizens afforded them a wide berth, unlike the town's many children who screamed and played happily amongst the men and the steaming piles of fast drying horse manure that lay everywhere. The soldiers, for their part, either ignored or else swatted at them amiably like irritating flies.

Jordan de Drengot surveyed the scene before them, his eyes searching. He very much doubted that the mighty Prince of Taranto would deign to shelter in a tent when there were any number of handsome and well appointed town houses to choose from. He noted one such on the far side of the square, a solid structure of two storeys, freshly whitewashed. Outside a collection of banners were erected, including the personal banner of the house of Hauteville, golden stars upon a field of blue. Two burly men with their halberds crossed stood at the entrance. De Drengot dismounted, handing his reins to an attendant. "You wait here," he brusquely told Gilles and strode off across the square to the house, scattering men as he went.

Gilles too dismounted, the rest of the group still backed up in the alley. He saw a man roasting lamb and placing it in pockets of warm unleavened bread. He realised he was ravenously hungry and bought food for himself and Benoit with a small coin. The Lady Zoe was escorted to a nearby house. Gilles wondered about her, her father, her future. The two men settled down in a companionable silence. They were still chewing, the juices of the lamb rolling down their chins, when they saw de Drengot leaving the house and marching towards them, he was scowling, and with a face like thunder.

"I am to leave immediately," he announced. "My Lord Bohemond has chastised me, openly, in front of others. It seems I have been remiss in not following his instructions to the full letter. I am to personally fetch your Lord and those others, and bring them to his presence." Gilles had not seen the man so angry, a type of restrained fury. He rose to his feet. "No, not you. This is my task. I have another task for you."

Gilles raised his eyebrows in enquiry, "if you would oblige me in this then I thank you and owe you a favour I shall return, some day. My worthless father in law, I am told, has already hauled his fat carcass here to Benevento." de Drengot's eyes blazed in a fury.

"It seems that he and my Lord are quite well acquainted. I go now to make my farewells of my wife. When I am done with her I would have you take her to her father. I would be grateful." And with that he was gone once more, calling for his men to assemble.

Gilles led the Lady Zoe through the main square, her eyes downcast and unseeing in that vast concourse of ogling men and their all too audible and complimentary remarks on her appearance. She did not look up until they were clear of it all, and them. Gilles attempted to converse with her across the swaying shoulders of their mounts. She favoured him this time with a single glance, a look that was neutral and quite without expression.

"I take you to your father," he said, quite unnecessarily. A barely perceptive nod of recognition.

"Yes," she said. "I know, and I am glad." Gilles continued to plough on. "Until such time as your husband returns to retrieve you."

This time Zoe favoured him with a slight smile, a smile such as one would bestow upon a servant in thanks after a service well done.

"Indeed," she said, "until such time. You should know then that my husband tells me that that is not to be yet awhile. He tells me," and here she leaned forward, almost conspiratorially, "he tells me that he too will travel with you on this Holy War of yours against the enemies of God." She smiled that rare and beautiful smile that he had only seen once before. "And I do not need to tell you, messire, that on such ventures better men than he have been known to die."

They continued on their way in silence. This was another matter altogether. He wondered briefly what strange combination of emotions had come upon the man for him to arrive at such a decision. A newly discovered piety perhaps? Gilles ruled this out almost immediately, bringing into account the personality and nature of the man Jordan de Drengot. He very much doubted any new discovered piety in the man. Had Bohemond shamed him into it in some way, perhaps? Cupidity, then, the opportunity of further riches. That was most likely to be it. Gilles knew that in all things Jordan de Drengot was something of a child, and one who thirsted for adventure. All this commotion and show of martial glory must quite have quite turned his head. So, for good or bad, he had now inherited the uncertain company of the man.

The girl broke his silence. "We have shared one big secret, and we shall have no opportunity to speak of matters further, you and I. So know this, messire. I shall delight in my father's company once more. I shall relish it and neither will I mourn unduly at any news of my husband's death." That, at least, Gilles could believe. "Should this happen," she continued, "then doubtless my father will be obliged to cast around for a fitting and suitable replacement for him." She pierced him once more with those beautiful eyes of hers. "And you, returned from God's Holy War, messire, all enriched and beautifully caparisoned and, who knows, ennobled? Why, my father might even then be tempted to cast his gaze in your direction?" She smiled once more, archly.

And then, ahead of them, there erupted an eruption; one of joy and welcome, of happiness and celebration. A crowd of jubilant people appeared before them, blocking their passage. In their midst a man, short, rotund and prosperous looking. He was beautifully dressed and his face, wreathed in beatific smiles, a face creased in pure happiness. In an instant, the girl was enfolded and swept up and borne off in noisy triumph. That was Gilles' last view of her as she was swept off in a happy aromatic cloud of good will.

The following morning the leaders of the mixed crusader army finally appeared, riding in some array and proud showing through that same decayed Roman arch that Gilles himself had entered the previous day, with de Drengot at its head. It took quite some time, given their number, for them all to pass through. In the van, of course, there came Duke Robert of Normandy. Jostling alongside him, shoulder to shoulder, came the great paragons of the crusading nobility, the Bishop Odo of Bayeux, notably and flamboyantly, of their number. Gilles nudged his horse into line to join them. Robert Curtmantle was in jovial and playful mood.

"Ah," he said, "Our absent peddler of languages joins us once more. And tell me, my boy, have you done and witnessed mighty things?"

Gilles thought, regretfully, of the charms of the Lady Zoe. "Indeed no, my Lord," he replied. "Nothing of note to report. Nothing out of the ordinary."

The playful mood was apparently infectious, for Odo leaned across and called out. "What? No feeding by ravens, or burning bushes, nor any rams with their horns caught tight in a thicket? How dull, boy, you disappoint."

Gilles, who like most people, scarce understood a word the good bishop ever uttered, simply smiled politely and inclined his head.

"You have been missed, boy," said the bishop and extended his ring finger to be kissed.

Gilles obliged, "I was but a few days away, your Grace. I understand that miracles often take longer to occur."

A space had been cleared in the main square for them to ride, through the soiled and torn linen and canvas tents of the army to a raised wooden platform placed against the wall of the Cathedral. There a group of men awaited their arrival. In their midst, like an ash in a colony of short and stubby olive trees, there stood an immense figure, arms folded across a brawny chest.

"And that," noted Robert, "will be our illustrious host and

benefactor, the Lord Bohemond of Taranto." He took in the immense and stately form.

"Quite so," murmured Odo at his side, "beyond a shadow of a doubt."

They were all obliged to dismount beneath the platform, to approach the meeting place on foot and through the cheering soldiery and a massed rank of cowled monks in grey and brown intoning psalms of joy and redemption in rising and falling harmony. They strode through wafts of expensive camphor, dissipated by the open air and as the bells of the Cathedral rang out. Upon some invisible command, a flock of doves was released, rising up in a pale cloud of white and powder blue. At the top of the steps the very tall man awaited to greet and embrace them, a herald announcing their names and titles as they clambered onto the platform. It was a very dramatic scene and one which gladdened the always theatrical heart of Robert, Duke of Normandy. He beamed with happiness as he stepped into the powerful bear hug of Bohemond de Hauteville. This welcome lacked all deference and a sense of protocol due to him, but Robert, elated and overcome by the moment, was only too happy to overlook it.

Bohemond de Hauteville stepped back from his embrace to view his latest acquisition; he had been collecting what he hoped would prove to be stalwart and faithful supporters for years. Thus far, the results had been decidedly mixed. He positively towered over the diminutive Robert, who stood there before him and sweating heavily from the heat and exertion. Bohemond, in fact, towered over most men. He was certainly an impressive figure, well made and proportioned and one who would turn the head of a Byzantine princess of the purple. He was muscular and well made, with slim legs, muscular chest and arms displayed to good effect in a short mailed vest. His face was finely chiselled, with prominent cheek bones and an arresting aquiline nose that thrust forward between a pair of far seeing eyes of icy pale blue. His hair was cut and cropped short in the old Norman fashion and with only the faintest suggestion of stubble showing on an otherwise carefully shaven and pumiced chin. His hands glittered with exquisite and ornate bejeweled rings.

One by one, the notables of the crusading army, jostled and shuffled onto the by now dangerously crowded and creaking platform to receive his welcome, a herald to announce them and call out their names. It was an assembly of some of the greatest names, a flowering of the finest blood of France and the lowlands. Bohemond, gravely, greeted each of them in turn, kissing the rings of the higher of the churchmen gathered. Like Robert, he basked in the heat and the warmth of the popular support. He then raised both muscular arms, signalling for a degree of silence. Into this silence there stepped the representative of Adelmar of Puys; the papal legate being absent hundreds of miles away. There followed a lengthy prayer of thanks and exultation, delivered first in Latin and then in vernacular French. A nod to an observer in the crowd and the signal was relayed back to the bells of the Cathedral which rang out once more in a joyful and triumphant paean of praise.

Even standing by the steps, Gilles had been able to catch only an occasional phrase of the welcome, or of the prayers that followed. Judging by the look on the Duke Robert's face as he cautiously made his way down the steps, a stumble here would be a public humiliation hard to overcome, but the man was content enough. Gilles joined Robert and the others as they were led in public display through the town and out by another gate onto the rich plains beyond. A camping site had been selected close to the walls, with easy access to fresh running water, for the ancient and once proud city of Benevento could simply not support such a large influx of additional men. To attempt this was an invitation to disease and the disorder that inevitably followed in the wake of such a gathering.

It was a well appointed spot, for sure, and clearly some forethought had gone into its selection, for there were stacks of firewood placed ready and a pen containing a herd of sheep, fine mutton for the roasting. Very soon, too, the place would act as a magnet for the inevitable stream of hucksters and purveyors of strong drink and a steady influx of supplies of bread and vegetables and other commodities from local merchants and the peasantry of the surrounding area. Inevitably, there would follow a tribe of harlots to meet and service other needs. The stay was more protracted than anyone had realised, as stragglers and contingents from other parties continued to arrive and the number of armed men there had risen to nearly six thousand, a restless and agitated collection of men and prone to disputation and the slightest possible perceived insult. By the end of the first week the provost marshals were hard at work dispensing summary justice and it fell upon Gilles too to exercise his own policing on behalf of his absent Duke, carousing in nearby Benevento.

Clearly, it was time to move. Rooted here, the army was losing all sense of purpose and sense of cohesion. Already there were desertions, though quite to where and for what purpose was never clear. Such men never got very far, instead they turned feral, breaking into hen coops or grain bins, their future ambitions not the pile of glittering gold they had dreamed of, but rather the end of a swinging rope in exchange for a fistful of grain or a couple of eggs.

Bohemond de Hauteville announced the decision, rising dramatically to his feet one evening at the supper board. All of his movements tended to be imbued with a sense of majesty. He cleared his throat and called for silence, all of the quality were present, they never missed a single opportunity to be present at one of his pronouncements.

"My good lords all," he announced to the packed hall of his

purloined town house, "the time has come for us all to move." He paused and was not disappointed in his expectation of a roar of acclaim. "Today I have been informed that the fleet of ships we require is now at Bari."

News indeed, in truth, though, most there had no understanding at all of what and where Bari was, or indeed had thought too deeply over quite how a vast host of men would conjure themselves over a vast and unknown expanse of water.

When Gilles himself heard the news the following day he was glad. As with all the others, he had become dangerously bored and jaded. He had little inkling then of the extent to which Robert had come to rely upon his presence within his small quarter of the unruly and riotous camp as a quieting and moderating influence. In the next few days Robert came to seek him out specifically with seemingly random instructions to attend to this or that.

The men, he was told, were indolent and overweight. Take a section of them on an all night journey to work some of the fat off them, to collect timber from the uplands or else collect fallen olives for a pressing. Here a coin to placate them, there a large measure of wine to dispel any ill feeling and to dull any abiding anger and resentment. Those horses need exercising, that grey in particular. A whole litany of tasks. The latrines are overflowing once again. Site them there, a stubby finger pointing. Gilles felt rebellious at this riding tide of onerous duties and almost squared up to him at one point. Robert subjected him to a steely glare, eying him coldly.

"You," he said, "will do exactly as I say, and know that you do it with my full authority." He stalked off and that was enough.

Gilles had come to understand that he had in some way become a preferred favourite. His authority was not to be brooked and that when he spoke, it was with the authority of the Duke of Normandy behind him. This became generally known and accepted.

On one occasion the bishop Odo was present at one of these listings of duties, staring around interestedly at the disorder and the seeming turmoil of the camp in preparation for the move, his heavily jowled face creasing in concentration and with his small pig's eyes darting about. Together, they watched Robert canter off in high temper at the end of it, scattering clods of earth in his wake. Odo sighed deeply.

"There he goes, my impetuous young nephew. His father always thought carefully, I recall, before making any move." He shook his head ruefully and turned to Gilles. "He values you, boy, more than you perhaps realise, my fine young Earl's son. He thinks much of you, this I know, for he has told me so. He will do well by you, so take heed."

Startled at this display of unsolicited frankness, Gilles bowed his head and mumbled his thanks. The bishop waved his hand dismissively, at the same time subjecting the boy to an unabashedly appraising stare, taking him in from boots to head. The proclivities of the bishop were an open secret and much commented upon.

"Almost time for a blessing, I feel," he said at last. "For I shall not be accompanying you, I fear. No, not I. The mysterious island of Sicily and the City of Palermo beckons and who am I to ignore the call? I have friends there, good friends, and colleagues." He chuckled to himself. "Perhaps I am grown old and weak, my boy, and not strong enough for escapades such as this. In Palermo, so I am told, there is much to my further advancement and interest. But what is this to you? And why should I be discussing such matters with you? As I say, I grow old. Yes indeed, I grow old. And now, it really is time for that blessing."

Startled by the bishop's shared confidence, Gilles thanked him and bowed his head. The bishop appraised him once more, taking in his young frame from his booted heel to the top of his head, subjecting him to that frank and approving stare that Gilles found disquieting. It was not part of the general way of things to enquire even lightly concerning the complexities of the life, public or private, of this perplexing man and his entirely worldly loves and interests. This knowledge was already the bawdy subject of many a camp fire. He had come to grudgingly respect the man, feeling it also inappropriate and dangerous to remind him of his earliest encounter with him in the cluttered and disquieting room of Queen Matilda in his childhood.

As if reading his thoughts, Odo continued. "Perhaps I shall rejoin this fine army at some later juncture, that, though, lies within the will of God." Somewhat irritably, Odo bid him to kneel and there, dutifully, Gilles knelt amongst the mud and straw and bustle of the camp and felt the heavy hand of the bishop upon his head to receive the Bishop's blessing and benediction.

"And so farewell, my boy. May God keep and guide you."

Without too much difficulty, the bishop mounted his fine palfrey, wheeled it and rode off towards Benevento. Gilles was never to see him again. Shortly after, Odo the bishop of Bayeux and half brother to the Conqueror himself, led his retinue away and to the south. In his time the man had flailed his deadly mace on that long terrible day at Senlac, he too had killed the English. Being a churchman, the sharpened edge of a sword was forbidden him and so, instead, he had used a heavy club of iron to shatter and splinter bones. He had plotted and conspired for all of his life in France and England, he had instigated rebellion and treacherous acts against his own brother, had grown all powerful and rich beyond all measure. He had been humiliated and imprisoned for his acts and had risen once more, freed by a pardon and William's death. He was now at the peak of his powers, lured to the city of Palermo where, surrounded by Christian bells and the wail of the muezzin, he would be struck down and killed by a fever.

A few days after this last encounter Gilles was himself summoned, to attend a council convened and presided over by the great Prince of Taranto himself. Leaving Benoit outside to guard the horses, he entered the large house in the main square of Benevento, his steps sounding heavily upon the stone paving, a very different sound to boots upon wet straw and squelching mud. It was a large hall with flooring that soon reverted back to hard and impacted earth. The place was soaring, with smoke blackened rafters and an upper floor reached by ladders. Predictably, the place was packed. Confident in his clearly expressed order to attend, he strode through the throng, elbowing his way and stood before a fine table of polished oak at the head of the hall. Here, obediently, he inclined his head downward, waiting to be summoned further. Gazing up through his eyelashes, he covertly took in the scene before him.

At the centre, an island in a sea of parchment rolls and documents and with a flurry of attendants buzzing around him like troublesome flies, sat the Lord Prince of Taranto seemingly engrossed in a particular document set before him whilst some person, a prosperous merchant by the look of him, leaned over his shoulder, prodding and jabbing.

To his right sat the Duke Robert, dwarfed by Bohemond. He was inclining in to listen, and, beyond him, a small assembly of some of the great enterprise's finest. The Duke of Brittany was there, Mortain, one of the de Grandesmil boys, others. Immediately to the left of Bohemond there sat a youth of about Gilles' age. He instantly recognised the breed and the type. The youth was tall and powerful looking, seeming as taut as a tightly pulled leather strap and fairly seething to be up and away from that table and doing something of a violent nature, whether on behalf of God or not. To Gilles the youth looked to be the very epitome of this restless tribe of Italian Normans. A killing man, Gilles decided, no doubt of it. His look reminded him very much of the man Jordan de Drengot and the thinly veiled threat that he represented. Clearly, another well born second generation scion of a group of dangerous robber barons who had seized this country by the ears and had largely made it their own. One to watch, no doubt of it. About and behind the table numerous servants and attendants scurried about on a variety of tasks and errands.

Glancing into the hall, Duke Robert noticed Gilles standing patiently there, slightly apart from the usual mob of litigants and petitioners. He murmured into the ear of the Lord of Taranto and motioned Gilles to come forward. Perhaps bored and welcoming a diversion, Bohemond subjected him to a long and appraising stare.

"My Lord," said Robert, "this is the man of whom I spoke. A good man who has earned my trust and favour. I commend him to you." Bohemond continued to rake Gilles with his long, contemplative, stare.

"Indeed?" He said at length. "Have him step forward."

Dutifully, Gilles took a few further paces and knelt. "And is he aware of his duties?" Bohemond asked.

Robert improvised, "Not fully, my Lord. Not until such time as you deem it necessary." His eyes flashed a silent warning to Gilles, who was wise enough and respectful enough, to say nothing until matters became clearer.

Bohemond bid him rise. "Well, let me have a look at you, boy. Your Lord Robert does indeed speak highly of you, to be sure. When, finally, we arrive in the lands of the Greeks, and may that be soon, you are to be both the eyes and ears to me and the Lord Duke Robert." He turned to the others at the table, "or one set of them at least." Obligingly, those around him chortled merrily.

"Doubtless, your Lord will furnish you with all the details in the fullness of time," again, Duke Robert's eyes flickered in warning.

"In the lands of the Greeks, I have no doubt," Bohemond continued, "you will be provided with local guides and a force under the orders of the Emperor himself. You will move ahead of us. As I say, you will be our ears and eyes. In the first instance you will accompany my nephew here." He indicated the baleful looking young man, now fidgeting with a belt buckle to his left. "This is my kinsman, my nephew Tancred, and much beloved by me."

The eyes of Gilles and Tancred met briefly before, bored, the youth looked away. Gilles felt he had been right in his estimation, a dangerous one, and to be treated with caution, for sure.

"Now you know my pleasure," Bohemond concluded, "and that of your own Lord to whom you owe loyalty and service. That is all, you may leave."

The town of Bari looked welcoming enough when viewed from a distance out on the dusty plain. Closer still and it lost something of its allure. It seemed alien and exotic with everywhere the influences to be seen of a very recent past of Islamic rule. This still vivid memory crowded cheek by jowl with an equally recent Byzantine past. It was a maritime port that simply could not handle this sudden influx of an army of thousands of men with all their unwieldy wagons and hordes of followers. Gilles, like all others of the host, settled down to an uncomfortable stay in an improvised encampment outside the town.

Just over twenty years ago Bari had been seized and taken over by the redoubtable Robert Guiscard, that guileful man, the 'Fox', and even now it bore the scars and had the feel of a frontier town, notwithstanding the fact that the bones of Saint Nicholas lay in a reverential shrine in the Basilica San Nicola, a belligerent fist of a building raised up in the main square. The bones of Robert the Wily, not long dead in his uneasy tomb, also lay there and the touch of his restless spirit was everywhere. The irascible Peter the

Hermit had been here too, one of the many places the visionary rabble rouser had visited and subjected to the vitriol and passion and inflamed oratory of his tongue. Here too had the Pope very recently been, had held his Council in an attempt to pour oil on the very troubled and complex theological waters that separated the Holy Apostolic Church and the Orthodox Church of the east. This had, almost inevitably, proved to be one task too many, ending in acrimonious theological dispute and failure.

Heeding the observation and the implicit advice of the bishop Odo and aware also of the esteem that Duke Robert appeared to hold him in, Gilles began to take an actual pride and pleasure in those tasks and duties that once he had held to be tedious and mere drudgery. Certainly, there were tasks and chores enough to occupy him the whole of the day and long after nightfall. There were men to be chided and scolded and praised, a flogging at the drawn halberds to be supervised, a palm to be be greased with a coin. In that unpromising encampment water had to be found and rationed. There were horses to be doctored, fresh leather to be bought and metal studs to be bought, polished and sewn into protective jackets. The tasks seemed endless.

Occasionally such duties took him into the town itself. Bari possessed a vibrant and very mixed spread of diverse cultures and peoples. Bari had always been a thriving slave mart and the trade had continued to flourish despite any change of masters. Entranced by the docks and the wharves that reminded him of his own Rouennais childhood, Gilles took every opportunity to explore and to observe with fascination the slave chains as they came ashore or laboured at the quays or on their way to the market. For the most part, they spoke no language known or understood by him. They were, he was informed, from many different places, from Illyria and the Dalmatian coast and a heavy leavening of people from further to the north and the east, Slavs, high cheek boned and powerful looking and, of course, women and children. They were destined for the most part for the voracious centres of the Saracen east, where there was always a market. They were the source of vast profit, these cargoes of human misery, and their transport and ultimate disposition fell largely to trade rich Pisans and Genoese and, most especially, the merchants of Venice. For the privilege, they too had to pay large amounts to the port authorities and, of course, to Bohemond of Taranto. In this all profited, save the hapless slaves themselves.

Equally entrancing was the massive bay and the harbour itself. Gilles was often lured here, inhaling the salt tang and the ripe aroma of fish far too long out of the water. And such a profusion of boats, great and small! Gilles marvelled at the sight each and every time he viewed it. At certain times of the day, the smaller craft lay at drunken angles, trapped by the stinking black mud before the water raised them up once more. These were not the strong tides that he had experienced off the French coast, but rather a subtle and almost imperceptible shifting of water.

The larger vessels, further out, bobbed and nodded serenely at their anchors. Each time he looked there were more boats arriving, under sail or entering using oars, weaving artfully between all the others. Looking at their large single square sails, they looked majestic. It was vessels such as these, Gilles assumed, that would ultimately take them all away to the lands of the Greeks, and to the Turk beyond.

Gilles would shrug and give the matter no further thought, striding instead through the crowded, noisy and foul smelling streets and thoroughfares redolent with the sights, sounds and smells of packed humanity and armed with his mental shopping list of requirements and provisions. The question of ships and shipping was, however, very much on the mind of Bohemond de Hauteville and the other leaders of the great enterprise as they continued to meet on an almost daily basis with a steady and constant flow of Pisan, Genoese and Venetian traders and adventurers. Vast amounts of money were being pledged in return for lucrative trading concessions and enticingly large tracts of land. Logistical issues of transport and provision were discussed at great length, with several of those present nodding off into sleep.

Bohemond de Hauteville, Lord Prince of Taranto, weighed all of this up with his customary self possession, balancing immediate loss against future possible long term gain. His own band of advisors, enthusiasts to a man, were, at the end of the day, largely unable to discern a greater pattern and scheme to things. Only Bohemond alone seemed to possess this skill as promise after promise made further inroads into his considerable wealth. Almost despite himself, he had grown fond of Robert of Normandy, though the man's bungling incompetence, explosive enthusiasm and frustrations and his distressing inability to see any wider picture occasionally preyed upon Bohemond's diplomatic nerves. The man, by turn was solemnly pious or else cheerfully profane, rambunctious and bawdy. At this moment he was monumentally bored, as was his own nephew Tancred, seated at his side and forever champing at the bit.

As the hours in council drifted past, men inevitably allowed their minds to wander, happily contemplating an evening to be spent with the dice and the consoling juice of the wine cup or, better still, the attentions of a comely and accommodating woman. Not so, the Prince of Taranto, his nuanced and complex mind set instead upon a higher purpose and one which, in time and all things being taken into consideration, would reap its own set of rewards. More immediate pleasures could wait. For Gilles and Benoit, meanwhile, surging through the seething markets of Bari and swatting at the irritating hucksters that surrounded them like a cloud of flies whenever the two appeared, there were more immediate matters to attend to. The price of the tiny iron rivets needed for a variety of purposes had soared. Likewise, the price for a cartload of hay or for a barrel of wine had become scandalous since the arrival of the army, crowded like squabbling locusts in the increasingly untenable encampment. In due course Robert would foot the bill, if not always cheerfully.

Bari was fast proving to be an illusion, a dangerous one. The autumn was setting in, the signs were visible for all to see. The trees, increasingly a rarity in a land where the soldiery constantly searched for fuel and construction materials, were red and russet and golden and the local peasantry noted the vivid red of the berries and muttered darkly of a harsh winter to come. It become increasingly clearer that the city and its hinterlands could not tolerate the presence of such a large number of men for much longer, it was being bled dry. Of equal concern to those who understood such matters, gales running in off the sea became more frequent, sudden and violent, rocking the boats at anchor in the harbour and the bay and sending others scuttling off in search of safety for the season. It became evident that no safe crossing to the land of the Greeks could be hoped for until the spring.

A particularly stormy meeting in Bohemond's much abused and put upon town house. Everyone with a vested interest in the success of the Great Enterprise, as it was coming to be called, was in attendance. At length, Bohemond rose to his considerable full length and screamed above the uproar and bellowing for silence. "Enough, my Lords all," he roared, banging the table for emphasis.

"We must all of us face the facts, as unpleasant as they may seem. Not for the intercession of the Virgin nor all of the saints in Heaven, will the winter stay away from us. It will soon be upon us, and all the signs are that it will be a harsh one. We can expect no sailing, and so we must disperse." By now it had come to be acknowledged that Bohemond was the ultimate authority on all things temporal, and that he should at the very least be heeded.

"So," he continued into the calm, "What is best to be done? Bari is exhausted. It cannot support us for much longer. I am taking my people south, to the port of Brindisi, and the lands about it. Perhaps, given better weather we can cross from there. You, my Lords, I recommend strongly that you move your arrays south too, into Calabria. You can winter there. The harvests, I have been told, are good there and, by the Grace of God, we can sail in the Spring." He sat down once more and reached for his drink. "We are done here. I suggest you all make your preparations." And the meeting was done, concluded in a brief sentence.

The rumours of the meeting spread swiftly back to the camp through those unofficial agencies that always governed such matters; from the ostlers, from the men who served the drink and carved the meat, from a variety of sources. In truth, the camp had grown bored and listless and in dangerous mood. Men of such mixed backgrounds and nationalities were bound to seek quarrels, food and strong drink had become scarce and the price for their services demanded by the women, sensing the removal of the source of their income, had risen alarmingly.

Robert had had a fine pavilion erected in the centre of the camp of his particular following. It was a brave and handsome affair, rarely used while the lights and delights of Bari beckoned, with the Ducal and personal banners permanently on display and a squad of extremely bored men guarding the tent and its contents. He rarely used it at night, but he was a frequent sight around the camp, indulging in his beloved horseplay and rough jokes, his common touch. Gilles was personally summoned there one morning. There was nothing unusual in this and he went, mentally prepared for the usual litany of complaints and unreasonable demands and a doubtlessly long list of tasks. He was well known to the guards, who let him pass without comment or hindrance. He ducked under the flap of the entrance and coughed politely to announce his presence, his eyes adjusting to the gloom of the interior. Unusually, the Duke was quite alone, even his personal scrivener was absent. Duke Robert was seated upon his leather fold stool, behind and above him stood the wooden cross bar bearing his chain mail hauberk and helmet and his sword, glinting dully in the poor light. Gilles had come to be able to detect Robert's moods with ease, to successfully detect the nuances that lay in his voice and in his actions, but here was something unusual. The Duke was clearly restless and unresolved on some issue. He greeted Gilles briefly and immediately rattled off a list of items he wished attended to. He paused and looked Gilles in the eye.

"For we are to move," he announced, "and don't act as if you did not know."

Gilles simply nodded and raised an inquisitive eyebrow. "Indeed, your Grace? Might I enquire when, and where to?"

Duke Robert emitted a heavy and annoyed sigh. "God damn your eyes, man. I don't rightly know, myself." He waved a vague hand in the air, "down there, down south, and soon." He sat back and the leather of his stool squeaked in protest. "There is one further thing." He peered at Gilles intently. "You are, in all things and in all ways, my man, Gilles. You are bound to me and it is your honour to serve me, in all respects."

Gilles nodded, and bowed formally. This was of course true.

"The noble Lord of Taranto," he continued, "is soon to leave us, it seems. And that nephew of his, Tancred. They are taking their following to Brindisi, a port south of here along the coast. There they will separate from us, to take ship to the lands of the Greeks."

So, thought Gilles to himself, the latrine rumours are true. "And so," announced Duke Robert, "in fulfilment of a promise given, and you were present to hear it for yourself, you are to place yourself under their command and travel with them. In this, and throughout, you remain my man. Is that understood?"

The Duke rose, and Gilles bowed once more. 'Quite

understood, your Grace, very clear. And may I ask, what my duties with them will be?"

Robert relaxed somewhat, even resuming his seat. "'That," he said at length, "is a pretty question, Gilles. Your duties will be as they have always been, to be my ears and eyes. You will send reports to me as often as you may so that I may plan and act accordingly. There is nothing ignoble here. I ask for nothing wrong or anything that carries deceit."

As he said these words to Gilles, his eyes conveyed a separate meaning, which he fully understood. If necessary then the good Lords Bohemond and Tancred need not know quite everything. Gilles, in fact, was considering another matter entirely. How was he, a mere supervisor of the construction of latrines and burial pits, a mere grocer, holder of horses and general dogsbody, expected to earn the respect of these noble and arrogant Norman warlords? Here, in this host, the ancient and noble lineage of his dead father counted for less than nothing.

But that day, for some reason, the normally obtuse Duke of Normandy appeared to have been endowed with the gift of reading minds. His mood changed abruptly to one of buoyant conviviality.

"And now, Gilles, will you take some wine with me?"

Gilles was startled, this was something new. He had never been offered wine before. Duke Robert rose and moved to a stout wooden chest in the corner of the pavilion. Two pewter cups and a flagon were among the many things resting upon it. With his own hand he poured out a measure into each cup and handed one to Gilles.

"I had almost forgotten," he said. "I cannot pack you off like some unwanted pot washer! The saints above, no! You have given me much service, Gilles. It is time to recognise the fact." He returned to his stool and sat, where he sipped his wine and contemplated Gilles. Finally, he snapped his fingers in a triumphant manner.

"Yes," he said. "I have it. Do you remember, in all our travels, a little place called 'Les Arbres Jeune', or some such. It is, as I said, a little place, strange name, just to the north of Argentan."

Gilles struggled to remember. He had, after all, been obliged to travel to many places in the wake of the itinerant Duke in his battered and besieged duchy. He recalled Argentan readily enough, a reasonably prosperous little market town in central Normandy, far from the hub of things and relatively untroubled and with a customary stronghold of timber and stone looming threateningly above it like some angry and festering boil.

"Well," continued Robert as he refilled their cups, "to the north of it is a fief belonging directly to me, with its own mesnie of men who serve. As I recall, it has some fine pasture land, with a good amount of forest too. Good for hunting, good for pigs. Yes, yes, I do remember too, now that I think on it, a good reputation for fine barley and the brewing of it. There's a good income there. There is of course a raised mound with a wooden palisade and tower, a wretched affair, that will need to be seen to rectified in these uncertain times, but there is too a half way decent manor house above the village and church. Yes, I remember now. Lots of work needs to be done there too."

Gilles listened patiently, Duke Robert took pride in his ability to recall details and it was not his place to interrupt. "Well, it is vacant, I have been told, and in need of a guardian. I shall enfeof you, Gilles, by God! Yes, you see if I don't. Now, we can't have you trailing after the good Lords Bohemond and Tancred with just your shirt and your bare arse hanging. Heavens, no. You shall receive your knighthood, Gilles, my boy, and carry a title with you." His voice was suffused with enthusiasm and warmth and he actually clapped Gilles heavily on his shoulder. "Now, what do you have to say to that?" This was typical of the man, typical of his extempore spontaneity.

Gilles bowed formally once more. "Your Grace, in truth, I do not know what to say."

Robert considered this reply and exhaled noisily. "Well," he continued breezily. "We must observe all the necessary observances and niceties of course, Gilles. Tonight, this very night, here in my pavilion and before my travelling altar you shall observe your Vigil, as is proper. And tomorrow, in the presence of witnesses, worthy men, and noted by clerics, you shall be knighted at my own hand and given the lands and the riches of 'Les Arbres Jeune'. You might like to consider the exact phrasing. Then you may travel with honour in the gathering of the Lord Bohemond, not as a servant, but as a Knight. More wine, I think. This I give you, this honour and title as my gift."

Chapter Nine: The Lord of the Young Trees

"Here were his famous colleagues, the glorious paladins, but what were they? There was their armour, proof of rank and name, of feats of power and worth, all reduced to a shell, to empty iron, and there lay the men themselves, snoring away, faces thrust into pillows with a thread of spittle dribbling from open lips." [Italo Calvino: *'The nonexistent knight'*]

That evening, at the hour of Vespers and as the sun dipped in the horizon to the west, Gilles, as instructed, entered the pavilion of Duke Robert, by the Grace of God, Duke of Normandy once more. He was accompanied to the very entrance by the silently sardonic Benoit, who left him there. He would assume his own vigil outside. The interior had undergone something of a transformation since his previous visit that morning. There was Duke Robert, waiting for him, booted and dressed up in his by now somewhat tawdry finery for some event or other in nearby tempting and beckoning Bari. From somewhere or other he had managed to conjure up two two grey monks, cowled and somewhat furtive and shifty looking creatures. Robert was still beaming and brimming over with evident good will, a satisfied master of ceremonies.

"I shall not," he announced, "be attending your Vigil, which you shall of course observe all night in the presence of our Good Lord. These two," he indicated the pair of monks with evident disdain, "will attend upon you. And now your sword, if you will."

To one of the monks, Gilles surrendered up his sword, tarnished and battered from much use. Only the other day he had used its leather wrapped hilt to hammer down some pegs in the horse lines. With a degree of reverence, the monk placed it upon the planking supported by two uneven rocks, Duke Robert's portable 'altar', upon which there burned a single large candle, admittedly of beeswax. Not for his prized man a shabby offering of foul-smelling sheep's tallow. There was also a simple wooden crucifix.

"And here," said Robert, "You will prostrate yourself before our Lord God. Now, I must be about other matters. I shall see you in the morning," and with that, he was gone.

Gilles looked about him, eyes now accustomed once more to the gloom. The departure of Robert made the place seem less bright and the flickering light of the single candle cast discomforting and eerie shapes of himself and the monks in distracted wavering patterns upon the soiled and tattered linen of the tent walls. Gilles had been present at enough investiture ceremonies in his time to know that this particular ceremony was altogether lacking in any sense of magnificence. He gazed upon the battered sword lying before the candle and crucifix before the makeshift altar and arrived at a decision. He ducked out of the pavilion once again and there was Benoit, whistling tunelessly as he whittled away at a discarded piece of wood with his knife.

"Benoit," he hissed, "a further favour to ask of you."

Benoit looked up enquiringly from his labours. Their own quarters were in fact only a short trudge away through the accumulating mire.

"My helm, Benoit, and my shield, such as they are. Could I ask you to fetch them for me? Also, a pot of water and a cloth."

Benoit grinned, a characteristically lop-sided affair. He and Gilles, of course, rarely washed, an occasional dousing in a river crossing or the consequences of being caught in the rain from time to time.

"Would this be," he enquired, "something of a ceremony we have here?" Gilles nodded briefly and re-entered the pavilion, to his candle and crucifix and monks.

The long, slow and tedious hours of the night passed very slowly as Gilles contemplated the objects on the altar before him and as he knelt on a rough padding of straw, hands clasped devoutly before him. His helmet was a rough composite and a shoddy thing; a cap of iron and a worn leather strap riveted to the inside. He recalled he had won it in a wager against a Breton man at arms back in France somewhere, he could not recall the place or the circumstances. The shield, too, was a ramshackle affair, circular in shape and of seasoned linden wood reinforced with iron rivets, with a metal rim and an inner handle with which to grip it. Benoit had duly fetched them all and handed them in at the entrance to one of the monks, along with a pair of mailed gauntlets that Gilles didn't recognise, a touching after-thought on the part of Benoit, who now shared Gilles' vigil, albeit at a small fire outside and where he could at least doze. Gilles shuffled, fidgeted and occasionally cleared his throat throughout the night, wondering, idly, where the monks had come from, and how much the Duke had paid them.

Gilles sporadically attempted to focus upon pious thoughts of a redemptive and spiritual nature. He attempted to ponder upon the Passion of the Lord as he contemplated the crucifix. In that uncertain and treacherous light, the eyes of the crucified Christ seemed to wink at him, a low and conspiratorial closing and then opening of one eyelid. He thought for a while of his strange mother, the perpetually sad Eloise, and then of the unbearably beautiful Zoe, of what had been and of what might yet be. He shook his head vigorously, this would never do! He attempted to concentrate instead of the honour of knighthood; the title, the land, the respect so long denied him. He thought of his dead father whom he had never known and of his illustrious Northumbrian past. He thought of fame and glory and the wealth he might gain in the fight against the Turk. He, no longer the discarded bastard son of a discredited Earl, but a man of wealth and power in the Great Endeavour set before him. Briefly, he contemplated what he could recall of the life and works of the blessed saint, Martin of Tours. He had always been led to believe that he was the man that military folk could call upon in prayer. Before long, the subject palled and, on his knees, he drifted off into sleep, to be only awoken once more by the gentle chiming of a hand bell and the sound of the monks breaking into a ragged unison of a chant to mark the passing of another hour.

The first hints of an approach of a grey and pink dawn in the camp, stilled and muted by the strictly enforced curfew. The first faint fragments of light through the frayed linen of the pavilion, the candle, much lowered now and resting in a pool of hardened grease, was guttering. One of the monks, quite frankly, was snoring. Gilles became acutely aware of how hungry and thirsty he was. Distant sounds of the camp stirring drifted over to him, the habitual dawn chorus of explosive coughing and retching, an iron pot falling heavily somewhere, an isolated shout of anger. Finally there came the sounds of the arrival of a number of horses and then, bursting in through the flap, looking much the worse for wear but still exuberant, came Duke Robert of Normandy. His smile was wide and infectious. He roosted out the monks, flapping his hands at them as he shooed them out of the pavilion like startled chickens.

The limited space of the interior was now a confusion of big, noisy men jostling for space, all of them much taken in drink, a jarring contrast to the secluded mood of only a short time ago. There, for example, stood the large and bristling form of the lord of Tosni, a particular boon companion and drinking partner of the Duke Robert. He and Gilles had shared more than one camp fire in the past months. Now, his wide, gap toothed grinning face wore an affable smirk. In his broad hand he held, dangling by a shining leather strap, a pristine new helmet, conical and beaten from a single sheet of iron with its distinctive strip of iron to protect the nose of the wearer. In it, Gilles would be identical to the greatest Lord. As a refinement, riveted to the rim at the rear was a brief curtain of chain mail to further protect the neck, a novelty that Gilles had rarely seen. Duke Robert pointed disdainfully at the beaten old sword, battered and dented and nicked, lying on the altar.

"Well, you won't be needing that any further," he said. "You shall receive something far more fitting." He whirled around and shouted. "Where is that damned scrivener when I need him."

A very little man eased his way through the crowded pavilion. He all but prostrated himself before the Duke.

"Mouse. There you are, you are so small, it is easy to overlook you," Robert said. "You have all your things necessary with you?"

The man indicated the large wallet attached to him by a length of cord. "Indeed, your Grace," he said. "My pen, ink, parchment and sand."

Robert nodded at him. "Good man, and no mistakes, mind. Such stuff is expensive." He turned to Gilles, "and you, have the goodness to kneel before me."

Gilles had been anticipating such a moment for years past as he had laboured and carried out the many tasks required of an unrecognised squire in the household of the Duke of Normandy. All those years spent in the mending of harness, the mucking out of stables, the many tasks required of him, ranging from the demeaning and mundane to the relative position of trust of recent weeks. He had, in his many musings, envisaged a warm and crowded hall, a stomach replete and satisfied and the admiring gaze of beautiful women as he received his reward from a contented Lord and with the murmurings of praise and mentions of his name echoing around the rafters. The reality, of course, proved to be very different as he knelt in the mud and straw of what was, in reality, a rather threadbare and shabby tent of linen.

Robert had drawn his sword from his mildewed leather scabbard. Instead of a resounding sound of metal there came a rather apologetic belch as he worked the blade free.

"Here," Robert of Normandy announced formally, "is my 'Benedictio Militis' to you." With the flat of his blade he touched Gilles lightly on first one shoulder, then the other. "And here is my 'adoubement'. My accolade."

Gilles had not anticipated the vicious rabbit punch that sent him sprawling, he could taste the iron tang of blood in his mouth and his eyes swam. There followed a bellow of laughter from the Duke, readily joined by all the others in the tent.

"Look at you there, sprawling in the mud like some landed fish," Robert said. "Up, up with you, Sire de Arbres Jeune, or whatever your name is, and welcome!"

Gilles clambered to his feet, wiping blood from his mouth, and was vigorously embraced by the Duke.

"Is all of that noted, scribe? Good. See that five copies are made. One for myself and one for the Sire de Arbres Jeune here. Have one sent to my Lord Bohemond of Taranto and one dispatched to my Chancery at Rouen. The other, well, to make up the numbers." He turned and addressed the small crowd that had gathered. "My Lords?"

The response was a hoarse acclaim of his name, "The Sire of De Arbres Jeune," followed by cheering.

"And now," announced Robert, "we shall all break our fast."

By now, as men crowded around Gilles and hustled him out into the cold morning air. The camp was fully awake and about its business. A full mug of strong wine was thrust into Giles hand and he was forced to drink. After a full and uncomfortable night of vigil, the alcohol went straight to his head as men alternately pumped his hand or slapped his back. Out of the corner of his eye he saw Benoit, saw his ever sardonic smile. Duke Robert was clapping his hands and bawling commands. Firewood was gathered and fires lit, trestle tables appeared, as if by magic, and a steady file of servers were somehow conjured up, placing bread and wine and cooked cuts of beef and mutton on the tables as the men crowded around, elbowing their way in to snatch at the free food and drink; a breakfast in honour of the Sire de Arbres Jeune.

"I think you should reconsider that name," observed Benoit quietly as he appeared at Gilles' side, "my Lord. It is, if I may say so, quite clumsy on the tongue and the ear."

The news was now being shouted about the camp. Robert, who had ever loved a crowd, ushered them in. There arose a single bark of a cheer. Gilles was already a well known figure, principally as an enforcer of the Duke's will, and not always popular as a result; but he was respected, and now he was a belted knight and seen to be high in the favour of the Duke. Sensing that the occasion for a drink would not be frowned upon, men brought their own to mark the event; fearsome stuff for the most part, a vicious combination of cheap local brandy fermented from dubious fruits, ale and wine. Before long the provosts would have to be called upon to beat them back for the celebration of Mass with their knotted rope ends, but for the time being at least Duke Robert tolerated it with good humour as gifts were presented.

Gilles choked violently on his home made apple brandy as an iron fist punched his back. "Smoother than a shaven eel," murmured Benoit urbanely, "ah yes, your gifts."

The nobleman Tosni was back before him once more, once again dangling the helmet before him. On his left arm, gripped by the enarme handles he held before him a handsome almond shaped kite shield, it was in fairly good condition. An external linen cover stretched over the treated, laminated poplar wood and with a rawhide rim. The centre boss of iron had been polished for the occasion. The shield was about three feet in height and its concave shape would protect him in the saddle from shin to shoulder. He recognised it, and the helmet, come to think of it. Tosni, forestalled him.

"Yes, yes," he said. "They are the possessions, or rather, were the possessions of the Sire de Fecamp. He is, as you know, now in Heaven with our Saviour." Yes indeed, the Sire of Fecamp, kicked in the head by a maddened horse he had been trying to pacify. "Can't let good things go to waste, can we now."

Gilles nodded at the truth of it.

"But," said Tosni who had assumed the role of a sponsor, "this is new, and made especially for you," he added magnanimously. Behind him, two men approached, carrying between them on a cross shaped pole on which was draped what appeared to be a full sized chain hauberk with mailed hood and stretching to the knee. It appeared to be brand new, an intricate affair of wire and linked iron links that seemed to gleam and shimmer like a fresh caught salmon in the uncertain light of the fire.

"Yes," said Tosni, appearing to read his thoughts. "It is, fresh made on the forge and fitted to your size and shape, more or less."

Gilles already owned his own gambeson, his quilted and padded coat. It was a wretched thing, torn and much patched. With this over him, he felt he would be invulnerable. He knew a woman in the camp who would make any necessary adjustments, for a price.

And, finally, that ultimate award, the sword. The sword, when finally it was presented to him, appeared in much the same way as everything else in this rushed and chaotic and improvised early morning with a full and proper Mass yet to be celebrated in the awakening camp. It was, of course, incumbent upon Duke Robert, as Gilles' liege Lord and sponsor, to make the presentation. By now the new Sire des Arbres was, like everyone around him, three parts drunk from the lethal combination of raw red wine and home-made brandy on an empty stomach and following a night of deprivation on his knees in the straw and with precious little sleep. Owlishly, Gilles attempted to focus and to concentrate as the Duke Robert stumbled into his line of vision once more. A scabbard and a trailing belt. Not just an ordinary scabbard either, but rather a fine piece of tooled leather, sleek with newness and embossed and punched with a swirling combination of marvellous shapes and designs. Robert, for balance, stood with both legs wide apart, rearing up before him, standing uncertainly like a man braced in a strong wind. With a fine and well oiled hissing sound, he removed the sword from the scabbard.

"Take it, hold it," Robert commanded.

Gilles took the sword for himself, it came to his hand like an eager lover. Even in his befuddlement he felt the fine balance of it; a three point blade of tempered steel that tapered, nearly two lengths of a man's arm, linseed oil still dripping down its central channelled groove. It was a weapon for hacking and for chopping rather than thrusting, as all good swords were, a weapon with which to cleave the head of the heathen Turk! He noted the hilt of the weapon, the usual shape of a crucifix and with the handle lightly wrapped in fine wire and ending in a pommel shaped like an almond. It was a fine weapon indeed, it felt like an extension of his own arm and the very personification of his new status and identity. This was an object, clearly, fresh from the forge of a master armourer. He felt that some kind of response was required of him. Holding the sword, he filled his lungs and yelled. "Deus lo Volt!" The cry emerged from him like a strangled croak.

Duke Robert seemed to appreciate the gesture, and the effort and clapped Gilles on the shoulder once more. "No further words are necessary," he told him. "None at all."

When all this has settled down," he indicated the chaos that surrounded them, "seek out Hebert, my horse master. He will take you to my lines and there you will pick out a suitable mount and to your liking. You will also, of course, need a squire. I have one or two suitable people in mind. Come attend me when all this is done."

Without a further word, he strode uncertainly off, calling for his retainers as he went, and leaving a bemused Gilles in his wake.

There was a marked difference in the way that people now approached Gilles, and treated with him in a camp that was now bustling with activity and the uncertain expectancies of the various preparations for a move to the good Lord alone knew quite where. He had grown used to ostlers and stable hands knuckling their foreheads at him, but now they bowed low at his approach and called him 'my Lord.' Gilles tried to make light of it, but could not, quite. He had shared a tattered and ripped canvas covering supported by sticks with Benoit for as long as he could remember. That had gone on the very morning of his elevation and in its place Benoit had instead led him to an infinitely superior construction of sticks and linen which from now on he would occupy on his own. It was cramped and he was not able to stand upright, but it was, Benoit assured him, for his sole occupation. There, with his saddle as a headrest, he slept heavily that morning whilst the encampment continued to erupt noisily around him. He slept through it all.

He was nudged awake by Benoit at some point in the late afternoon. He emerged out of the fog of a deep and unsatisfying sleep full of disturbing images. His mouth felt like he had been eating mud. He attempted to focus, uncertainly. He had no real clear recollection of where or indeed who he was.

"There are people here to see you," said Benoit, making no acknowledgement of Gilles' poor frame of mind. "They have been waiting for some time, now." Gilles groaned, staggered to his feet.

"Water, Benoit, for the love of Christ." He poured the offered water down his parched throat and stumbled out into the open.

Outside the tent stood three men wearing the insignia of the Duke and a boy. They all politely inclined at the waist at the sight of him, something that Gilles was still not used to.

"Well," he enquired, "and how might I be of help?" It was a simple enough question, but nonetheless it seemed to catch them all unawares.

One of them cleared his throat and fumbled in the wallet at his side. "I have here something for you from his Grace, the Duke," he said. "These others are here as witnesses, to see it done."

So saying, he produced a sizeable leather pouch with draw strings. He placed it in Gilles' palm, it felt very heavy. Gilles stared at it in bemusement and then loosened the strings and peered inside. He plucked out a single coin, one of many. He held it up to his eye, a thin object approximating to a circle. On one side a rough cross with Latin inscriptions, on the obverse what appeared to be a rough approximation of an angel or eagle with spread wings.

The man coughed again, deferentially. "I am to tell you, my Lord, that there are one hundred and twenty of them. Ten shillings from his Grace, the Duke. Please to make your mark here," he produced a scrap of parchment with more Latin written on it.

Dutifully, Gilles produced his dagger and scratched a cross at the bottom of the writing. "There, my Lord. I thank you. Some scribe will doubtless fill it in with ink."

A further deferential cough, this time from Benoit, and a raised eyebrow, advised Gilles to make no further comment. He had never seen, let alone handled, such a sum of cash in his whole life. Explanations could wait until such time as he saw the Duke in person once more. He suspected it to be a down payment of sorts on his newly acquired property. The three men knuckled their foreheads once more and then left, leaving Gilles and Benoit standing there.

Only the boy remained. Gilles looked him over, a long and painfully thin beanpole of a boy. He would be very tall, if he lived. He was shabby and unkempt and with holes in his hose and a dirty jerkin. He lowered out from beneath a lank mop of unkempt black hair that hung to his shoulders, staring out with startling black eyes, shining with an ill suppressed pride and a perhaps misplaced sense of pride. He looked as if he hadn't eaten in a week. Gilles was conscious of having seen him around, since before Italy, even; occupied with the whole variety of things that men of quality set young boys in service to do, such as the lighting and tending of fires, the grooming of horses, the scouring of pots.

Gilles sighed. "And you are?" he enquired, "what do you want?"

The boy drew himself to attention. "My name is Raoul," he said, "and I am here to serve you."

Benoit let out a bark of laughter and Gilles, too, smiled. "Are you, indeed?" he said. "And on whose authority?"

The boy's reply was almost defiant. "I am here," he said, "Because his Grace, the Duke of Normandy, bade me to. I am your bound servant, in all respects, and here to serve."

Gilles nodded to himself. First the knighting, all the gifts made and still to come, the huge amount of money that had come so easily to his hand, and now this. It was about time that he began to live up to his new found responsibilities.

"Well," he said. "Right now you look like nothing other than a drowned rat, boy. Benoit, get him something to eat before he ups and dies on us. Then, Raoul, if I have that name right, my horse needs grooming, feeding and exercising. After that, find me a money changer and bring him here. Can you manage all that?"

In the late evening, staring into the fire, Gilles felt more content. He and Benoit had shared a shoulder of mutton, roasted in the fire by the boy Raoul and now sat in a companionable silence, sharing a flagon of wine. Gilles' old horse almost shone with the currying and grooming it had received from the boy, who had also taken it out for exercise far beyond the encampment. Now it dozed contentedly at its picket, a belly full of oats. A money changer had been located and told to attend him first thing in the morning and he had also received a message from the Duke's horse master to call upon him at his convenience. Life was looking good, for the time being.

At last Benoit broke the silence. "If it is all the same to you, Gilles," he began. Gilles started, the man had never referred to him directly by his name before. "If it is all the same with you, then I shall stay, for the time being at least."

Gilles chose his words carefully. "Then that is fine with me too, Benoit. Though I am not sure what I can offer you in return."

Benoit considered his answer before replying. "Well," he said. "You have a new name and a new reputation to make. I shall do as well with you than I would with any other man who has nothing to prove." He passed Gilles the near empty flagon, "to the making of reputations then. We shall do well enough, you and I."

They both lapsed back into silence one more.

Another day rich in promise. The first of Robert's fellow leaders were busy in the arrangements to move location. By the end of the day the first of them had begun to move off, a move south to the promised better fields, better harvests and better weather of this place called Calabria. A series of short moves to a final new muster, the exact location yet to be arranged. Small parties of noblemen and their retainers made their noisy and disgruntled exits. For Gilles the day began with a half way decent breakfast, warm bread, cheese and olives provided by the boy Raoul, he was appearing to be most attentive and anxious to please, speaking only when addressed directly. Shortly after, the first of the day's tasks, a novel one, to be performed.

On Benoit's advice, he had recruited two of the more unpleasant looking men Benoit could find, and in that camp he was spoiled for choice. They were paid in coin and at his disposal for the entire day. Their task was far from onerous, being required simply to be there and to exude an air of menace and look ugly. He took one of his silver coins and hacked it in half, handing each their half portion and thus establishing a reputation as a good payer. Further service would of course ensure further payment. It was mid morning before the money changer, a Jew of Bari appeared. He was mounted on a donkey that carried also all the impedimenta of his trade, for Aaron Ben Shimat was also conscious of his status and bearing. Strewn about the donkey was a small wooden table, a canvas folding stool, a complete set of weights and measures and various other pouches. The money changer too was clearly conscious of security, for he had his own bodyguard of two men with him, as equally unpleasant as Gilles' own two men. Gilles could feel the hackles of his own men rising.

Ben Shimat dismounted, bowed and bestowed the most charming of smiles.

"I believe, my Lord, that we may well understand each other," Gilles nodded.

"I do believe so," he said, watching as one of the money lender's men set up the stool and the table.

The money lender eased his well dressed bulk into the stool with a satisfied grunt. Benoit provided an upturned log for Gilles to use. The two men sat, the table between them. Gilles was not prepared to break the silence, inviting the man to speak.

"My name is Ben Shimat, first name Aaron," he finally said. "I am, as I imagine you have already surmised, a Jew." He spoke the French of the camp, passably well, but with a very strong accent that was difficult to follow. "I have been summoned from Bari and I am here at your service, my Lord. How then may I be of service? But, forgive me, will you take wine?"

Gilles nodded and the man gestured to a servant, who produced a flagon and two pewter cups from a pannier.

"And this," the money lender said, "is of the best quality, such as I serve to honoured clients." His eyes glittered with a genuine good humour, provoking Gilles into a response.

"I," began Gilles, "am the newly appointed Sire des Arbres'. I have been named and endowed as such by my Lord, his Grace, the Duke of Normandy. It is a great honour and carries many riches." As he spoke, he realised how pompous he sounded, but Ben Shimat responded with a soft voiced murmur.

"A great honour, indeed, my Lord, and how may I serve?" The man's manners were impeccable.

Gilles motioned Benoit forward to place the heavy weight of the kidskin wallet on the table. Gilles released the drawstrings and allowed a few of the silver pennies to spill out. The money lender's eyes widened momentarily at the sight.

"May I?" he enquired and picked one of the coins up and held it up to his eye, feeling the weight in his mind. He placed it on his brass scale and added a weight. Finally he said. "It is a silver denier, my Lord. It is of the correct weight and is of an admirable quality. Minted in France, I would judge." His eyes drifted to the wallet and the spilled coins. "And may I ask? How many of these do you possess?"

Gilles calculated, numbers were not his strong point, he had never had a schooling in such matters. "I have," he told the money lender, "ten shillings, taking away one coin which I have already used."

He felt uneasy in discussing such matters, he had never been rich before, uncomfortable at discussing such matters with a complete stranger. The money lender was evidently well used to such uncertainties on the part of a client.

Ben Shimat pursed his lips. "A tidy sum," he said, "much too much for you to be carrying around with you, my Lord. I take it that you will be embarking on this, ah, 'Grand Enterprise'?' Yes, I thought as much. Well, my advice to you is that you return the half of it to your good Lord and ask him to keep it safe for you. He will have any number of churchmen happy to do him the service of minding it. But, be sure to ask for a document of surety. Politely, of course. That advice I give you freely and at no charge. As for the rest, you should keep it with you. Where you are going you will need all the comfort that a coin can bring. Believe me, I know. So, for a fee I can give you coins of a lesser value but amounting to the same in total. Thus, you will also have ready money that is appropriate for the purchases you will need to make, without paying too much. I can also advise on how to spend it to the best purpose and how to recognise the people you will need to trust. I have been to those places that you plan to visit, yes, as far as the Great City of Constantinople itself, should you get that far, which is, I regret to say, by no means certain." The man looked genuinely regretful for a moment, pursing his lips and then sighing deeply.

"But that," he concluded, "is not for either to us to know. We both live in the present moment, and we must make of that as much as we may. The important thing is to make as much of what we have when we have it. This is my profession, my Lord. It is the reason why I sit here before you. I see that your cup is empty. Will you take more wine?"

This was deep thinking indeed, and too deep for Gilles to cope with at this present time.

"You mentioned a fee," he said.

The laughter was back in the money lender's vivid dark eyes once more. "Indeed I did, my Lord. It is, I assure you, a mere token, a gesture. For the price of four of your silver pennies I will convert half of your wealth, for the other half of it you must return for safe keeping to your own Lord. I will change your money for portable smaller coin of the same value in weight and silver. I will also provide you with pouches and, perhaps my greatest gift to you, a letter to those of my brethren and profession that you might encounter in your travels. They will help and assist you and you can trust them."

Gilles considered this offer. In truth, the weight and all the responsibility of all that money was a burden to him.

"I accept," said Gilles.

Ben Shimat appraised him speculatively. "Then drink up, my Lord. Come to me at my place in Bari this time tomorrow, your boy knows the way. I shall await you there." He bowed, rose and his men rearranged all the various tools of his trade on the donkey.

He bowed with utter courtesy once more, and left,

A brisk walk through the camp, a chaos of arrivals and departures to the horse lines. He found Duke Robert's master of horse bent double over a horse's forelock, swearing foully as he scraped at the hoof of a far from passive horse, his mouth full of nails.

"Son of a bitch," he muttered. "This sodding mud will do for all of them if we don't take a mind to it." He straightened up at Gilles' approach and spat.

"So, it is yourself," he observed. Gilles grinned.

They knew each other of old, these two, from years back. He had learned much of the mastering of horses, and had received more than his fair share of cuffs and kicks from this man now grown old and grey in the Duke's service.

"Should I bow, or can we take that to be unnecessary?" News had travelled fast.

"No, that will not be necessary, Hebert," he said.

Hebert removed a few nails from his mouth. "Just as well, it would be a long time coming." He wiped his hands free of dirt vigorously. "You would be here, I imagine, about a horse. His Grace has informed me." He strode off and Gilles fell in beside him.

"Two more also, in fact, in addition to the gift. I have a man and a squire now in need of something serviceable."

Hebert paused and nodded. "Aye well, his Grace said as much. He clearly values you, young Gilles, for that too can be arranged. A good serviceable mount for each of them, but for you something of a different quality, I think. Let us go and take a look over at what we have."

He led him off to a ramshackle stockade of rough timber hammered into the uneven ground with strands of pliable willow woven between the posts, such as a basket maker might weave. It was a large space surrounded by incurious and idling men who parted as Hebert cursed and shoved his way through. Contained within the space were about a score of horses, either standing idly or else dipping their heads to snatch a mouthful of the panniers of hay tethered to the posts, miserable fodder to horses more accustomed to oats and barley, but these were pressing times for man and horse alike.

Hebert pointed at one, occupying a corner for itself, clearly having made a space in which the others feared to intrude. The creature was a handsome bay of some sixteen hands, perhaps eight years old.

"That's a right bastard, that one, and no mistake," said Hebert. "Been with the herd since France. Scarcely no one can get near him, he's that difficult. A stallion, not gelded. Will you look at the fine sight of him, now. That's the one I have in mind for you."

Gilles allowed his eyes to feast upon the creature. It was a strong, fighting horse, strong and powerful hindquarters rippling with muscles, a short back, well muscled loins, strong boned with a well arched neck. Its neck was strong and with a firm jaw and a good width between the eyes. A flash of white between the eyes, a star.

"Earandel," Gilles breathed to himself, 'morning star' in the old English, "that is your name. It is fitting."

Hebert would have been unmoved by any such sentiment. "Son of a bitch will need a rope," he said.

Gilles travelled into Bari for the discharge of two further details. He gained admittance to the town house of Duke Robert with no difficulty, indeed with a certain amount of ceremony. He found the Duke himself in the hall, and far from the affable mood of the previous morning. Doubtless, he was nursing one of his vicious hangovers. He was also extremely harassed, with a constant flurry of servants and aides clamouring for his attention as he prepared to move his command south, a scrivener with pot, ink and parchment a constant presence at his side as he barked orders and commands. No offer of a drink on this occasion.

"Gilles," he said, for old habits died hard. "As you can see, I am very pressed for time. I do, though, have one or two things that need to be said. You may begin, for I can see that you are here to thank me," he paused to snap at the helpless scrivener and to shout out a command at a person at the far end of the hall. "No, no, the candlesticks first, dolt, and wrap them in linen, mind," He turned back to Gilles, "you were saying?"

Gilles bowed low. "Your Grace, my Lord. I thank you for all of the gifts you have given to me. I thank you also for the boy, Raoul, and I thank you especially for the gift of the horses. I am, in all ways, your man and here to serve."

Robert, appeased and soothed, managed a brief albeit wintry smile in acknowledgement in all that chaos. "Well, yes, and so you might. Is there anything else? For I am pressed for time."

Gilles produced the heavy kidskin wallet of coins. "My Lord, I must thank you also for this. I fear that it is too much of a responsibility for me to carry it with me into the fight with the Turk."

Robert's eyes narrowed. "So, what is it you would have me do?" he asked.

Gilles thought carefully before answering. "Your Grace, I would have your clerk here count out the half of it and for me to return it to your care until such time as things are clearer for you and I, and that I may then reclaim it."

Robert considered this. "It is well considered, and well said," he decided at length. "I agree. You, clerk, count it out here before us and remove the half of it for our safe keeping."

He turned to Gilles, "You would require a receipt, I take it."

Gilles swallowed, "Your Grace," he replied, "that would be most welcome, I thank you again."

It had been a worrying moment, his Grace, the Duke of Normandy, had made it all very easy. He drew a deep breath.

"See to it," Duke Robert ordered the clerk. He drew Gilles to one side, leading him off to a corner of the hall, waving aside all of the others.

"A word in private, Gilles, my boy," he said. "The boy Raoul is of fine stock, I made a promise to his father, see to it that you keep him as well as you may in the times ahead. I shall hold you to this. In these harsh times I fear he has had a harsher start than most. Do not remind him of it and treat him with kindness, I have made a pledge upon my honour to his family. And now," he said briskly, "to other matters. You must have a following. You are to recruit five men, as well as that great beanpole who is forever hanging around you like a bad smell, and the boy, Raoul. Their expenses for the time being will be met by me until such time as you can meet them for yourself. You will then present yourself to the Lord Bohemond. Saving myself, you shall now be his to command. You will, of course, remember our particular understanding."

Gilles bowed once more, "My Lord, your Grace. I do."

Robert nodded. "Good, good. And now here is that man of mine with his parchment and the rest of your coin. May God protect and cherish you, Gilles. We shall of course meet again, the saints grant that it may be soon." A brief grasp of Gilles' arm, "and now begone. I have no further time for you."

A journey, now, to a far less salubrious quarter of the teeming city of Bari, with Benoit and his new two henchmen. Raoul led the way with confidence, guiding them through the jostling crowds. The money lender occupied a booth screened by a tarpaulin from the street. One of his guards, muscled and intimidating and with a practiced scowl, stood outside, arms folded. He held a vicious looking blade that looked capable of taking off a man's head in an instant. He recognised Gilles and wordlessly beckoned him in. Ben Shimat rose from his seat in wide armed and effusive welcome.

"You have the money, my Lord? Good, good. To business then."

Gilles produced the by now much lighter purse. He placed it on the table between them.

"I have here, he said," my silver pennies of the highest quality. I am told that there are fifty eight of them, tested and verified. My understanding is that I must pay you as a fee four of these. If you have any further services to offer me, and if they are of interest, then I shall pay you for these also. Otherwise, I shall thank you to give me smaller coins, and to the same value."

The smile on the face of Ben Shimat broadened even wider.

"Admirable, admirable," he said. "This is the work of a moment. Please to note the fine quality of the containers I have for you." He busied himself once more with the scales, his hands blurring with speed. "These here, my Lord," are silver pennies. Some are quartered and some are in halves. The quality of silver, I assure you, is excellent. And now, if I might?" He counted out five of Gilles' pennies, weighed them against a number of half pennies.

These he weighed, once more, with solemnity and with a protruding tongue in concentration, and placed the half pennies into a pouch. Gilles' coin disappeared into the depths of his lap. He repeated this several more times, Gilles' pile diminished and the pile of wallets before him increased.

"And now for the quarter pieces," he said, and repeated the process. "There, we are done. Might I suggest you retain five of the pennies for, shall we say, larger purposes?"

Gilles nodded in agreement.

"Then we are done," repeated Ben Shimat. "If I may, I shall now claim my four silver pennies." Carefully, he made to remove his fee. Gilles nodded to him. Ben Shimat clapped his hands and called for wine. "And now, some advice, if I may."

In truth, Gilles was beginning to tire of this man's advice, but it was being given freely and he was, at heart, a tolerant man.

"Very well, then. But I need to say that my time is short," he said, somewhat brusquely.

"To be sure, to be sure," Ben Shimat agreed. "Only this, then, my Lord. In all matters relating to money, know that each man you encounter is potentially your enemy. He will prove to be your friend only if he makes some gesture to show that he might be trusted. What that gesture might be, I know not. It will arise out of the circumstances of the moment." Gilles was largely unimpressed by this.

"Is that it?" he asked.

Ben Shimat, first name, Aaron, bowed low once more.

"Yes, Lord, that is it. Where you propose to travel now will be perilous, enemies will surround you. Beware the advice of great men." He produced from within his tunic a folded parchment. On it Gilles could make out a strange script, a confusion of heavy blocks and whirling curves. "I am, as you know, a Jew, my Lord. We are an oppressed people and in all that we do we must tread carefully." He handed Gilles the parchment. "Take this for surety, for I am known. If you meet any person of my race and background and you feel that he can be trusted, then show him this."

Again, the courteous bow. "Go with God."

The newly appointed Sire of the Young Trees was now a man of authority, wealth and stature. He did not know how old he actually was, could only make educated guesses. He was in many ways very emblematic of this army of this Great Enterprise. In rude health, brawny and resourceful and in possession of additional skills earned in the Duke's service, he was to all intents and purposes illiterate and ignorant of the world. Gilles was a young man full to the brim with the beliefs, superstitions and prejudices of his time and class and with little time for any philosophical niceties or any undue delicacy. He was aware of his station in life and of the reverence due to his betters. He had had his own history in his experiences with women and had behaved as all others of his kind ever had. He had killed a man in a knife fight and had followed orders scrupulously in the execution of others in obedience to his Lord's will. He had never been involved in anything other than brawls and scuffles, let alone a full blooded encounter with the Turk, but he had no reason to doubt either his confidence or his ability. Gilles was conventionally pious and had no doubts that God would provide. He believed utterly and with all sincerity in the old war cry of the Norman warrior class, 'God Wills It."

Gilles, then, had every reason to feel confident as he rode out under the orders and in the service of his Lord Robert Duke of Normandy to take up whatever duties the Lord Bohemond, Prince of Taranto might require of him. He did not come alone like any other ordinary servant, not this time. Riding at his side was Benoit and, slightly to the rear, his peculiar and newly acquired young squire Raoul, each of them proudly astride a new mount and with Raoul leading the spirited war horse Earandel, a creature that had already drawn many admiring glances. Gilles had yet to ride him himself. Benoit led another horse, a sumpter, laden with all the paraphernalia of Gilles' war gear, his helmet, his chainmail, spear and kite shield and his personal possessions. Gilles' new sword was strapped firmly to his waist. He turned in the saddle to look round at his new command, trudging through the mire behind him, for he was a freelancer no longer. Five men and another two heavily overladen sumpter horses that clattered and tinkled like a tinker's cart with all of the things strapped to them. As he looked, an iron kettle fell loose and into the mud. Clearly, they would need to acquire a cart. He sighed heavily, it was hardly the vast retinue and panoply of a great lord but, he supposed, it was at least a start.

Five men, either recruited or actually pressed into service. Ralph, from the uncertain badlands that separated the Norman and Breton borders, appeared to be a natural leader of sorts. Benoit had found him, the Lord alone knew where, or knew anything of his history. At some point in his life he had clearly fallen foul of the authorities, for both his ears had been cropped for some offence; two red and livid webs of scar where once his ears had been. Perhaps for blasphemy and for the size of his tongue, for his insistent whine of a voice could be heard all over the camp, usually giving voice to some lurid and often heretical statement. He was giving tongue now as he laboured along the ruts created by heavy wagons in the heavy mud.

The others clearly found him entertaining, though Gilles

suspected that his own patience might soon pall. Next to Ralph, himself rather a slight man, there strode a veritable ox of a man, tall and powerful looking, named Arnauld, a large and shambling creature, heavy browed and with small black eyes that glimmered out of a brutal looking face just discernible beneath a forest of hair and beard. Benoit had selected him personally, too. He knew nothing of his history.

"But you would not believe the strength of the man," he had assured Gilles. "I have seen him bend a horse shoe with those great hands of his. Very dependable man, very loyal, he'll come in very handy at some point."

Gilles had personally taken possession of the other three from the Duke Robert himself, sweepings, the detritus from within his host that he clearly no longer had any use for, if indeed he ever had, and whose wages, such as they were, he had met himself. Two of these, unremarkable and nondescript in every way, were the men named Ernoul, from the slums of Rouen and an equally ill favoured individual, Jacques, 'the weaver', apparently from Artois, wherever that might be. Neither man appeared to possess any particular skill in anything or anything that suggested the promise of great things. The Duke's final gift was a strange looking foreigner, almost a midget in size, very muscular and bandy legged, bald as an egg and covered in a pelt of thick black hair. There was a single golden ring in his ear by way of adornment. Gilles could not but be amazed that he had managed to hang on to it, the company he must have been keeping.

The man was the colour of a ripe nut and had a face full of either merriment or devilry, depending largely on one's point of view.

"Watch that one," the overseer had advised. "A natural born thief and born to be hanged. He could have the shirt off your back before you could draw a breath."

The man introduced himself as Reynard. By his speech and accent he was from somewhere far to the south in France. How he had fetched up under the Duke's command was anyone's guess.

"Full of little tricks," the overseer had added, "but some of them might prove of use."

Gilles took one further look at them as they straggled along. He sighed once more, imagining the impression they would make upon the haughty Duke of Taranto, they could barely understand a word of what the others spoke. Some of them he had yet to hear speak at all. Still, beggars could not be choosers. These were the men he would lead to fight the Turk.

The Lord Bohemond had led his command away some miles south of Bari and along the infertile land as it met the Adriatic. It was unpromising terrain, to say the least, but his Norman army, free of the taint of the other European commands, had moved in clear order and cohesion and with a purpose only to be expected from the tough mercenaries and adventurers under his leadership, men well inured to the dunes and bitter salt marshes and other vagaries of the local geography. All along the route Gilles encountered armed and well appointed and disciplined pickets who required to know his business. This he explained, with much waving of the official and impressively sealed documents with which Duke Robert had provided him. In each case he was allowed through with no further questions and to complete his next progress along the bleak and sterile coast. The next and final interception came when Gilles and his motley little command had actually come in sight of the pavilions and tents and campfires stretched out along the strand in this now wholly Norman led affair.

The final intercepting patrol, larger and more imperious than the others was led by a familiar figure. Gilles' heart sank as he recognised the leader, none other than his old acquaintance, Jordan de Drengot. The man reined in next to Gilles.

"So," he said quite unnecessarily, "it is yourself."

There was no fondness or glad recollection in his tone. De Drengot cast a sneering glance over Gilles' ragged little following, his face a picture of contempt. "These, er, men. They are yours?"

Gilles felt entitled to a sense of stung pride. "They are my following, yes," he replied.

De Drengot allowed himself a little smile. "Your following? Oh yes. I had heard something of the like. My congratulations... my Lord. Well, we all have to start somewhere, I suppose. The horse, though, is fine."

Without a further word, de Drengot motioned for them to follow. He led them through the tall coarse grass and the dunes and the horse lines through the camp. Incurious faces eyed them as they passed. They arrived finally at a pavilion larger than the rest. Surrounded by a group of men, Bohemond de Hauteville himself sat outside on a canvas and leather stool, demolishing a capon. Gilles recognised of old that the man did so absently, simply as something merely necessary as his startling eyes focussed on something else. He did not rise, of course, as Gilles dismounted and knelt before him.

"My Lord," began Gilles formally, "I bear greetings and messages from the Lord Robert, Duke of Normandy. He..."

"Yes, yes, yes, to be sure," interrupted Bohemund impatiently, "get up man. Enough of all the fawning. You have written messages? Give them to my clerk here." He snapped his fingers. "You there, de Drengot. See that these people of his," his tone was equally contemptuous, "have a place to settle."

De Drengot's face stiffened and darkened in anger, but he bowed curtly and left to attend to the needs of Gilles' new command.

Bohemond discarded the bone he had been gnawing on, threw

it over his shoulder and wiped his hands down his jerkin.

"Now then, my new found Knight," he said. "To the present matter. You are now here and under my present pleasure. You may consider yourself as within my household. As such, you will eat at my board and at my expense. In all respects you must consider yourself mine to order whatever might be my will and to be sent wheresoever I might wish. I trust that that is clear enough?"

Gilles nodded, "it is, most certainly, Lord," he said.

Bohemond considered him with that chilling and far sighted stare. "Good, good. Remember this. I repay loyalty to excess, and I am swift to anger in my disappointment. You may go."

Within a fortnight the whole army of Bohemond moved further south to the outskirts of the ancient port of Brindisi for its winter quartering, leaving Robert and all the other commanders to seek their own salvation elsewhere. Bohemond was a far stricter task master than the more relaxed and easy-going Duke Robert had ever been and Gilles only had brief visits to the ancient city itself. Like Bari, it had the febrile air of a frontier outpost, despite its antiquity. Finally seized by the Normans barely thirty years earlier, the menace of their military presence was everywhere, cowing the mixed Greek, Albanian and Moslem population. They went about their daily lives carefully and with circumspection, a city under military occupation.

The city was crumbling and fly-blown, but the harbour was safe and the harvests from the surrounding districts plentiful. In the winter weeks within the camp, Bohemond made sure that Gilles, along with everybody else, was kept fully occupied in a whole series of tasks infinitely more varied and demanding than those imposed upon him by the Duke Robert. In accordance with his future duties, Bohemond was keen to have him work on at least a practical understanding and command of Greek. To this end, he had Gilles sent out at least once a week to see the Prince's authority maintained in the countryside, the reading of proclamations, attendance at local court sessions and other, more forceful, duties, related usually to money.

In these frequent excursions his more or less constant companion was a wizened old Greek cleric named Demetrios, an ancient and unkempt figure who looked as if he had been left to dry and shrivel and turn to raisins in the sun for far too long. The man was dry, pedantic, utterly lacking in humour and an insufferable bore. Perhaps under instructions, he refused to speak to Gilles in French as they laboured along the treacherous coastal paths or inland among the rocky hills. He spoke only in Greek and in this way and in very short order Gilles began to acquire first a broad vocabulary for objects and then a greater sense of fluency as he listened to the old Greek's demands of his various audiences and the outraged patois of their protests. Demetrios was also, it seemed to Gilles, excessively pious. Perhaps all Greeks were like this? In any event, the old clerk, missed no opportunity in hauling his scrawny carcass into every Greek Orthodox shrine or church that they encountered on their journeys. Sitting or standing for hours on end as the solemn chanting of the old Greek Mass rose and fell and swirled about him, Gilles was absorbing far more of the language than he realised.

Occasionally he would ride out on Earandel on some of these expeditions, to grow accustomed to the creature and to allow it some knowledge and experience of him. Mostly, though, he rode his old mount, for Earandel was a horse bred for other purposes. Occasionally, also, Benoit would accompany him, but for most part he and the clerk had the company of five or six grim faced and taciturn mailed men as support whilst Demetrios extorted and made his demands. Demetrios was, of course, literate, and never travelled without the tools of his trade and the keys to his portable strong box.

Benoit kept a firm and strict order amongst the men, reporting back on their doings and, more frequently, their misdoings on a regular basis. The gigantic Arnauld rarely spoke, but was biddable enough, Ernoul and Jacques the weaver were a pair of feckless, idle bastards who needed to be constantly watched and the man Ralph was forever provoking fights in the camp through his ungovernable tongue and irreverent wit. It also transpired that, amongst his many other talents, the 'gypsy,' Reynard, was a cook of no little talent and capable of taking away anything not actually firmly nailed to the ground. Through his efforts they were never short of supplies and had through some means acquired a small cart and donkey. Reynard was reticent about the source of these things and Benoit never pressed him unduly.

The boy Raoul was a concern. He was perhaps thirteen years of age. The boy's attention to his service and duties was faultless He was up before anyone else and went to bed later than they. He was attentive, obedient and assimilative and the men had learned to deal with him with a rough fondness. But the boy was clearly unhappy and Benoit had caught him on a number of occasions in silent tears. It was most unlike Benoit to show an undue compassion.

"That boy has a story to tell," he informed Gilles one evening as they shared a fire. "Something is burning him up, but he won't tell me. I think you should try and worm it out of him."

But Gilles' had little time to spare on unravelling any personal issues of his new squire. The demands of the Prince of Taranto were too exacting for that!

Chapter Ten: Bari and Beyond

"A crusade army was, in effect. A loosely organised mob of soldiers, clergy, servants and followers heading in roughly the same direction for roughly the same purposes. Once launched, it could be controlled no more than the wind or the sun." [Professor Thomas Madden: *The Concise History of the Crusades*]

For the most part, the city of Brindisi and its superlative port was forbidden for idle visits and pursuits. For the occasional public meetings and assemblies, however, Bohemond preferred the selection of one church or another where he could be raised up and seen and heard by a crowd, far more preferable to the confusion attendant upon any public assembles before his pavilion. Messengers would go about the camp announcing the chosen venue and the time and who was and who was not required to attend, Bohemond frowned upon any possible confusion or obstacles to his desired aims.

Gilles had yet to witness any of the man's temper tantrums, but they were held to be legendary. On this particular Sunday in November, lest there be any doubt of the venue, the Prince of Taranto personally led those bidden through the camp and then the ragged fringes of Brindisi to the very steps of a Church yet to be built. The space was just open wasteland with here and there signs of evidence of the work of masons and carpenters. The Normans were, after all, relatively new to this land and had yet to make their full mark in aspirations of towering and intimidating stone. The ancient and discoloured raised steps to some ancient and derelict pagan temple, however, would suffice for the purposes of Prince Bohemond of Taranto. Gilles stood in the open space in the company of a few score chosen men waiting for Bohemond to say what he wished to say. It was a mild day, a blustery wind, but not cold, it hadn't rained in a week. November. Gilles suddenly recalled that a year before he had been struggling in the Alpine passes at Pontarlier, flinching and shivering in the sleet. Where, he wondered idly, would he be a year from now? Perhaps Bohemond had the answer to that, raising his arms for silence and preparing to speak.

Gilles, arms folded, braced himself and set to picking out the bones of such of the speech that he could hear. In truth, he had heard similar on previous occasions. All was good and set fair, he heard. The harvest was good and food and supplies guaranteed for the winter months, which promised not to be harsh. Agreements had been made and terms set for transport to the land of the Greeks at the first Spring sailing. A consortium of Venetian, Pisan and Genoese merchants and traders had guaranteed to fill the excellent harbour of Brindisi with all the shipping and transports and provisions they would require by the end of the winter. The Emperor of the Greeks has sent his loving care and thanked them all for their Christian devotion in this time of need.The Emperor looks forward to welcoming them all to his land and then to conveying them at his own expense to the land where our Saviour had lived and died. Our fellow warriors, from France and the Lowlands, from Greater Germany and beyond, are busily making their own plans. We shall meet at Constantinople! And that, largely, was it. There followed the usual string of exhortations and dire threats regarding the keeping of order and peace, and then a list of names of people to attend upon him at his pavilion. With a start, Gilles realised that his own name had been called.

Gilles duly presented himself at the pavilion of Bohemond, as instructed, on the evening of the following day, there to witness the machinery of personal rule. For reasons of space, Bohemond summoned his followers in groups of ten or so, summoned not to listen to general proclamations but rather to receive specific and detailed instructions. It was, Gilles had learned, how Bohemond liked to conduct affairs and there was little scope for either confusion or individual interpretation .Dutifully, he waited in line as others more exalted than he received their instructions and were dismissed, Bohemond did not encourage any undue questioning. A little further up the coast, Gilles learned, there had come reports of something that could well turn into a mutiny of sorts in a collection of fishing boats requisitioned for ultimate mobilisation, minor acts of piracy and the theft of sheep. A rape and a murder had also been reported. Clearly an uncompromising stance was required, and who better for the task than the far from diplomatic person of Jordan de Drengot himself? Bohemond wagged an admonishing finger at de Drengot.

"And no half measures, mind, de Drengot. I want this firmly nipped in the bud. If you find ringleaders, then hang them and be done with it. No loose ends." He pointed also at Gilles. "And take that Frenchman, or whatever he is, with you. He could do with some exercise instead of sitting around on his arse and getting fat at my expense. I understand that you are, er, old friends. Take fifty men. A show of force is needed." He waved them away, that characteristic flick of the wrist indicating that the interview was ended.

Outside and away from earshot, de Drengot was, predictably, far from happy with the arrangement. Nothing, it seemed, would ever please this fiery man and Gilles could sense his resentment. He had been summoned from his previously happy and independent life as a hill ruffian and translated into the role of a glorified domestic servant. This, clearly, was not how he had envisaged the life of a Holy Warrior. He positively snarled at Gilles.

"Be ready at daybreak to move out. Don't bring any of your rabble, just that man of yours and your squire. I shall provide the men we need. Keep out of my way as much as possible, just watch and learn."

Gilles nodded in agreement and understanding, de Drengot was, after all, a master in the gentle arts of persuasion.

"We shall need some bags," de Drengot mused aloud, a form of note to self. "My Lord Bohemond likes to see a head or two for his pains."

The whole affair took just over two days. The group convened at dawn and rode out through the camp, a long double file of grim faced men in full armour heading north to the scene of the disturbance and following the rough and desolate track along the fringe of the coast. Naturally, no person disputed their passage. They saw very few people and in the few miserable settlements that they did pass through the inhabitants stood in fearful and sullen silence as they watered their horses and purloined food. In the mid afternoon they were joined by a guide who, as the light began to fail, led them to a secluded place amongst high sand dunes. They watched the first twinkling of lights out in the bay from a group of five fishing vessels and, on the shoreline, frenzied activity as men scurried hurriedly from beached boats to the supposed safety that lay inland. Watching them, Benoit sighed heavily.

"Well," he observed, "devil a doubt but they have seen us. I wouldn't put money on catching any of them now."

There was nothing further they could do that night, so they settled in, grumbling, among the dunes and the biting sand flies.

In the first flush of the early morning the fishing boats were still there, rocking gently but seemingly abandoned. The guide led them at a brisk trot to the nearest of the villages and the men of Jordan de Drengot rousted out in a far from gentle manner as many of the inhabitants as they could discover and marshalled them into an open space before a ramshackle church. Gilles sat astride his hose and silently observed, wishing heartily he was elsewhere, Benoit, equally stone faced, beside him. There arose from the crowd of forty or so people corralled closely together a hair raising keening sound from the women folk, mixed with the dreary crying of young children, the unearthly calling of gulls and the alarmed sounds of the few cattle they possessed in a nearby pen. There was an overwhelming stench of drying and putrefied fish that overwhelmed everything, that and the unmistakeable metal tang of recently spilled blood, for already there had been casualties and the bodies of two men lay sprawled in the dirt. The guide was shouting to make himself heard above the general noise. He was, Gilles recognised from his travels, screaming in Greek, for French or even Italian was clearly not recognised in this community. Already, torches had been applied to the thatch and the crackle of burning was added to the background din.

"It would be better for you," shrieked the guide in Greek, "to surrender up the guilty men we seek. Far better by far. You are all of you under the punishment of our Lord, the Prince of Taranto. Your punishment will be all the less."

Clearly bored with the whole situation, Jordan de Drengot barked a brief command to three of his men. They dismounted and elbowed their way into the pen, shouldering their way amongst the livestock. De Drengot indicated a heifer, a milk giver and clearly in better condition than the rest. One man drew a wicked looking knife and, whilst the other two secured it by the shoulders, cut its throat. A collective moan of dismay arose from the crowd as the beast sank to its knees.

De Drengot muttered an aside to the guide who then proclaimed to the crowd, "The rest will follow, unless you produce the guilty men." There was no response and de Drengot swore violently.

"Enough of this," he said. "de Hauteville will require heads." Briefly, he scanned the crowd. "Him, and that one there, they'll do."

Gilles felt moved to protest. "My Lord, we have no means of knowing that these are the men we seek."

The man's answer could not have been simpler. "They are here, aren't they? Did I not tell you to watch and learn? You may be sure that there will be no more trouble after this."

Clearly, de Drengot felt that too much time had already been wasted in this rather futile exercise. No time for any hangings. A log was produced and placed in full view of he crowd. Gilles watched silently as the two men selected were led to it and forced to kneel. De Drengot had had the foresight to bring a specialist along with him, a monstrously large man in a studded leather jacket and armed with a large two handled axe. Experimentally, he swung the axe about his head, making an ugly whooping sound in the air. The first of the chosen men, securely pinioned by two others, braced himself for the expected blow. When it came, his severed head fell to the ground in a welter of blood and bone, coming to rest and staring up accusingly at his executioner. A further collective moan rose from the crowd, forced now to shift position and away from the burning buildings. The second man, little more than a youth, knowing what was coming, struggled. A mailed fist stretched him out senseless upon the ground. The executioner botched the job badly, requiring four blows to separate the head from the shoulders before kicking the body aside in frustration at his own incompetence.

"The heads," commanded de Drengot. "Put them in the bags. And slaughter the rest of the cattle. Take what we need for food."

A single stray chicken had appeared to take up position on the shoulders of one of the decapitated men, pecking randomly at the severed tendrils. The boy, Raoul, leaned over the withers of his horse and vomited a thin, acid bile, for he, like all of the others, had eaten nothing. The stray chicken was shooed off by a group of hysterical, screaming women as they gathered about the body.

Gilles felt his own gorge rising as he watched the heads of the two dead men placed in bags and placed over the withers of a horse. The order was given to leave and the soldiers hacked frantically at the bodies of the slaughtered cattle to secure some final cuts of meat. Riders rode in among the villagers to break them up as the village continued to burn about their ears. De Drengot gave the order and the column wheeled their horses and headed south once more.

With Benoit at his side, Gilles rode in complete silence for a very long time, watching de Drengot ahead of him rise and fall rhythmically in the saddle to the rhythm of the trot as he led his men home, the panniers of his bannerman beside him containing the bouncing heads. It was clear that, as far as de Drengot was concerned, the task was completed. He rode now to continue his work as a holy warrior. What had occurred was of no consequence to him whatsoever. The guide and some appointed men had remained behind to secure the boats and wait for a more trustworthy crew, de Drengot's task was at an end. Gilles had considered himself inured to violence, but this incident had affected and troubled him more deeply than perhaps it should have done. Doubtless, he reflected, he would see far worse in time, but they would, surely, be Turks and thus damned to the pit of Hell already. The people of that unfortunate village, on the other hand, had been Christian, albeit of an inferior quality.

Benoit leaned across to him with a flagon of wine. The taste of bile was still in Gilles' mouth. He spat out his first gulp and wiped his mouth, muttering his thanks. Benoit took a long drink himself without comment. It was not until some considerable time later that he made a simple statement. "An ugly business," he observed. And to that, Gilles had no response.

Late February of the year 1097. The army of Bohemond had returned to Bari and had been in quarters outside the city for months past, all through the winter. The season had not been unduly harsh and neither had they gone short, for Bohemond was a truly accomplished provider and exercised a heavy hand with the rationing. There were times in the long winter months when Gilles dearly missed the riotous disharmony and anarchy of life in the camp of Robert of Flanders and Robert of Normandy, for all its many faults. Bohemond of Taranto, on the other hand, ruled with a rod of iron.

There were very few opportunities for unbridled debauchery and drunkenness; such as there were were carefully weighed out with the eye and the measured hand of a miser. The army was kept from straying. Bohemond kept his men as active as possible, with regular expeditions inland to forage inland to collect firewood, competitions with handsome rewards for displays of strength and fortitude and on occasion carefully regulated feastings and displays of largesse. Not noted especially for any outstanding personal piety, Bohemond insisted upon regular attendances at Mass within the camp and defaulters were fined and otherwise punished for any detectable transgressions.

Bohemond kept his impetuous chief noblemen on a very short rein and it was required of them that they do likewise with their own commands. The army of the winter of 1096 and 1097 was, as a consequence, unduly pious, permanently exhausted and monumentally bored, surrounded by a cowed and subservient population.

News from the outside world and from the other major contingents was sparse and usually contradictory. The combined armies of Robert of Flanders and all the others of the main French force were themselves still encamped nearby and likewise waiting for the opening of the spring sea lanes. Occasionally there was an exchange of messages, usually delivered by itinerant priests, and sometimes by escorted noblemen.

Gilles was afforded no opportunity in that closely controlled encampment to talk directly to any of them, nor to pass any messages on to the Duke. In truth, there was nothing to pass on that he would himself not already know. He made himself his own assumptions, that the Duke would be hard pressed for money and that his patience would be at full stretch. The much smaller contingent led by Hugh of Vermandois, the brother of the excommunicated Henry, King of France, had arrived in Bari in their absence and, against all advice, taken ship to Greece in hastily commissioned vessels, only to be shipwrecked on the wild coasts of Albania.

The supremely arrogant Count of Vermandois, who had sent an overwhelmingly arrogant message to the Emperor demanding full recognition of the importance and the honour of his visit and which had caused much offence and ribaldry in a court more sophisticated and cultivated than he could possibly envisage, found himself instead shipwrecked for his pains and had been rescued and conveyed safely to Constantinople. Those battered remnants of his expedition who had managed to once more reach land in Italy subsisted on the fringes of the encampment, keeping body and soul together on scraps and charity whilst their leaders were occasionally granted grudging access to the more than adequate table of Bohemond.

It was known that the army of Godfrey of Bouillon, Duke of Lower Lorraine, had already arrived in Constantinople without major mishap, having wisely taken the long land route down through Hungary. Raymond of Toulouse, Count of Toulouse, on the other hand, had led his army of Provencals and the men of the south of France down the Adriatic coast of Illyria, causing immense mayhem along the way and was at last report also said to be approaching the great city of Constantinople. Of the hordes of scarecrows who had earlier followed the Hermit to the east nothing further was known.

As far as it was possible, Gilles spent some time there, stranded in Bari, in at least attempting to understand the separate natures of the men that he had in some way inherited. He felt it to be his duty and his responsibility. It soon became clear that in some instances there was nothing of note or interest actually to be discovered. Arnauld, massive and unkempt, he of the terrifying strength and the ham like fists, was monosyllabic to the point of being a mute. Gilles had witnessed any number of examples of the man's stupefying strength and, understandably, men left him well alone. He was a source of endless fascination, on the other hand, to the hordes of camp children, either local or else those of the pilgrims who had survived the long march through France and down into Italy, and whose numbers had been savagely decimated by disease and privation.

The man was patient and allowed them to take extraordinary liberties with him, liberties that an ordinary man would simply not tolerate. They pulled his beard, made faces and attempted to trip him up, to all of which he reacted with an amiable tolerance. As he had suspected, Ernoul was feckless, a wastrel from the dockside stews of Rouen. The Rouen of Ernoul, however, was not the Rouen of Gilles' own remembered childhood.

There was no real connection or point of contact and, in the end, Gilles stopped trying to find one. Benoit had formed an active dislike of the man and regularly assigned him the most onerous of tasks, the digging of latrines and the mucking out of horses and the like. Jacques the weaver had the long almost deformed fingers and permanently bent back of his trade. Not physically strong and afflicted with a fearsome stammer, he was generally held to be feeble-minded and it took no real amount of deep thought to discover why the Duke had been only too happy to lose him.

Quite early on in their relationship, Gilles found it necessary to take the man, Ralph, aside and talk sternly to him. For some time past he had been finding his ceaseless prattle irritating.

"You have no ears, Ralph," he said. "I would know why they were removed, for what offence, and where."

Ralph smirked knowingly. "It was in Caen," he said, "Five, six years ago? I can scarce remember. It didn't half hurt, though, I can tell you."

Gilles suppressed a smile. "I can well imagine," he said drily. "And your offence?"

Ralph shifted his feet and licked his lips. "It was an innocent enough remark, my Lord, a compliment, really."

Despite himself, Gilles felt compelled to ask. "And the nature of this, er, compliment?"

Ralph smiled reminiscently. "Ah, well," he said. "There was this woman, see. And she had a bosom the size of, the size of..."

He was clearly searching for some suitable point of comparison.

Gilles helped him out, "I would imagine that it was large?" he offered.

Ralph nodded gratefully. "Yes indeed, Lord, as large as..as large as...." He trailed off for want of a comparison.

"Yes, well. I can imagine," Gilles said. "And you made some remark?"

Ralph smiled his broad smile. "Aye, that I did, Lord. And she found it to her liking, and laughed, like I had meant her to."

Gilles was beginning to tire of the conversation.

"But somebody else didn't, I take it." Ralph grimaced, "quite so, Lord. Her husband, God bless him, did not find it in the least bit funny when she told him." He looked directly at Gilles. "Turns out that the man was the leading cloth merchant of the city, a man of great power, you see."

Gilles had had enough. "And he had you marched off to the pillory in the main square and..."

"Yes, Lord, you have the right of it. Chop, chop," Ralph interrupted him.

"Now see here, Ralph," said Gilles sternly. "You are liked well enough. You are popular, but I require you to stop that tongue of yours. No good can come of it and, well, you know the consequences."

Again, the broad smile, "Right you are, my Lord, from here on in. As the tomb," and he mimed the sewing together of his own lips. Exasperated, Gilles turned on his heel and walked away from him.

The man Reynard had always been a curiosity, a puzzle to Gilles. As with all the others, he had become accustomed to the unexplained appearance within their allocated section of the camp of rarities, of vegetables hardly mildewed, sacks of barley nearly full and only slightly sprouting, for the horses; a barrel of wine, fresh bread and, on one miraculous occasion, a little dog cart in its entirety! Reynard was the source of all these fine things and he offered no explanation for either his frequent and protracted disappearances or for the arrival of these valued objects. The others had long since learned not to ask and, anyway, when Reynard did speak, a rare event, it was virtually impossible to understand him.

Amongst his many gifts, it transpired that Reynard was a more than competent cook, insisting always on taking on the task himself, invariably adding handfuls of onion and garlic, dried herbs that he had gathered from somewhere himself. A further peculiarity of his was that he carried about him always a small and slender flute of bone, or rather of yellowing ivory. This he would play at odd and quiet moments and in the evening, seemingly to himself; strange music the like of which Gilles had never heard before. It was trilling and lilting, in some way eerie, the music of mountains and wild and high open spaces. The others always stopped to listen.

The man had other habits that marked him out as a further oddity. He could juggle, almost in an absent minded manner, with any object to hand, pottery, small stones or, alarmingly, knives. His hands seemed to possess a consciousness of their own, forever darting and weaving. They were gifted hands that could steal away a prized possession or else produce something, seemingly from the owner's ear. This skill would be bound to bring trouble down upon Reynard sooner or later.

Matters came to a head one morning when Gilles was returning from the horse picket lines where he had gone to cast a proud and possessive eye over Earandel. The farrier there also operated as a general blacksmith when required and a short file of slaves had been gathered there, squatting in the dirt whilst the man was making some necessary and very loud adjustments to their chains. And there too was Reynard, likewise squatting, and in apparent conversation with one of the chained slaves. The man was old and wizened, with a shock of white hair, and very dark. The conversation between the two appeared animated and Gilles unobtrusively edged nearer to listen. The language was completely alien to him, sounding like a succession of harsh guttural outbursts and strange clicks. It sounded almost as if they were arguing, but this surely could not be. At the very end, Gilles observed Reynard, in a very swift movement, pass the slave a single curled iron nail, which the man then secreted in the palm of his hand. That done, Reynard stood up and walked away without a further word. Clearly, a transaction of some form had taken place.

That evening Gilles took Reynard aside, ostensibly to discuss fresh barley for the horses. When that was concluded he said directly, "Reynard. Where is it, exactly, that you come from?"

Reynard squinted up at him, his single gold earing twinkling in the firelight. "I doubt that you would have heard of it," he replied. The man meant this simply as a statement, not because he might feel affronted or was making a proud and defiant challenge.

"Be that as it may," said Gilles, "but tell me."

Reynard shrugged, an acquiescent rolling of the shoulders. "I come" he said, "from a place midway between Bayonne and San Sebastian. It is high up in the mountains, and in the middle of nowhere."

Gilles was struggling, for he had not heard, in truth, of either place. "You are not, then, of the Languedoc, though you speak a French, of sorts."

Reynard allowed himself the faintest of deferential smiles. "Lord," he said simply, "I speak many languages, of a sort."

Gilles considered the remark. "To be sure, you do, Reynard. And that slave with whom you were talking this morning down by the horse lines, what language was that, then?"

Reynard remained completely undisturbed by the fact that he had been seen, and heard. "The man was a moor," he said. "Where I come from the place is full of them, and the language was Arabic, of a sort," he added. Reynard did not look as if he were disposed to add further comment.

"You mean to say that you speak Arabic?"

Reynard smiled modestly. "Like I said, Lord, of a sort."

There was still the matter of the exchange of the small iron nail. What of that? Reynard did not seem inclined to elaborate.

"Merely the matter of the exchange of some information. It was nothing of any importance. As for the nail, well he might use it to break clear of his chain. And what good would that be to him?"

Reynard spread his hands to indicate the bleakness of the scene around him. Perhaps wisely, Gilles did not seek to pursue the matter. Sufficient unto itself that he had a man serving him who spoke Arabic, of a sort. That might well prove useful in the future.

The boy Raoul, another mystery in his midst. The boy was polite, deft and ever courteous. He took to his many duties well and was clearly a swift learner. Gilles' chainmail was kept burnished and free of rust through the daily application of sand and a chamois leather, his sword regularly dripped linseed oil and kept sharp and Earandel and the other horses in the boy's care positively gleamed with health. But the boy remained silent and withdrawn,

Gilles judged him to be about thirteen years of age, scrawny and lanky and likely to grow very tall. Finally Gilles asked him directly to tell him of his family and his background, as Benoit had advised him. The boy squirmed under his direct scrutiny.

"My family," he told Gilles, "own land in the Cotentin, near to a place called Picauville, near to Sainte-Mere-Église. Good growing land, good barley, a fine living." He spoke with pride. Gilles could not recall any Picauville, but he had visited Sainte-Mere- Église on a number of occasions in the retinue of the Duke Robert. The man had seemed to have a rather strange fondness or fascination for the place. Gilles recalled a number of mistresses there, one in particular.

"And your family?" he prompted the boy. Raoul shifted uncomfortably.

"I am the youngest of three sons," he began. My father is dead, killed in a dispute with the men of Henry when I was small, he died in the service of his Grace, the Duke. My oldest brother, he inherited the land, He too is now dead. My other brother is in Holy Orders somewhere, I know not where. His Grace now holds the lands of Picauville directly and owing nothing to any other. I am his Grace's man and for him to dispose of as he sees fit. This is how I now come to serve you, as his gift."

Gilles was beginning to understand, was filling in some of the missing details for himself.

"And your mother," he asked gently, "does she yet live?"

There was a flash of pride once more from the boy. "She does indeed, Lord. She is now a Prioress of great sanctity, and living in good estate in Sainte-Mere Église, a fine place."

Gilles' eyes narrowed, yes, he knew the very place. Indeed, he had been kept waiting in the courtyard on a number of occasions whilst the Duke conducted business, doubtless of an ecclesiastical nature, within. He had even seen the woman on a number of occasions. She had been tall, he recalled, as tall as young Raoul standing here before him. Beneath the sombre head dress there had been, he now vividly remembered, a violent shock of black hair. He recalled a striking, not to say, beautiful woman who had towered above the Duke until he had mounted his horse to leave.

Gilles was by no means an overly imaginative youth, but he was beginning to form a picture based on the known facts available to him, that and a number of suppositions on his part. What he beheld then, in the shy and gawky and diffident youth standing before him, was nothing less than the bastard son of his Grace, Robert, Duke of Normandy. The more he thought about it, the more it made sense. He felt overwhelmed by a deep and an unavoidable sense of responsibility.

"Well, my boy," he said, his voice still gentle, "We must make your mother proud of you when we return from our Great Enterprise, and, of course, his Grace, the Duke of Normandy, who has entrusted you to my care. Now, it is growing late and you have worked hard today. Go and sleep. Doubtless, there is something in Reynard's pot for you."

On that particular day a full and solemn Mass had been celebrated in the camp on the feast of the Saint and martyr Polycarp. The name of the saint, obscure even within that massively overcrowded calendar of saints, barely raised a disinterested eyebrow or a casual comment, but the event was impressive enough, for the event was also a divine blessing on the expedition, for it had been made known that they would finally sail to the land of the Greeks the following day. They had all of them taken the knee, taken the Sacrament and been blessed. Bohemond had then issued a ration of wine and elderly mutton and an extra ration of bread. For days past the camp had been a riot of activity. More ships had been arriving in the harbour for a week past and the space there and out along the coast was crowded with vessels of all size and description.

The harbourside was packed with jostling and foul mouthed seamen as they and chained coffers of slaves conveyed materials, equipment and supplies to the waiting ships. The taking of the horses onboard was a particular trial, and Gilles and Benoit had spent an extremely vexing day in getting Earandel and all the other mounts and their little cart aboard their allocated vessel, in the process being obliged to part with a few of his silver pennies in bribes to ease the way as much as possible. The whole process of getting the mounts into an open boat, conveying them to a small flat bottomed, clinker built cog and aboard it and then settling them down in the dark hold took almost the entire day and all of the energy and patience of Gilles and his men.

Being landsmen, all of them had of course treated the strange, foul smelling and creaking vessel with alarm and suspicion and their fears were far from alleviated by the mixed crew of Italians, Greeks and north Africans. Neither had the master, a one eyed mariner from Genova, in any way allayed their fears. Gilles barely understood a word he spoke, but the language of money was sufficient to smooth the way. He was able to discover that besides himself and his men, at least a further score of men and their possessions would somehow be crammed into the tiny vessel. Gilles had at last managed to ask the master how long they could expect to be at sea, and to make himself understood. In reply, the man had simply grinned, shrugged and then spat.

They now sprawled, exhausted, on the beach, waiting for the dawn and embarkation. Jacques the weaver, Ernoul and Arnauld, slept. Arnauld slept at every opportunity that presented itself, his snoring could wake the dead. Gilles couldn't see Ralph clearly, but by the silence, Gilles judged him to be also sleeping. Raoul likewise slept, someone had considerately placed a rough blanket over him. Reynard the Gypsy lay, arms behind his head, staring up wide eyed at the heavens, thinking the Good Lord alone knew what.

There was no more wine to pass around and the last of the mutton had been chewed down to the bone. About them lay satchels and flagons containing their provisions and for the voyage and the immediate days after, should they be successful in surviving the voyage; stale bread, water, an amount of flour, a small container of dried peas and a bag of shrivelled raisins. It was not a sight to raise the spirits. They were surrounded on every side by men experiencing the same emotions and conditions. Marshals appointed by Bohemond passed by regularly with their clubs and knotted rope ends to ensure that order was maintained. Gilles imagined that he could have spent the time carousing with the other lesser knights, he could hear the sound of their festivities nearby, but he felt no real compulsion, preferring instead the company of the men he led.

"Then you are a fool," had said Benoit frankly, earlier that night. "That's where I would be, were it me."

Gilles stared at the man, squatting on his haunches and scratching away at the rust on a discarded stirrup he had found. Benoit never threw anything away he found if he thought he could find a use for it.

"Well, Benoit," he snapped. "You are not, and that's an end to it."

Benoit shrugged and smiled pacifically. "And that is for sure," he said, adding 'my Lord' after a suitable pause. "Have you, may I ask, given thought as to what is next?"

Gilles had learned that although Benoit voiced his opinions very rarely they were rarely idle thoughts and should be encouraged. He relented. He still knew very little of this man, this drifter from the badlands up on the border.

"Please, of your courtesy, do continue."

He realised that he had come to depend upon this laconic and seemingly rootless man who had somehow casually entered into his life some months ago.

Benoit shifted position, stretched himself out for greater comfort and laid the stirrup aside.

"Well," he said. "The way I see it is this. We are all of us off to fight the Turk in the morning and to rescue the Kingdom of God, or else win eternal salvation for our troubles. It is not for me to question this unduly, though for myself I hope that I have lots of women on the way and also become very rich. But you, my Lord, if I might make so bold, will require something else. You may in time come into possession of your new holdings, a happy and successful man, and I hope there will be a place there too for me, grown fat and prosperous." He allowed himself a low chuckle at the thought. He sat upright and looked at Gilles directly. "But you, you are under the direct obedience of his Grace, the Duke of

Normandy. At this present time you are also under loan to the Prince of Taranto. Great men, the two of them and it is not my position to judge what value they hold you in. But consider for a moment, my Lord. Great men, forgive them, can fail and fall too. You are younger than I. In this great enterprise of ours, look to yourself. Make yourself great, against the time that they may no longer be relied upon to aid you. And now it is late, by your leave I shall sleep now."

Benoit turned on his shoulder and closed his eyes. Soon there came the sound of a deep and rhythmic snoring. It had been a long speech, longer than any Benoit had ever uttered in his presence. It gave Gilles much to think upon. He tried to sleep, but sleep eluded him, and so the dawn found him, surrounded by sleeping and restless men on the morning that they were to sail to the mysterious land of the Greeks and to the great unknown beyond.

Continuandum

Follow the continuing tale
with Julian de la Motte's upcoming novel

"The Road to Redemption"

On the eve of his departure to the Holy Land and the liberation of the Holy places, Gilles Fitz Earl, recently knighted and owner of lands that he has yet to see, is a young man of great promise and with the trust and favour of his lord and with so much still to learn. Now he must command his own men in battle and lead them through the bloodstained turmoil of the march all the way to the goal of the holy City of Jerusalem itself and the carnage and its despoilation in one last savage act!

The Road to Redemption is the sequel to *The Will of God.*

* * * * *

Prologue:

"The surest way to work up a crusade in favour of some good cause is to promise people that they will have a chance of mistreating someone. To be able to destroy with good conscience, to be able to behave badly and call your bad behaviour 'righteous indignation' - this is the height of psychological luxury, the most delicious of moral treats." {Aldous Huxley]

****

In the grey and pink of the false Adriatic dawn there was little of the flatlands surrounding the ancient port and fortified city of Dyrachium to inspire any sense of wonder or of beauty, only the very real sense of relief at the prospect of standing on firm dry land once more. Like a collection of relieved and tired ducklings heading for home, the bedraggled squadron came about, nudging for sea room as it headed for the harbour beneath the dark, austere outline of the castle.

On one of the lowliest and most foul smelling little tubs in the entire flotilla, Gilles and Benoit stood side by side, incurring the wrath of the scurrying mariners. As they prepared to come alongside the crowded quayside, a hive of activity, loomed ever closer. Benoit spat over the side and swore colourfully and at length. It had, in truth, been a very long and taxing crossing, full of the fears that all inexperienced landsmen could possibly experience added to the nausea and sheer fatigue such a terrifying encounter with the unknown could conjure up; a time of sleeplessness and of coping with the needs and requirements of terrified horses less qualified even than they for the crossing. They had been a full day and all of the night at sea and neither of them felt at their best. In time, and with a jarring thump that caused both of them to wince, the boat finally nestled next to the quay. Whistles were blown and ropes flung ashore for waiting men to gather up and secure to stone bollards. The Master's language, constant and unrestrained, achieved new depths of imagination and profanity.

"Well," observed the greatly relieved and recently ennobled Gilles of the Little Trees, "we are arrived, and that would appear to be that." Benoit grunted in the fine morose manner to which Gilles had become accustomed in their time together.

"Well, thank the good Virgin and all the saints above for that, at least."

Not for the first time in that voyage, the Master broke in on their shared contemplations of the enormity of the task ahead.

"Well, as you can see, my Lord," he announced, "we are here, and I'll thank you to get your arses off my boat, soon as you like. Time is short, and I have things to be doing."

It was fair to say that in their brief time together, the Master and his reluctant passengers had failed to grow fond of each other. Gilles inclined slightly at the waist, affording the Master a courteous small bow. Aping and parodying the language of his superiors, of which he had made a close study all of his adult life, Gilles replied. "It shall be our deep pleasure to comply. I thank you for all your many kindnesses."

While the Master absorbed this, Benoit added with an ill suppressed sneer, "Yes, it has all been immense fun. We must be sure to do this again sometime." The Master spun on his heel and strode off, muttering.

As was his customary habit, the boy Raoul, he of the troubled past and the mysterious parentage, was no further from Gilles than the length of a kick. Just beyond the boy, hovering expectantly and in various degrees of sea sickness, were the rest of Gilles' ill favoured and motley command; giant and patient Arnaud, the shifty Ernoul and stunted little Jacques, the arthritic weaver, Ralph, with his usual air of innocent mischief and the ever enigmatic gypsy Reynard. As they all regarded him, Gilles, not for the first time, experienced a wave of anxiety and self doubt, and of deep responsibility.

"Well," he snapped at them with a sudden anger, "See to it then, all of you. As soon as the planking is down, I want the horses ashore, and all in one piece, mind. Any harm that may come to any of them and I'll have the hides off your backs." Benoit sucked his teeth, but made no comment. "That done, I want you all on that quayside with all your gear, and no straying!"

As with the embarkation back in Bari, now one hundred and thirty five sea miles away, disembarkation proved to be a very lengthy and frustrating task and took considerable time and effort to achieve, the horses proving to be, as expected, the greatest difficulty. At length, Gilles' inconsequential command; with shivering horses, their equipment and possessions and their dismantled little cart, were finally assembled in a foul tempered little huddle on the quayside as, all around them, various commands of various size also gathered themselves. There was little order to be seen in that crowd of ill tempered men, despite the hoarse shouts and imprecations of various marshals and provosts. It had begun to rain, gentle and insistent, adding to their discomfort in the early morning. Gilles suddenly realised just how hungry he was. Immediately he felt guilty, his men must be experiencing the very same sensation. He turned to Reynard, ever their unofficial quartermaster.

"Reynard," he said proffering a coin from his purse, "see what you can find."

The man nodded once and ducked and disappeared into the growing crowd. Ships were continuing to arrive and the milling men and horses added to the confusion. Ultimately, a harassed and understandably irritable provost moved them off the jetty and up a rough ramp leading to the castle. There they were brought up short by a rank of alien cavalrymen and, before them, a knot of official looking men. These, clearly, were their new allies in their great and noble Great Enterprise to rid the Holy Land of the godless infidels; their first contact with the servants of the great Lord and Emperor of Byzantium. Shouldering his way and in obvious high temper through the growing crowd, Gilles noted the gaunt, uncompromising and towering figure of Tancred, beloved nephew of the Lord Bohemond and notional leader of this particular gathering. He strode forward now to meet the gathered Byzantine officials.

Gilles shrugged. None of his business, after all. He had his own particular cross to bear, in looking after his own men and attempting to rationalise and determine his own role in this present Great Enterprise. It had, all in all, been an exacting and demanding year before ever he had fetched up in this particularly uninspiring corner of the mighty and much vaunted Byzantine Empire, upon which the rain continued to fall upon his sodden shoulders, this last bastion before the deprivations of the pagan Christ abusers.

Gilles Fitz Waltheof, now the Lord of the Young Trees, a possession he had never in his life visited, had been raised since boyhood in the chaotic, nomadic court of Robert Duke of Normandy, the oldest child of William, he who had destroyed forever the power of the Saxons. He had not had an easy time of it, being obliged for the most part to fulfil the lowly tasks of the household and the stable. In all of this he had steadily mastered a number of essential skills, serving at the table, despatching chased down animals at the hunt, preparing meat for the feasting and the elementary principles of doctoring horses, all of this whilst being subjected to the usual blows and beatings, which he was obliged to endure and put down to experience. Thus, in their avoidance, he learnt also valuable lessons in cunning and had developed an acute awareness of the various natures of humanity and how best this understanding could be deployed and capitalised upon. In short, Gilles was a survivor. In time he had slowly risen in stature and in the estimation of his Lord Robert, who had developed an affection for this half English boy, seeing in him skills that could be fostered and put to good use. Gilles was thus a minor rising star in the firmament of the insecure Norman Court when, late in the year of 1095, Robert of Normandy, for excellent practical and religious reasons of his own, decided to involve himself in the rising clamour for a Holy War against the infidels and to liberate the places where the earthly Christ had walked and preached.

Thus had Gilles accompanied his Lord, making the difficult journey all the way from Normandy and northern France, through and over the high and inhospitable Alpine passes and down into the rich, fat and fertile lands of Italy to the point where he now stood, gently steaming in the rain, here at this alien dockside, his tousled and unruly thatch of straw coloured hair plastered to his scalp. Still in his early twenties, Gilles, robust and well built, was no virgin, having been seduced by the beautiful young Greek wife of a very dangerous man. He had also killed a man and seen violent death come to many others in the course of his epic journey. More important still, he had earned the Duke's trust and had indeed been knighted by him one very drunken morning and awarded land he had yet to see, and a rich purse with which to maintain himself in appropriate manner. He had received the dubious gift of an ill assorted collection of men to command and, of course, was gifted by the invaluable presence of the highly experienced Benoit. More recently, he had been given over to the command of Tancred, Norman adventurer and nephew of the all powerful Count Bohemond, ostensibly for his flair with foreign languages, as scout and liaison officer between Bohemond and Robert; though the latter had made clear to him that he would value any further information that might be of value and use to him.

And now all he was required to do, he reflected, like that unruly mob of men gathered around him, was the mere task of a gentle ride to the Holy Land and there to liberate the sacred city of Jerusalem.

COMING SOON FROM HISTORIUM PRESS

Bibliography

The History of the First Crusade, and indeed of all of the subsequent Crusades, has of course generated a huge range of valuable and original research on the part of historians and authors. Specifically, the author is indebted to the following and recommends these to all readers wishing to study the subject further:

A History of the Crusades: [volumes I-III] Steven Runciman
Armies of Heaven [The First Crusade and the Quest for the Apocalypse]: Jay Rubinstein
Crusades [An epic history of the fight for the Holy Land]: Dan Jones
Crusading and the Crusader States: Andrew Jotischky
The Crusades: Thomas Ashbridge
The Crusades: Ashley Bridge
The Crusades: Zoe Oldenbourg
The Crusades: Archer and Kingsford
The Crusades: Hans Erbhard Mayer
The First Crusade: A New History: Thomas Ashbridge
The First Crusade [The Call from the East]: Peter Frankopan
God's War [A New History of the Crusades]: Christopher Tyerman
The Kingdom of the Sun: John Julius Norwich
People of the First Crusade: Michael Foss
How to Plan a Crusade: Christopher Tyerman

Julian de la Motte is a Londoner. He graduated from the University of Wales with a degree in Medieval History. He was further awarded a Master of Arts qualification in Medieval English Art from the University of York. He studied and taught in Italy for nearly four years before returning to the U.K. and a career as a teacher, teacher trainer and materials designer before taking up a new role as a Director of Foreign Languages and of English as a Foreign Language.

Married and with two grown up children, He is now extensively involved in review writing and historical research, primarily on medieval history.

"The Will of God" [the first of two books on the subject of the First Crusade] is his third novel.

Other books by Julian de la Motte:

"Senlac: A Novel of the Norman Conquest – Book One"
"Senlac: A Novel of the Norman Conquest – Book Two"